Fate Moreland's Widow

STORY RIVER BOOKS

Pat Conroy, Editor at Large

Fate Moreland's Widow

| A NOVEL |

JOHN LANE

Foreword by Wiley Cash

The University of South Carolina Press

© 2015 John Lane

Published by the University of South Carolina Press
Columbia, South Carolina 29208

www.sc.edu/uscpress

Manufactured in the United States of America

24 23 22 21 20 19 18 17 16 15   10 9 8 7 6 5 4 3 2 1

Library of Congress Cataloging-in-Publication Data
can be found at http://catalog.loc.gov/

This book was printed on recycled paper with 30 percent
postconsumer waste content.

ISBN 978-1-61117-469-4 (hardback)
ISBN 978-1-61117-470-0 (ebook)

For my mother, Mary Brown Lane (1926–2005)

Before all had happened that has happened since
And is now arranged on the shelf
Of memory in a sequence that I call myself.

Robert Penn Warren, "Covered Bridge"

CONTENTS

Foreword ix
Wiley Cash

1988 1

PART I
The Evictions 5

PART II
Malice Aforethought 67

PART III
The Last Flying Squadron 131

1988 169

Acknowledgements 179

FOREWORD

You learn five-dollar words such as *liminal* when you go to college—at least that's where I learned it. Maybe you already know what it means, but for my purposes here I'll define it as "a place that is betwixt and between two separate, but definable, states." Perhaps John Lane, author of *Fate Moreland's Widow*, learned the word *liminal* while growing up in Spartanburg, South Carolina. If not, then he probably learned it at Wofford College or in graduate school at Bennington. I can't speak as to whether or not John was thinking about this word while he wrote *Fate Moreland's Widow*, but I believe you should think about the word *liminal* and its definition while you read it. I know I did.

Fate Moreland's Widow is about a man named Ben Crocker who is being pulled in many different directions. He was born to millworkers and raised in a mill village in Carlton, South Carolina, but now he balances the accounts for the mill's owner, George McCane, and before he realizes it, he's also balancing his boss's guilt and innocence after McCane is charged with murdering three people just north of the South Carolina line.

There's a good chance that Ben Crocker wouldn't know the meaning of the word *liminal*, especially having been raised and educated in a southern mill village in the years between World War I and the Great Depression. But I have no doubt that Crocker knows what *liminal* feels like; after all, he's stuck "betwixt and between" countless "separate, but definable states," the two most obvious being the states of South Carolina and North Carolina, since he burns up the Asheville road between Carlton and Huntersville, desperately trying to influence public opinion in favor of McCane's innocence. Back home in Carlton, he's stuck between social classes, and both sides are demanding his allegiance. The folks who live in the mill village of his youth want Crocker to stand with them as McCane evicts residents and shutters the mill in order to "modernize" it, a development that will demand higher output from fewer workers. But Crocker is pulled in the opposite direction by George McCane, who expects Crocker's absolute obeisance in the name of progress, even if that progress requires him to turn his back on his own people. And you can't forget about his being stuck between the domestic sphere, represented by his life at home with his loving if insistent wife, Coleen, and the very volatile sphere of public opinion as the legal drama unfolds while McCane evicts his employees from the village.

Crocker's relationship with—and connection to—these states grows ever more tenuous during the course of the novel. He finds himself confronting Olin Campbell, the mill village version of Tom Joad—a man whose impulses Crocker can understand, even if he can't quite trust them. But it's not until Crocker finds himself in cahoots with George McCane's mercurial and morally bankrupt brother Angus that he begins to question his own impulses, especially in relation to the beautiful and mysterious Novie Moreland, the young widow who lost a husband and son under George McCane's hand. Crocker's interests in Fate Moreland's widow come to haunt his life, leaving him perpetually stuck between unanswered questions of his past and any chance at happiness in his present, never fully living in either.

As the novel unfolds, Ben Crocker and the anxieties born from his various predicaments come to symbolize the evolution or, as some would say, the devolution of the southern mill village in the years between the World Wars. Rural people who'd come down from the Appalachian mountains to find work in the mill towns of the South Carolina upstate and North Carolina piedmont were torn between the agrarian lifestyle their families once embraced and the promises of consistent pay and communal living promised by the mill owners. As the Great Depression took hold and the need for cotton began to shrink, more and more regretted making the trip down from the mountains, and many of them found themselves stuck: unable to afford to make the move back home to the mountains, but too poor to continue to live the life of the mill worker. If that's not *liminal* then I don't know what is.

John Lane deftly captures the hardscrabble plight of the southern mill worker and the ambitious greed of the southern mill owner in *Fate Moreland's Widow*. But he does an even better job of capturing the quandary of Ben Crocker, the man precariously stuck in the middle, right there in that liminal state.

You too will find yourself in a liminal state as you're caught between the book's opening and final pages if you read it through in one sitting as I did. Rest assured, it's a place you won't mind staying for a while.

Wiley Cash

| 1988 |

A porch rail makes for a poor defense against the past, but I sat behind mine and watched with some curiosity as Mrs. Edna McCane parked her late model Cadillac in front of my house and walked into the yard. I had not seen Mrs. McCane since George McCane's funeral. She looked like she was dressed to go lunch down at the Club, but then decided to take a side trip to Morgan Heights, a deviation in her daily routine we might both come to regret. She wore her hair pulled tight in a bun, and a single strand fell awkwardly to one side. She was maybe ten years younger than I, and I always imagined that the infirmities that have besieged me also restricted everyone else in old age. But not Edna McCane. She was thin, but she moved with grace and ease to the bottom step where she stood and looked up at me.

As she approached I had the odd thought that maybe she was trying to sell something, so I made a joke about an old man on a fixed income. "Ben, you were Mr. McCane's personal assistant for forty years. You know who I am."

"Personal assistant. That's a title I never officially held," I said. "But now I could use a little assistance myself."

Despite the compliments I was pretty certain that Mrs. McCane wasn't on a social visit. She mounted the two steps to the porch with the authority and confidence of someone on a mission.

"Would you like a glass of tea?" I offered as she stepped up on the porch.

"No thank you," she said. "May I sit down?"

I gestured to the empty folding lawn chair beside me and she settled down lightly like a bird on a nest. Old Mrs. McCane was so genteel it was hard to make out what she wanted until she was in her chair and she pulled an envelope out she'd brought in her black pocketbook. She opened it and unfolded two fragile newspaper clippings and held them before her. She turned and looked straight at me. Her eyes struck me as what I'd call mockingbird gray. I took in the rest of her fine face and noted the prominent high cheekbones of the well bred. My

1

cheekbones had been collapsing downward for decades, but the structure of Mrs. McCane's face was still sound, feathered lightly with a coral blush.

She handed me the clippings. "You'll see these are from 1935 and 1936."

"That's a long time ago."

"I found them going through an old desk I'm giving to one of the grandchildren. They appear to have been published in the Huntersville, North Carolina, paper. If you will, I'd like to talk with you about them."

There was nothing I'd rather talk about less than those two articles but I took them anyway. The old paper smelled like pipe smoke. I glanced down. I wondered why George McCane had kept them, and wished that he had not. At the center of the first clipping, taken from the front page filling a whole column above the rotten fold, I saw the familiar face of Novie Moreland among a group of solemn bystanders. The lake was behind them. I knew what its depths contained the day the picture was taken. Seeing Novie's face caused my breath to catch as I held the picture and studied it, then I finally breathed a little deeper and handed the articles back. I didn't need to read on. The stories harbored more than the memory of Novie's face—the salacious content, the description of the dead bodies pulled from the lake in the longer piece and then the brief legal notice in the second when Mr. McCane was indicted for murder a few months later.

"Years ago George flew into a rage at a party up at the lake," Mrs. McCane said, as if just remembering the incident at that moment. "He threatened our neighbor Dr. Simmons, and told him never to bring up his brother's name again. I thought it was odd. Dr. Simmons had not brought up George's brother. He'd referred instead to some incident on the lake. I asked George about it later, but he brushed it aside. All he ever told me was there was an accident up on the lake and he'd been involved. I asked around but no one was willing to talk and they acted like they knew little about it. I never heard the whole story and then I found these clippings."

I didn't respond. We both sat in a lull of awkward silence and looked at the street. Mrs. McCane sat still for two minutes. I know because I glanced down at my watch at least every thirty seconds. I tracked the passing of three cars and stared as one of my neighbors walked an obedient dog on the other side of the street. The opposite empty porches were shadowed as the afternoon sun hid behind the oaks and high-pitched roofs behind us.

"What happened?" she finally asked when that eternity ended. She smiled as she released the question she'd had since turning up the two brittle yellowing clippings, but the smile did not seem sincere. She held the articles with her gloved right hand and shook them a little as if my answer might fall like a ripe persimmon from among the printed sentences. I shook my head slightly, but did not say anything.

"It says George was indicted for murder. Could that be?" she asked. She wasn't giving up easily. "There is nothing here about a trial. Was there one?"

"It was settled," I said, picking up my iced tea glass from the table between us to take a sip.

"But did it go to court?"

"The case was resolved."

She waited for me to continue, but I wasn't going to say anything else.

"Those clippings were from ten years before we were married," she said. "I was younger than George. I'd just graduated from Agnes Scott and knew nothing of this place or its ways. I was so young."

If Mr. McCane had meant for you to understand, he had decades to tell you, I wanted to say, but the words seemed impulsive and a little insensitive for someone of my social station. I knew they would sting, and that was not my style.

"You know, he was not well," she said. "He did not have the clear mind you seem to possess in your old age. He spent much of his time in his final years up at the lake. I usually stayed down here."

What did Edna McCane know of my mind? That was one of the longest conversations I'd ever held with her, and it consisted of picking at an old scab of an injury I'd managed to forget was a wound until that day.

She pulled a tissue from her purse and at first I thought she would daub away a stray, unexpected tear, but instead she wiped a half-smile of condensation off the table top from where my iced tea glass had sat before she arrived, then she placed the clippings between us. "Well, I guess that's that. Ben, let's have lunch downtown at the club when you're ready to talk a little more. I'll be glad to send a driver to pick you up."

| PART I |

The Evictions

Hey boss man won't you hear me when I call?
You're not that big you're tall that's all.

—*Popular song from the 1930s*

| 1 |

"Crocker, I'm closing the Carlton Mill," George McCane announced, walking over to my desk in late summer of 1935.

"Close the mill?" I said, looking up from the ledger book where I transcribed receipts each month, this time for August's raw cotton purchases. McCane handed me a folder of papers.

"Tomorrow," he said. "I'm shutting the mill down for a few months. All the details are here. Carry them out."

"This will create hardship for our people out there."

"That's the way it has to be. Draw up a memo to Bobo. We'll keep some supervisors on to help with setting up the new equipment, but those we lay off will have to be patient."

I had no hint of the closing until that moment and so the immediacy of the plan took me by surprise. I'd seen invoices for new machinery appearing on my desk for a few weeks, but when I had asked Mr. McCane about them he had simply said, "That's for our next project."

"There are over three hundred employed up there at the mill," I finally said. "How will they live without work?"

"Tell the company store to extend credit," McCane said. "Assure everyone that when the construction is finished the mill will be one of the few air-conditioned plants in the South. Tell them it will be a showcase, some place they can work with pride. And besides, getting the humidity out of the air will improve our productivity. There won't be so many threads breaking on the looms."

Then McCane turned, looked more serious, and removed two small sheets of paper like stationary from his coat pocket and unfolded them. "One more thing, Crocker. Here's a list of fourteen houses we'll be renovating, and a sketch of which houses are assigned to which workers. We're going out there tomorrow and help them get out. Tell your wife you'll be home late." McCane looked down and read off all the names, and he paused on Olin Campbell.

"These men are all union," I said. "I'm sorry but that's not right, Mr. McCane."

"Not right?"

"It's illegal, Mr. McCane."

"What's illegal about renovating your own property?"

"There's a code Mr. McCane—The National Recovery Administration."

"I know about the textile code. It doesn't have anything in it about construction."

"But you're putting out the workers. They have some rights."

"I'm not putting out anyone. I'm simply modernizing. They can keep those blue eagle NRA posters in the plant windows for all I care."

McCane walked over to the big front window and looked out at the street and spoke with his back turned. "Wasn't Olin Campbell the one who drove the lead vehicle over to Honea Path that first week of the big strike last year?"

I knew what Mr. McCane was getting at. Olin Campbell had been a lead driver back during the big strike when the flying squadrons appeared. They'd been wild roving bands of striking mill hands who drove from mill to mill to call out workers from plants that hadn't yet unionized or where plants were still in operation.

"Yes sir, Olin was the leader in what they say was the biggest flying squadron of the whole strike."

"Flying squadron," he said. "I've never liked that term. Do they know how military it sounds? No wonder Governor Blackwood sent in the National Guard."

"They didn't have an army, sir. The flying squadrons were just a line of rattle-trap cars and old trucks."

"The flying squadrons shut down some mills. That's good as a frontal assault on someone whose interest is violated."

"You know Olin's father worked as a handyman up at your lake cottage," I said, taking another angle.

"I know," McCane said. "And I also know my father gave the boy his first job here at Morgan Mill, but then Olin Campbell left to hide out up in Carlton when the union trouble started."

"With all due respect, Mr. McCane, it's against the law to fire them because they're in the union," I said and added, "besides, Campbell's one of Carlton Mill's most valued mechanics."

"I'm not firing anybody," McCane said, handing me the two sheets. "As far as I can see there's very little of value in that mill. Carlton kept it running until my father bought it, but just barely. You can read the balance sheets and see what I mean."

I was beginning to get a little mad, but was determined not to show it. McCane didn't simply want to renovate the mill. He wanted me to do his dirty work. He might not be willing to say "fire," but what was to guarantee folks would be hired back after the layoff, especially Olin Campbell? I'd never been placed in such a situation before and things were moving too fast to sort through where they would end up.

McCane turned, took two strides over to my desk and handed me the papers and then without saying anything else walked back into his office. I looked down at the papers one by one. The names were not written in McCane's hand and neither did he draw the map. Mr. McCane had to have someone else help him with both. Mr. Carlton? Mr. Bobo? I knew McCane's thin knowledge of the village wouldn't carry him very far.

In a minute McCane came back out. "Crocker, I'm not firing anybody. I'm not breaking any laws. I'm laying off people and moving them out so I can improve my property."

"Yes sir," I said.

"And one more thing before you go home. I hired you to balance my books," Mr. McCane said, "You leave the thinking to me."

| 2 |

Walking home that night I passed the mill and then I crossed the railroad tracks. I wandered on through the familiar town, but I didn't really see a thing. There could have been a hurricane blowing and I wouldn't have noticed. I was too angry, simply following gullies and crossing the streets when needed, moving along like a blind man or an idiot. The scene in the office with McCane handing me that list and map played out in my mind over and over, and in it I repeated the line I'd said about breaking the law like I was an actor in some movie, like I was Hoot Gibson delivering his lines in a Western. But I wasn't in a Western. I was a young man working in a mill office and McCane was my boss.

What would this mean to me? This was an expansion of my duties—dare I think responsibilities?—in the mill office. Mr. McCane had never asked me to carry out any task beyond keeping his books before that moment. I thought I knew what was expected of me, and I knew my response wasn't an appropriate one for a laborer to make to a boss. If your boss says jump, the answer should be how high, not why am I jumping? So what would this new request mean for me?

I was soon home and I probably shouldn't have, but I decided I'd keep the evictions to myself. I was uncertain about my own feelings and I wasn't ready to bring in another point of view. There was no doubt in my mind my wife Coleen would have one. She was even younger than I was and more impulsive, and she had plenty of opinions, especially concerning the way the bosses ran their mills.

I'd met Coleen, a red-headed Irish girl, when she was working downtown at the café, soon after I'd gone to work for George McCane. The first time I sat down she'd joked, "Can't you read? Booths are for two or more customers."

I'd come back with something as best I could on such short notice. "How do you know I'm not meeting a pretty girl?"

"If you're going to sit by yourself and eat, you need a stool at the counter where the coffee's closer."

I came back every night after that. I liked her sassy ways. She'd kept my cup full and I'd enjoyed the attention.

One thing led to another and after about a year Coleen and I got married. I wasn't even thirty years old back then, and Coleen was only twenty-four. We talked about starting a family right away. I thought my life was laid out the way it would be for a long time. I had the job in McCane's office and it would provide enough for us to live comfortably in town, so Coleen quit her waitressing, cooked, and kept the house, but the family didn't come. Instead the Depression came.

When I got home Coleen was sitting in the living room reading a magazine. All the windows were open, but it was still hot in the house. Coleen was pretty as a penny sitting in that easy chair with her legs crossed, her hair in a bob, wearing a blue print house dress open at the collar. One slipper nodded in a nervous way as she pumped her crossed leg and she cooled herself with a church fan. Her little dog Snowball sat in her lap. When I entered the room Coleen looked up and smiled.

I walked over and kissed her, then shuffled to the couch and flopped down like I was dead tired. Coleen inspected me and said, "McCane's working you too hard." When Coleen spoke Snowball raised his head, yawned, acknowledged me, and then curled his lip and let out a rattling little growl.

"Why doesn't that dog like me?" I asked.

"Snowball likes what he likes," she said.

I tried to change the subject. "What's for supper?"

"Too hot for anything but cornbread and buttermilk," Coleen said, putting down her magazine on the coffee table.

"Couldn't we have some chicken sometime besides Sunday dinner?"

"You sure are in a good mood," she said, getting up and disappearing into the kitchen.

"There's a lot going on down at work," I yelled, sitting up straighter.

"We're living on a cornbread budget," she said, handing me a glass and a spoon. "Go shoot a squirrel and I'll fry it."

I sat the glass down on the coffee table and picked up the issue of *Silver Screen* she'd been reading. It fell open to a spread on Loretta Young.

"Let's go see this movie *Clive of India* this weekend," I said. "Ronald Colman and Loretta Young."

"I'd rather have chicken than a movie," she said, sitting back down in the chair with Snowball on her lap.

"Well, if I shoot a squirrel we won't need any chicken."

"What is going on at work?" she asked. "What's McCane up to now?"

"He's just working on his boss man dreams," I said.

"Do those dreams include a raise for you?" she said.

"You know times are tight," I said.

"Don't you think a raise should come with your added work?"

"Should maybe, and will someday."

"I just want the best for you," she said.

"In five years I've come up to be what some might call McCane's right-hand man," I said, taking a spoon full of cornbread.

"Then he should pay you more," she said. "That's my only point."

I looked down at the magazine and ignored her last comment. I spread back out on the couch and closed my eyes, mulling over the day. Mr. McCane was right. I thought too much, but I also knew a lot when I was young, maybe even more than George McCane did. I thought back then that where you came from mattered a great deal more than I do today. I knew the McCane family history stretched back three generations in Morgan County, and I'm pretty sure he couldn't name my parents.

"How much do you know of the McCanes?" I finally asked, opening my eyes, deciding that if I wasn't going to talk about the present with Coleen I should at least talk about the past.

"I know enough," she said. "What should I know?"

"It's from my daddy I learned most of what I know," I said, and then I told Coleen how over Sunday dinner Daddy often repeated the beginnings of the McCane clan as if the details had come down to him straight out of the Bible, how he said the Good Book teaches us that a persecuted people need storied patriarchs and not everyone gets an Abraham, Isaac, or Jacob. 'We got a steady run of McCanes,' my daddy said, 'and in that rests both our blessing and our curse.'"

"They must have been rich a long time to have stories told about them," Coleen said.

"McCane's grandfather Josiah McCane died in 1895 at age fifty when he was run over by a wagon at his mill."

"He died young. What's he remembered for?" Coleen asked, petting the dog.

"He's remembered as the first man to get rich off cotton yarn in this cotton mill town."

"And George McCane's daddy?"

"Josiah left behind one ambitious son, George, and in time, George McCane begat three sons of his own," I continued, sounding like my daddy, repeating the details of the story I'd heard so many times. "His eldest son, Cyrus, attended Annapolis, but to his daddy's disappointment settled on a distant career in the Navy. The second son, Angus went away at sixteen to Sewanee, a tiny college in the hills of Tennessee, where the challenges of the family's cotton business could (and would) remain far from his mind for at least four years. Angus studied classics and mastered reading Roman poetry in the original Latin, a detail none of us on the mill hill cared much about. He did mostly whatever his family asked of him, and not much else. What separated him from us was that he had more choices. He had a college degree, even if it was in something useless and curious like Roman poetry."

"Doesn't Angus McCane live at Lake Whitney in the family compound?" Coleen asked, showing a little more interest.

"'Drinking moonshine and chasing whores,' that's what my daddy liked to say Angus McCane spent his time on."

"Sounds exhausting," Coleen said, yawning. "So with a brother like that how did George McCane, Jr. get where he is?"

"His daddy assigned him to a post in the Morgan Mill card room and then, a few months later," I explained, "the spinning room, erecting machines."

"Honey, this history is all very interesting, but I'm tired," Coleen finally said, yawning. "I'm going to bed."

"OK, I'll be in later," I said, happy to be left with my thoughts.

Coleen and the dog went back to the bedroom to go to bed and I stayed on the couch listening to the late summer sounds outside the open windows. Cicadas pulsed in the oaks and, closer in, crickets whispered in the shrubs. Once I got to know George McCane, Jr., I often wondered if there was an innate knowledge of societal ascent and passed-on privilege. Were they a common inheritance of the rich? My daddy seemed to have a knack for predicting the way things would go in the world and he wasn't rich, but I didn't. I didn't seem to have it. Things seemed to always creep up on me, like what had happened at the office that very day. That feeling of surprise was part of what I was trying to avoid thinking about.

I flashed back to McCane's announcement of the evictions. In my version of the scene McCane knew I was right and was ashamed and took the folder back and even apologized. But in reality I knew it didn't happen that way. It happened more strictly by the book, the way someone with knowledge of the mill business back then would expect it to unfold. I said, "It's against the law" once and I froze up like a slab of ice. I had worried once those words were out that McCane was going to fire me on the spot.

"It's like Mr. Roosevelt warned me," I said, aloud to the empty room. "I'm afraid of fear. That's how I came to get into this eviction mess."

| 3 |

The next morning Mr. McCane picked me up and we drove out to Carlton to oversee the eviction of the fourteen families. Though it was Saturday, Coleen didn't think it unusual when I left the house for work. Back then the common schedule included at least a half a day on Saturday, but what was a little unusual was that it was Labor Day weekend. I knew from experience that didn't mean very much to the mill owners. Looking back over my shoulder, I saw her standing at the door with a dish towel. I'll bet she was wondering why the boss man was picking me up in his big car though. "I'll try to be back in time for the parade downtown," I said, though I knew that was doubtful.

We didn't talk much as we drove. I thought about the parts of the McCane story I hadn't told Coleen the night before, how in late October not long after he made the deal to buy the mill, George McCane, Sr., and his wife died in a car wreck in town. There were two competing stories about the accident. In one, a local drunk runs a stop sign and plows into the Buick sedan. In the one my father favored, it was McCane himself who failed to yield and the accident killed two drunks headed in cross directions. Whatever the truth, the accident was big news, bigger really around Carlton than the mill changing hands or the stock market's crash.

Everybody speculated on whether the older brother, Cyrus, would quit the Navy and come home to run the company, or whether the drunk second son at the lake, Angus, would sober up and take the reins. "It's a shame them dying and all," my father had said when he heard the news, "and he sure will be missed in town by the people who depended on him." He added, "You mark my word, Little George" (what Daddy always called George McCane, Jr.) "will be the next president of the company. That will be the way it goes."

In a week George McCane, Jr., was the new Morgan Mills president. As the youngest of the three McCane boys, George McCane, Jr. was the one most would have considered least likely to take over the family business upon the untimely death of George McCane, Sr., but take over he did. The gravity of the times—the social turmoil, the growing economic and social crisis of the late 1920s—worked as a good mask for George McCane, Jr.'s, youth and insecurities. Once in a moment that was probably overstepping the line, I asked my boss if he was surprised his brothers hadn't made more of a play for the company when their father died. I remember that Navy officer Cyrus barely came home for the funeral, and Angus was drunk that week and entirely absent. All Mr. McCane said was, "I don't think about it much at all. It just is."

Daddy soon heard McCane was looking for someone good with numbers to be an office assistant. Daddy talked me into applying, and I did. McCane hired me on the spot. I took the job and I was working behind McCane's head bookkeeper. Until I became a man with his first job I didn't know much about the politics in town because I grew up on a mill hill outside of Morgan, in the village called Carlton. Though only ten miles from the McCane's Morgan Mill, Carlton ran to its own timepiece, one set ticking in a slower rhythm inherited from the farming people who first worked the outlying factory. We Crockers traced our line back to the American Revolution in that isolated corner of Morgan County. My father's father left the farm and rose to shift manager in the Carlton Mill and my mother's mother was the first teacher at the village elementary school, and so they knew everyone. My parents met in the mill and I grew up on A Street, right in the middle of the village, and all through childhood I had a front row seat to all the comings and goings at shift change every day. The whistle blew at four and the mill doors opened and everybody poured out through the main gate. Back then everybody wore hats and I remember how many different types the men wore. In the summer there were flat-rimmed skimmers and boaters and newsboy caps. In the winter there were fedoras, bowlers, and heavier caps. I also remember the men and women looked happy before the labor troubles and the hard times hit in the 1930s.

To help us out with the evictions I'd asked Elray and Oscar Ponder, two brawny loading dock boys, to meet us. They had pulled up in front of my house in the company truck, then followed us in McCane's Buick out of town.

When we neared Carlton we approached the mill league baseball field.

"Wasn't Olin Campbell a ball player?" McCane asked as we passed.

"He was an East Carolina league all-star pitcher," I said, "Some of the old-timers say he could have been the best who ever played in Carlton. Pretty good hitter too."

"Could have been?"

"Remember that fire that burned the Carlton warehouse in '29 just before y'all bought the mill? Olin went in after his cousin and burned his hand and arm—his right pitching hand—so bad he ended up losing two fingers."

"I remember reading about the fire. I don't remember reading about anybody injured."

"Olin's the kind of man who probably didn't even report it."

"Did he get the cousin out?"

"He was OK," I said. "Mr. Carlton lost 200 cotton bales."

"Hard to throw a curve ball with two fingers," McCane said. "But I'd expect it doesn't hurt his organizing skill. Probably helps him out. You know, the sympathy vote."

"Olin Campbell doesn't need anybody's sympathy," I said.

"You're a little sensitive about this, aren't you?"

I realized I had let my voice rise a little, and I laughed. "We were all close out there in Carlton."

"You live in Morgan now."

"I know I do now, but Carlton's where I was born and where my people are from."

"Did you ever play?"

"I was a manager one year. I had a good seat to see Campbell pitch."

I didn't explain to McCane how, unlike so many of my childhood friends, I didn't work in the mill. Instead I labored close by. My mama and daddy insisted I help on an uncle's farm just across the railroad tracks in a loose area of affiliated farmsteads we called New Canaan. The area was called New Canaan because all the folks who settled there were from Canaan, a river valley up in the mountains, the one flooded out by George McCane, Sr. for his Lake Whitney power project. After the lake filled up folks moved down from the hills and settled just outside of Carlton. I chopped cotton on my relatives' New Canaan farm fields in the summer and fed their chickens every morning before school rather than sweeping floors on second shift, or tying broken yarn together on a loom. I learned the value of a dollar by earning one, but I stayed clear of the year-round lint and July heat of the big Carlton Mill.

After high school I moved into Morgan with an aunt so I could ride the trolley back and forth to the nearby junior college where I completed a number of practical business courses but no degree. When the first opportunity presented itself, I moved back up to Carlton and acquired a job checking behind the main accountant in the mill office. I thought I'd go back to college someday and finish an associate's degree, but I never did, and in early October of '29 news spread quickly that George McCane, Sr., had bought the Carlton Mill, and my destiny would cross George Jr.'s desk soon after.

In the village of Carlton everybody had an opinion about the change in ownership. The owners up until then had been the Carlton family, and Carlton was their only mill. That mill was a shaky operation in the best of times and folks knew that the McCanes would shim it up. The factory had been built by Carlton in the 1880s on the site of an old iron works. Most folks liked Emory Carlton. He had made enough money out of the mill to live in Morgan on the same street as the McCanes and a few other mill owners, but he never put on airs when he was in the village on business. The day-to-day management fell on Harvey Bobo, the superintendant, and word was the McCanes would keep Mr. Bobo on.

McCane parked his car and the two dock boys walked up to the window on the driver's side. Mr. McCane handed the list to one Ponder boy and a street map to the other. "Y'all go on down the row, house by house. Be courteous but firm. I want 'em out by nightfall," he said.

"What if they ain't home?" Oscar said, staring at the list.

"What if they won't leave?" Elray added.

"Don't expect trouble," McCane said. "But if it comes, you just point down here and Crocker will go up to remind them who owns these houses."

"Nightfall?" I asked.

"They need to be out so we can start evaluating these structures first thing next week. We can't let it linger."

"Why don't you wait until after Labor Day? What would that hurt?"

The Ponders looked to me for direction and Mr. McCane noticed. He became more forceful in his orders. "Move 'em along, boys," he said. "Get this business underway."

We sat in Mr. McCane's Buick at end of Chestnut Street as the Ponder boys headed for the first house. I looked up the barren, dusty hill I knew so well at the parallel lines of shoddy mill shacks (house was too fancy a word for them) that made up what the former owner Mr. Carlton had named New Town when he'd had it hastily constructed in 1920 during the last boom time. The path leading up the hill was still dirt and the shacks had no underpinning.

There was nothing wrong with the idea of renovating the houses. In the years since their construction they had never been repainted and some of the windows had cardboard on them to keep the wind out. A single line of light poles snaked up the hill toward the mill, providing one raw electric wire to each house. There was little grass in the yards. For shade a line of chinaberry trees spread their bright green leaves.

I had been gone a few years but as a child I'd played on the broomsedge hill where those streets had been laid out. However, I didn't know all the people now living in the shacks. I did know how they'd feel when they answered the door. I wore a tie to work each day and I was far from them in income and interest, but my attitudes and values had been formed in the shadow of that mill. My daddy had kept his nose clean during the strikes and held on to his job. I also had an uncle, an aunt, and three cousins in the village. I imagine McCane knew somebody in my family would suffer from the layoffs.

The fourteen families McCane was asking to leave were all in New Town except for Olin Campbell. I figured McCane would deal with Campbell last, since his house was in the mill village proper, in a line of sturdy singles next to the best houses known as "Boss Line" where my mama and daddy still lived as well. I watched as the dock boys found each shack and knocked on the door. I imagined the women answering would look just like my aunt. They'd have their hair pulled back in buns. They'd be wearing cotton housedresses hanging down loosely like sacks. Each time they'd open a door there might be little barefoot boys and girls clinging to their dresses.

I could see from where we sat in the Buick that it didn't take much to clear everybody out. Most of the first thirteen families didn't have anything—a chair or two, a dresser, an old pie safe, beds, mattresses, a rickety table, and most of it went quick. Nobody fought back.

"Ma'am, is your husband home?" I imagined McCane's boys asking, looking past the doorframe to the business at hand.

"He's on the second shift up at the mill," the woman would say, the children clinging tighter to their mama's legs.

"Well, this is his last day," the dock boys might say. "Mr. McCane's closing the mill next week to renovate. He's also got work to do on these houses. Your husband's laid off until further notice and if you'll step back we'll move your furniture out for when he returns. Mr. McCane expects you off the hill by nightfall."

"Are you moving everybody out?" they probably asked.

"Well, not everybody since the renovations will be performed in shifts."

"Why are we first?"

"That's just the way it fell."

That would be it. I watched as the two dock boys moved furniture from the last of the line of houses into the dirt path in front of the shacks. The removals went fast with no hitches. Even the few men who were home kept silent once the dock boys pointed out McCane himself sitting in his dark Buick at the bottom of the hill.

After the dock boys finished with New Town, McCane cranked the car and followed the pickup up to Campbell's house in the Carlton village proper. Around noon he turned down Tenant Street and found the number on the porch's support post. Campbell's house was on a steep hill with a rock retaining wall holding back a short front yard bisected by a set of five steep wooden steps. There was a burgundy '29 Ford coupe on the street out front. "Campbell must have done all right with that union," McCane said. "He's driving."

McCane sent the dock boys up the steps. This time I thought they slinked a little like dogs as they mounted the porch. They rapped on the frame, and Olin answered. He wasn't more than fifteen feet above us. He was taller than both the Ponder boys, but stooped a little and gaunt. Even from the car I could see his cheeks were creased and what looked like a day's growth of stubble covered them, but it could have been a shadow. He was about thirty but he had been carrying a big burden for years. The union work mixed with the mill had made him old and worn like the shacks.

We could hear Campbell exchanging words with the dock boys and at first he was smiling, and then Elray pointed down to where we waited in the car just below and he wasn't smiling anymore. I rolled my window down and gave him a half-hearted wave.

Just as quick as the front door opened it closed, and the Ponder boys walked back down the steps and over to McCane's driver's side window.

"Campbell says you can't fire him," Oscar Ponder reported. "He says it's against the law."

McCane looked over at me but I didn't let on to anything. "What else did he say?" McCane asked.

"He asked to see the eviction papers. He said he wasn't going nowhere unless you had legal papers from the sheriff," Elray said.

"One of them men behind him said tell that boss man to go to hell," Oscar said, his voice gone squeaky with the excitement.

McCane's face flushed and he leaned back in the seat. "They told me to go to hell?" he said.

"Yes, sir, not Campbell, but that's what that other man said," Oscar confirmed.

"Crocker, you go up there and tell Campbell what kinda mess he's fixing to get into unless he's gone by sundown."

I didn't want to go up Campbell's steps, but I also didn't want to start into my newfound responsibilities in the company by disobeying a direct order from my boss. I opened the car door and walked slowly up and the Ponders followed. Once we'd made the porch I looked off in the distance. The village of Carlton is on a high rise and I could actually see a long way from that hill. Down below I could see the lights on in the mill, like a castle. I stood on the porch with the Ponder boys behind me and knocked on Campbell's door.

Campbell had a little smile on his face after he opened the door and saw it was someone he knew. "I heard he's laying off the whole village. I was hoping it was George McCane at the door, but I should have knowed he'd send somebody else to do the dirty part." He reached out and I shook his hand and with the missing index and middle fingers it made for an odd fit.

"We know Mr. McCane has his weaknesses," I said. "But I've found fairness to be one of his strengths."

"Fairness? You think throwing families out with no legal papers is fair?"

"He's remodeling the houses," I said. "Everybody has to go for a little while."

"So we're coming back?"

"I think that's Mr. McCane's hope, that he can reinstate as many as possible after the renovation."

"Ben, you know as well as I do that once he gets us out, we're gone for good."

"I have not heard him say that."

I glanced into the house and Campbell's wife and his three girls peeked out from the kitchen where she was making dinner. "Hello Hattie," I said, nodding in their direction. The two men sitting on a sofa in the tiny living room behind Campbell to his left ignored me. The shorter of the men still hadn't taken off his fancy fedora, though the taller one had removed his newsboy cap and put it in his lap out of politeness. The men were dressed in casual, dark suits and in the light of the living room's one bare bulb their faces looked haggard. Neither of them smiled.

Then the men rose from the sofa and edged up into the doorframe. One had a bad eye that crossed when he looked at me, then spoke without introducing himself, "You tell your bossman he's breaking the law."

"Ben, these are my colleagues. They've come down from Charlotte for the holiday weekend," Campbell said, nodding behind him. "Dan, John, this is Ben Crocker."

I stuck out my hand but neither man would shake. "Well, pleased to meet you anyway," I said. "I hope you are enjoying your time in Carlton."

"The big strike's settled over a year, Ben. McCane ought to let it rest," Campbell said.

"This is not about the strike," I said. "It's about improving the village." I thought I was probably lying. In the long-run throwing all those people out was all about the big strike and the union.

"I didn't expect you'd be the one serving it up cold like this," Campbell said after looking me over and glancing down the hill again.

"Why don't you just let these boys help you and your family vacate company property?"

"It's like I've already told these boys, McCane can't fire me for being in the union," Olin said. "And he sure can't throw us out without legal papers. It's against the government settlement."

"This house is his property last time I checked the deed," I said.

"The union says he can't throw them out and the President of the United States says he can't," the taller man said, joining Olin and the other one in the doorway.

"I agree with John here," Olin said. "We're staying if there is any hint that McCane is breaking the law. You tell him to come back with the sheriff. My rent's paid up. I don't have anything to fear."

"Mr. McCane would say Mr. Roosevelt doesn't run this mill, he does. Olin, you need to step aside and let these Ponder boys do their work."

"Mr. McCane might say that, but what would you say, Ben? You know the difference between right and wrong, between a rule book and playing sandlot." Olin stood his ground, and the two union men moved up behind him.

"You listen close," the tall man said. "Them boys ain't coming in and nobody's coming out. It's against the settlement."

"You heard 'em, Ben," Olin said. "You might as well get back to town and have supper."

"Come on, boys," I said to the Ponders as I stepped off the porch, "You're on the clock." We walked down the steps.

"Olin Campbell's got two big men up there with him," I said when I got back in the Buick. "And he's not going anywhere unless you draw up eviction papers and bring up the sheriff. They know the law."

"Union men?" McCane said.

"Maybe."

McCane flinched a little like he'd been stung. "You go back up there, Crocker," he said. "You get them out of my house."

20

"There's nothing we can do today, Mr. McCane," I said. "Let's just let Olin stew over Labor Day weekend. Maybe he'll come to his senses."

"Labor Day, hell," McCane said.

| 4 |

On the drive home McCane broke the silence. "So what do you think about all this, Crocker? Don't just sit there sulking."

"It's a big mess," I said.

"You can do better than that," McCane said. "Tell me something that will ease my mind."

"The Sunday before last I heard a preacher at the Methodist church blame all the troubles on the Yankees. He said there wouldn't be any call to reform our mills if it wasn't for them. He said there were public floggings of the union organizers in the strikes up at Gastonia in '29. The preacher said they got what they deserved, and that didn't set well with me."

"Blaming it on the Yankees doesn't ease my mind one bit either," McCane said. He let loose of the wheel of the Buick with one hand and swept it toward the expanse of cotton fields on both sides of the road we were driving down. "Look at these ruined fields, Crocker. You think somebody's going to make a living growing crops?"

"No sir. I'm not that stupid."

"Well, out there, that's the only alternative to factory work." After he spoke McCane sat silent for another moment waiting for me to say something and then started into a dissertation. "I am no lover of line work in a mill but there are abandoned tarpaper shacks out there as far as you can see in the distance. This is what they had, and now they enjoy running water, indoor plumbing, and a living wage." McCane gripped the wheel again, and smiled. "It was even worse where most of them come from up in the hills around Canaan."

"Everybody gets what they deserve in the end. We all pay for our sins one way or another," I said.

"Quite theological of you, Mr. Crocker, but you're avoiding the issue of whether you agree with me."

"If you're asking me if I'm on your team or off, then I'm on it, but I've got uncles and cousins in the union."

"We'll set them straight. Anybody can change."

"The night after the big strike ended I saw workers from all over the county gathered on the square marching behind an American flag," I said.

"That flag means the New Deal to them," McCane said. "To me it means a chance to vote that son-of-a-bitch Roosevelt out in '36."

"They held a rally to celebrate. I watched as they climbed in cars and drove out in every direction to all the other villages. They thought they'd won," I said.

"Won? You only win if you have a job, if you can make a living. You won, Crocker."

"They're my people," I said. "It's always complicated when your people are involved."

"Your people need to remember how good they've got it. Our people won't be living in tar paper shacks when we get the remodeling done. Our people won't sweat so much when they work. The economy's coming back. We'll make it through Roosevelt. There will be jobs and grits and fatback at the company store for our people. And Crocker, our people are your people."

"Let me know before you go home," McCane said when we got back to town, and then he walked into his office and closed the door.

I sat at my desk for an hour or so thinking about Coleen and her damn dog Snowball and how the dog ate at more regular hours than I did. I'd missed the noon meal and we'd miss the parade I promised to take her to and I wouldn't have anything until the evening. I looked at my pocket watch, then took up the company store's leather ledger book and flipped to the last column entered in the Morgan storekeeper's neat compact hand the day before. The last entry before the store had closed for the Labor Day holiday was an odd one. It showed someone paying $3.15 for nine gallons of molasses at 35 cents a gallon, $7.74 for 43 gallons of gas at 18 cents per gallon, a dozen oranges for 20 cents, and finally a cup of coffee for 10 cents. What was someone doing with so much molasses? Making illegal whiskey?

There were a million different ways you could break the law in Morgan County, from speeding to high crimes like murder or kidnapping. Where did George McCane's evictions fall on the scale of crimes, and where did I fall by way of association, my compliance in carrying out his orders? I never came up with any answers, but later in the afternoon on the other side of the frosted glass partition that separated us I heard McCane on the phone. He came back out and announced, "I know it's late but we're going back up to Carlton."

"Should I call the Ponders?"

"No, we're going to meet my brother. Angus will take care of this," McCane said.

We drove the same route back to Carlton and as we approached the Boss Line I could see a Ford pickup parked at the bottom of the hill. There were three men sitting on the front bench seat smoking with the windows down. We pulled up behind the truck and the driver opened the door and walked back to McCane's window.

McCane's brother Angus leaned in, swigging at a half pint pulled from his pocket. The McCane clan was mostly of medium height and weight, but Angus was built like a troll with stubby hands and short powerful legs and arms. I'd never seen him close up until that day and his face struck me as the oddest shade of red I'd ever seen, not beet-red like the face of a drunk, but with a ruddy complexion like strawberries not fully ripe, or rusty red calico cloth faded in the sun. His hair matched his hide and he kept it cropped short like a boxer and unlike the rest of us, he wore no hat or cap. His eyes were round like quarters, but with more luster. There was always something deep within or behind them that betrayed the impulse of those who locked gaze with him to dismiss him as a sot or a ne'er-do-well.

"Who is that with you?" McCane asked his brother.

"Friends I recruited."

"Angus, you know Ben Crocker," McCane said, gesturing toward the passenger seat.

"You want a pull?" Angus asked and gestured toward us both with the bottle.

"No thanks," McCane said.

"Oh come on, little brother," Angus said. "Share a little fellowship. It's Labor Day weekend. Nectar of the surrounding hills."

McCane took the bottle and turned it up for a shallow pull. "That's strong stuff," he said. "Crocker, you want a pull?"

I took the bottle and tilted it back and the moonshine burned down my throat. Angus would probably know where all those gallons of molasses were in use.

Angus leaned even deeper into the window. "Oh come on, Ben, that's not a pull, that's a swig."

"That'll do me," I said, "I'm drinking on an empty stomach." I handed the bottle back to McCane, who handed it to Angus who drained it with another long pull and tossed the bottle into the ditch behind him.

"What is it Campbell said to the Ponder boys?" Angus asked, wiping his mouth.

I spoke out of turn: "Campbell said what we're doing is illegal. He says we need legal papers."

Both McCane and his brother looked perplexed.

"What we're doing is illegal?" Angus said.

"Moving people from our own houses? When has that become illegal in America?" McCane added.

"Campbell wants to see papers."

"Sounds like our man Crocker has a soft spot for the continuity of textile mill culture," Angus said.

"It's understandable. Crocker grew up with Campbell," McCane said. "He knows him pretty well. He's a fan."

"Then why couldn't he talk some sense into him?" Angus asked.

"I can still try," I said. "I can come up here and see Campbell myself tomorrow."

Angus leaned with his elbows on the window frame. "Brother, you want us to do this or not? It's Saturday evening. I got some thirsty men waiting in the truck."

"Get him out," McCane said.

"Let's go, fellers," Angus sputtered through the truck's open window, and two men in slouch hats unfolded out the door on the other side. They wore denim overalls and their faces were all ridges and shadows under the greasy hat brims. They looked like ill-kept country drunks.

We scrabbled up the steps in single file with me taking up the rear. The burgundy Ford coupe was still parked on the dirt street. A single bulb lit up the front room of the house and the light leaked out the window. Angus rapped on the doorframe a couple of times with the butt of his open hand and Campbell answered. An oval scrap of yellow light fell on Angus's feet on the stoop as the door cracked open. Campbell surveyed the four of us and spoke to me, bypassing the other three men. "Ben, surprised to see you out so late. Hope Coleen ain't worried too much."

From where I stood on the top step I could see the two union men were still sitting on the sofa on one side of the room playing cards in their shirtsleeves. They glanced up to see who was at the door, then continued with their hand.

"Good evening," Angus said, tipping his hat. "I understand you needed some help clearing your belongings from our house."

"Mr. McCane," Campbell said.

Angus stepped into the doorframe and pushed into the living room and Olin backed away. Campbell's wife and kids peeked out from a cracked kitchen door. "Evening, Mam," Angus said, glancing their way.

"Close that damn door," Campbell spat, and the three heads quickly disappeared as the kitchen door slipped shut.

I stepped up on the porch and waited just outside the circle. The two drunks, one short and one tall, followed Angus into the front room like they'd done this all before. The three men huddled in Campbell's living room, and by the time the union men stood and approached the door they'd spread out in a line.

"Where's George McCane? In the car below?" Campbell asked.

"My brother sends his regards, and hopes you'll enjoy your vacation."

"You tell McCane it won't slow us down," the short union man said, putting on his fedora and stepping forward.

"'It?' What's 'it'?" Angus asked.

As the shorter man in the fedora edged closer to Angus the tall drunk pulled a billy club from his front pants pocket and slashed upward. The braided leather club snapped forward, hitting nothing but the union man's fedora brim as he leaned away. His hat flew off. This didn't seem to surprise the union man, who made no other sudden moves and caught himself before he stepped backward. The drunk pulled out a blue bandana and wiped his nose. "I don't think your friend here got Mr. McCane's point about the vacation," he said.

"I got the point," the man said, picking up his hat. He stepped back and the taller union man in the cap stepped forward and the second drunk pulled out a stub-nosed pistol. Everybody froze and seemed to pay closer attention. "I'm just not interested in your point."

"Hold on, I think we all understand just fine," Campbell said.

"Good," Angus said. "The Roman poet Horace said, 'Anger is a short madness.' I think we would all agree he was right even though he said it two thousand years ago."

"The only one mad is that drunk with the gun," Olin said. "Put that away and we can talk."

"Put that pistol away," Angus said and the drunk slipped the gun back in his pocket.

"It's against the law to throw them out for union organizing," the union man said. "And besides, you need legal papers to evict them."

"We don't need your legal opinions here," Angus said.

"Union?" the drunk asked.

"Union boys?" the other drunk with the billy club repeated, and flared his nostrils like a hound. "I wondered about that smell."

Campbell stepped forward and Angus reached for his own blackjack. I could see the dark leather handle and the strap twisted around Angus's right hand ready to emerge from the pocket. I stepped between them.

"What the hell?" Angus asked. "Ben, whose side are you on?"

"We can work this out without beating folks up," I said.

"It's a little late for that," the union man with bent fedora said. "Look what damage they've already done to my hat."

"Get the hell out of here," Angus said, easing his blackjack back down into his pocket. "Go wait in the car with George."

"Campbell, can you get out by tomorrow afternoon?" I asked.

"It's against the law," the taller union man said.

"Well, Campbell, if you think it's about the law, get yourself a damn lawyer," Angus said, smiling. "Take us to court, I'm sure your associates here know somebody. But, in the meantime haul your worthless shit to the sidewalk."

| 5 |

Coleen wasn't asleep yet when I got home but Snowball was. The dog snored in the chair where my wife always sat to read her magazines. He woke up and growled as I slipped in, and then Coleen walked in from the bedroom. She was a good-looking woman, glossy haired and slender. "Are you hungry?" she asked, not a bit surprised to see me.

"What you got left?"

"Some beans and a piece of chicken."

I sat down at the table and ate the leftovers straight from a pan off the back of the stove.

She sat down on the empty chair across from me. "What have you been doing?"

"Helping McCane with his figures," I said. "That, and helping with some of his union troubles."

"What sort of troubles?"

"Asking some workers up at Carlton to leave their houses while we renovate."

"Like who?"

"Some union workers is all. Olin Campbell and some others."

"My grandfather was in the union up in Lowell," Coleen said, "and my father joined up when we came down here. As his daughter I can tell you, hungry kids don't know nothing about a union. You tell George McCane he ought to leave those good people alone. They're trying to make a better life."

I gnawed the last gristle off the chicken leg. "Little good telling a McCane anything."

"You don't like him, why don't you quit?"

"Everybody's out of work. What good would it do to quit and add to the misery?"

"What's he like?" Coleen asked.

"McCane? You've met George McCane. You don't like him."

"No, not George McCane. Campbell."

"Campbell?"

"Yeah, Olin Campbell."

"You say his name like he's some sort of hero."

"He is a hero. He was a baseball star. He saved that boy from the fire. He drove that lead car over to Honea Path. People say he's not giving up even though everybody thinks it's over."

"What people?"

"The ones I see on the mill hill when I go see Mama and Daddy," Coleen said. "The ones I see when I go to the café."

"Not people like me, huh?"

"No, not like you," she said. "The ones that don't wear a tie."

We undressed and I put on my bedclothes like most nights, but then when I pulled back the bedcover I saw Coleen's naked shoulder. She smiled and rolled over on her side to cover herself with one arm. She could tell I was surprised. "I saw the way you looked at me when I came from the kitchen," she said. "Put the dog out in the living room before you get in bed."

When I was naked and settled in next to her she said, "I know I'm tough on you, but I don't mean to be. We've got a good life but we can't forget the others. Ever."

"You and Daddy won't let me," I said, and I pulled her close.

"Your daddy's always looked out for you, but you need to be looking out for him now."

"I know what's right and wrong," I said. "Remember, they taught us that in Vacation Bible School."

"It's not difficult knowing. We don't need Bible stories for that. It's as plain as the nose on your face."

"But sometimes it's difficult to know what to do even if you know the difference."

"Will you talk to me? Don't keep me in the dark except times like this," she said and reached over and cut out the light. Snowball scratched at the door, but we ignored him like he was just a ghost branch ticking at the outside of our temporary dreamy pleasure.

On Sunday morning I received an unexpected visit from my father. I'd just heard the Morgan Mill whistle in the distance when he rapped on the doorframe—so I knew it was 7 a.m. sharp. The whistle always blew, even on Sundays and holidays. I thought of it as a mournful sound, how all over town that whistle would remind the men, women, and children of how little work they had. I remember asking McCane why he didn't discontinue the whistle and he said it was important to carry on with regular things even if we had cut back. Those were hard times for all working people.

"What are you doing down in town?" I asked as Daddy walked up on the porch. He'd put on his old black suit coat over his tan work shirt. He always dressed up when he came to town.

"I hear you were up on the hill last night," Daddy said.

"News travels fast," I said.

Coleen walked out behind me. "Oh hello, Mr. Crocker," she said, wiping her hands on her dish towel. "You're looking sharp this morning. You want some coffee?"

"Yes, that would be good," he said, and Coleen went back for the cups.

"You should have stopped in to say hello," Daddy said.

"It wasn't social," I said. "You heard what happened?"

"Heard Little George is closing the mill."

"Only for a few months to do some remodeling."

"I heard McCane's remodeling houses in the village, not just the mill. And I heard they're starting next week."

Coleen came out with two cups of coffee. Snowball stood yapping behind the screen. She handed a cup of coffee to us each, keeping the dog inside with her foot against the door. "What brings you down from Carlton?" she asked. "There's no trouble with Mrs. Crocker I hope."

"No Coleen," Daddy said, "the trouble's with McCane."

"Trouble?"

"Ask your husband."

"Daddy," I said, "you're making a big deal of nothing."

"Ben, what's he talking about?"

"Ben helped workers in Carlton to leave last night."

"Throw them out?" Coleen said, trying to figure out what was going on.

"Him and the McCanes threw them out in the street," Daddy said, "And some of them was close to his own kin."

"Why didn't you tell me this?" Coleen asked. She was still standing in the threshold.

"I told you a little of it."

"And I expect it's a coincidence that the families Little George threw out last night are in the union?" Daddy said.

"Daddy," I said, "you know McCanes have always done things their own way."

"Big George McCane knew a lot about mill work," Daddy said. "Big George McCane even walked the floor to see how things were going. What does Little George do, sit in his office and pour over blueprints and make plans?"

"Have you heard whether Campbell got out or not?"

"Campbell's holed up in that house like it's the Alamo. I went over there and asked him about leaving and he said he wasn't going nowhere without a sheriff delivering proper papers."

"He'll find his way," I said. "He's a good worker. There's a job for him somewhere. He just needs to leave."

"Does McCane care there's kids up there who don't have enough food and no roof now?"

"Campbell was going to be in some trouble if he's not out today."

"I'd put my money on Olin taking care of himself and his own."

"We've got a mill to get back on line so those kids can eat."

"Son, whose side are you on?"

"You got me this job. You put me in the middle. What else am I supposed to do?"

"Stand up," he said.

"I'm standing so you'll have a job when all this is settled."

"I'm not going back into that mill when it fires up again," he said.

"What?"

"Community Cash is hiring in the meat department."

"Daddy, you've got seniority," I said. "You want to come in at the bottom in a grocery store?"

Coleen listened and finally spoke. "I can't stand behind this foolishness."

"You listen to your wife," Daddy said. "You need to stand up, boy. Stand up for yourself and for your people."

After Daddy left Coleen asked, "What is going on? You're not telling me everything."

"The trouble in Carlton wasn't as bad as Daddy made it sound," I said. "We've just got to get this behind us."

"There is no 'us.' It's you. Your daddy says you just helped the boss man throw families out of their own houses," she said. "There is no getting behind that."

| 6 |

The next morning, Labor Day, I answered a knock on the door and this time I was surprised to see Angus McCane standing there. He looked sober and stern, dressed in a pressed shirt. "Ben, my brother's been arrested up in Huntersville," he said. "I wouldn't be bothering you, but I need some money for bail." I wouldn't have been more surprised if he had told me George McCane was on Mars.

"How long's he been in jail?" is all I could come up with.

"They've held him overnight," Angus said.

We didn't talk much as we drove over to the mill. I was afraid to ask what had happened. I figured if Angus wanted me to know what his brother had done, he'd tell me. I had a big knot in my stomach and suddenly the whole Olin Campbell issue in Carlton didn't seem so important.

Why involve me if this affair? I'd have thought there was enough McCane money around not to have to pull in a bookkeeper like me. The intimacy of it all frightened me. I felt like I'd tripped on the top step of a dark staircase and I didn't know if there was a bottom.

"Get $300 out," Angus said as we pulled up out front of the office.

Once inside I twirled the round bronze dial in the middle of the big right door of the wall safe, then gave it a counter twirl, another twirl back in the other direction, and heard the tumblers click into place. Then I reached down and rotated the handle to slide to the bolts open. The smooth action of two heavy doors opening made little sound.

Once inside the safe, I negotiated another set of cast iron doors, but there was no lock to engage. Only a latch held them closed. These doors were painted with a large cardinal sitting on a nest on a blossoming dogwood branch with a banner of script—Morgan Manufacturing Company—flying above her. The graphic was nowhere else but on the interior of the safe. McCane told me once that the cardinal was his grandmother's favorite bird and his grandfather had had it painted there.

Behind the double doors we kept neat stacks of bills divided by denomination. Usually there was at least $3,000 in the safe, but because of the renovation of the Carlton Mill it held considerably more. I reached behind the cotton bag of silver dollars and pulled down a stack of crisp bills and counted out fifteen twenties for Mr. McCane's bail, but then before I closed the safe I counted off ten more. I'd need some money for a contingency fund, I thought to myself.

Contingency fund? For what? I didn't really know, but I tucked the $200 in my inside coat pocket anyway and I put the bail money in the front.

After I closed the safe I counted the bills again in my mind and let it wander to an incongruous image of George McCane in jail. My father always knew I had my own ambitions and he probably speculated this was why I'd end up doing McCane's bidding. "You like to talk too much," he said. "On the floor now you don't have time to talk. You yell at each other if you talk at all."

I closed the office and went back out to the car. "OK, let's head up to Huntersville," Angus said. I looked at him hard for the first time. I could tell he'd been drinking afterall. He wasn't drunk, but I could smell whiskey on him now that I was conscious to my surroundings. I also noticed he was in Mr. McCane's Buick. Angus drove too fast and I gripped the dashboard as we slipped a little going around a curve. As we approached the state line he said, "Ben, I'll bet you drive like an old lady."

"I would on a curvy road like this, Mr. McCane."

"If I don't speed they'll hang George before we get up there."

"Hang him?" I still had no idea why McCane was in jail.

"There's probably a pack of vigilantes gathered outside the jail by now," he said. "That family George drowned was from a valley near Huntersville called Canaan. You know, mountain people. They still believe in backwoods justice."

"A family drowned?" I said.

"I'll tell you about it as we drive up there. I need a beer. How about you?"

We parked in the dirt lot out front of the Flats, the juke joint, just past the state line. Angus went in. He brought out two bottles of beer. "An appetizer," he called them. He tried to give one to me, but I didn't take it. "Come on Ben, you aren't on the clock with me," Angus said, pushing the bottle my way. "And no more of this Mr. McCane formality. Call me Angus like the rest of the civilized world."

The drinking cheered him up considerably. As we drove he finally filled me in on his brother's predicament. He recounted the details of a boating accident that had happened on Sunday morning. He said his brother was out for a joy ride alone and had the boat up to speed when he saw another boat on the lake. "He said he throttled back but he saw the other boat roll in his heavy wake anyway. He saw bodies thrashing. He says there was nothing he could do," Angus said, taking a swig of beer.

The story Angus told was deeply troubling, and even more so, he recounted it as if his brother had drowned three muskrats tunneling into the dam.

"Were there were other folks in the boat or did everybody drown?" I asked, still trying to get clear what had happened.

"There was a women and a young girl and two other men."

"Sounds like they had a full boat. Are the woman and child and the men alright?"

"They'll cause some trouble down the line."

"Trouble?"

"They'll go after our money like yellow jackets after rotten plums."

My stomach felt even more uneasy, and I wasn't even drinking. Angus talked about those dead people like the story had no connection to him at all and it seemed callous and indifferent. I knew I probably needed to keep my mouth shut though, so I asked a series of simple automatic questions about his brother's situation. First I asked about the rescue. "As I understand it, George might have hesitated before he turned the boat around. By the time he got there those folks had gone under. But he did pick up the survivors and take them to the Lakeside Inn where they dried out," Angus said. "You know what the Romans said about bravery? 'Fortune favors the bold.' Good thing we already have our fortune before George got the reins of the company."

"Why did they arrest Mr. McCane?" I asked, and Angus continued: "In an hour the Huntersville police were there. I'd been asleep at the cottage and I missed it all. George says the wife of one of them that drowned went hysterical when she saw his boat coming back across the lake like he was going to run them over. George waited with the four survivors, but he waited on his boat at the end of the dock. Afterwards the sheriff talked to that woman—it was the drowned man's wife, named Novie Moreland."

"What about the bodies?"

"By the time I got over there they'd already brought in grappling hooks but didn't find anything. The deputy said the missing were a man named Martin, the Moreland boy, and his daddy. They're all still down there."

"So when did they arrest Mr. McCane?"

"Sheriff came back with a warrant and arrested him yesterday evening. We had dinner together at the cottage and George didn't say a word about the accident. I found out after I saw the commotion across the lake and went to check it out."

"This is terrible," I said.

"The cops told me if they had the bodies they'd charge George, and based on what the woman was saying, it sounds like that sheriff wants murder."

"Murder?"

"The goddamn sheriff had him arrested on a phony warrant for causing an accident so he could hold my brother until the stinking bodies came up." Angus gripped the wheel tighter and his face shook a little. I could tell he was very upset and I hoped he didn't accelerate and run off the curvy road. "They simply stopped by Judge Tucker's cottage. They had George right there in the judge's lakefront living room. 'Take him in,' the judge said like he was picking up a stray dog," Angus said. "He set bail at $300 because he figured George McCane wasn't going anywhere further than down the mountain, seeing we own half the county.

"I can't believe it," I said.

"I wouldn't worry. I'd say it's manslaughter at worst. You know what that daddy and his boy's names are? Fate Moreland and Fate Moreland, Jr. A New York novelist couldn't do better than that."

If Angus seemed unconcerned about the victims of the accident he certainly was concerned about his brother. We were silent for a few minutes as we drove into the mountains and finally Angus said, "I said not to worry but if George's luck fails it might be murder yet. I don't trust that sheriff or the solicitor or Judge Tucker. The charges might stand with George running back across the lake once a grand jury gets hold of it. Once that solicitor gets the local passions roused it might quickly become more difficult to detach someone even of George's social standing from such a predicament."

"Who are they?" I asked. I was having some trouble following the story.

"You mean the people involved? You want the short list of the clowns, or the ones with the peanuts waiting in the bleachers to see the big show?"

"The short list will do."

"First there's the sheriff with three missing bodies, then there's a local lawyer or two probably sees something to gain by trying a McCane, and there's the solicitor, and there's Judge Tucker who always had a grudge against our daddy. You name it. There's plenty of people up around the lake who would like to see the McCanes in a pinch."

"How did Mr. McCane get on the bad side of a Huntersville County judge?"

"Daddy ramrodded the lake through. It wasn't pretty. Daddy needed the power for his mill and so he spared no effort to acquire the five thousand acres of the Upper Canaan Valley. A few local boys saw it as their chance to get rich quick, but a few held out. I think Daddy had a number of spirited disagreements about what the land was worth and some of the good old boys, including Judge Tucker's daddy, lost. There's still hard feelings about the deal, although it was almost twenty years ago. The judge's daddy finally went along with the lake. That's how Judge Tucker got that nice lot down near the Lakeside Inn."

"Bystanders sitting in the bleachers?"

"You know, peckerwoods, hillbillies, cooters, grits," Angus said. "The unwashed hordes my granddaddy rose out of and only by the grace of God that we now rise above. They all hate us up there. We built the mills and drew the best of them down to the flatlands, and the ones that are left, they're ungrateful. They'll be standing around when we get up there. It's good we're springing George. If we waited until they found the bodies I believe it would take all the resources you and George could muster just to get my young brother out of jail."

"What about the drowned ones' families?" I asked. We'd hit a straight stretch and my hands were relaxed beside me and my eyes were straightforward.

"I wouldn't concern myself with them. They'll do alright. They got their church and their kinfolk."

"But what about Mr. McCane? What about the jail?"

"I'd say my brother has paddled himself a few hundred yards up Shit Creek."

Angus turned off for the lake and followed the winding road around to where we could see a big crowd. When we pulled up, there were four police cars parked along the narrow road, probably all that Hunter County had. Angus pulled the car behind them and we joined two dozen observers behind a ski rope the officers had stretched between two trees in front of the dock. A hundred yards out on the lake the police had hauled a floating dock and anchored it. Three men stood on the platform pulling heavy ropes.

"That's the best they can make out where the three of them went down," Angus said. "Those are grappling hooks they're working with. They'll bring something up."

The crowd was perched like buzzards at all the high points along the shore of the lake, waiting for something to come up.

Where was the regret in Angus McCane? Where was the sadness I'd expect from any human being over the death of not one but three people? I shook my head a little from side to side but thought better of displaying emotion when I realized Angus might detect on my face the depth of my discomfort.

While we were standing there one of the men hauled in his hook and from a hundred yards away I could see the apparatus was covered with ghostly black brush and sticks from the bottom. He untangled the snarl of rotting vegetation on the hook and cast it out once more into the lake.

"I'd say that my prurient rich neighbors have the best seats in the house," Angus said, pointing to five expensive powerboats anchored a safe distance away from the scene. "They'll let us know if they bring anything up. They'll probably starting honking their horns."

"That's disgusting," I said.

Angus laughed. "Don't have much of stomach for the drama of the classes, do you, Ben?"

"There are dead men out there in the lake," I said. "This is no high school play."

"Well, they won't have any peace until somebody snags 'em and brings 'em to shore. Might as well enjoy the natural spectacle."

"I don't profit from other people's suffering."

"You're missing it, Ben. There is a drama here and it's Greek. Over there is the chorus," he pointed to the crowd gathering behind the ski rope, "and over there in the motorboat sit Oedipus, Jocusta, and Creon, not even knowing what fates await them in act three."

"The only Greeks I know run the diner in town," I said.

"There I go, just a Sewanee classics major talking over your head."

"Oh, I got your joke," I said. "I had a year of freshman English at the junior college and we read *Oedipus Rex*."

"Well then, suffice it to say it's just a hell of a story we got developing here, Ben," Angus said.

One of the sheriff's deputies spotted Angus and walked over to speak. He was a lanky mountain boy with freckles. He wouldn't look Angus in the eyes. The whole time the deputy stared off toward the dock floating offshore.

"Mr. Angus McCane," he finally said, his face cocked toward the distance. "You got your brother outta jail yet?"

"We're headed that way now," McCane said. "Ben Crocker, this is the good deputy Abner Petty."

Deputy Petty turned and looked my face over for a second too long, as if he wanted to make sure he'd recognize me if he ever saw me in a police lineup. "This is the first McCane we ever had in the county jail." He continued as he turned from staring at me, "Well, the first besides Mr. Angus McCane here."

"Those boys out there have got a lot of rope," Angus said, changing the subject.

"It's deep. Could be seventy-five feet where they went down."

"What's next if the hooks don't catch something?"

"They'll bring up a diver from Charleston," he said. "The sheriff wants those bodies out of the lake."

"A diver? Who's paying for that?"

"We asked the family, but that lady said all their money's at the bottom of the lake. You want to make a contribution in your family's name? The church is taking donations."

"Crocker, you got any money with you?"

"Twenty dollars," I said, taking a bill out of the extra stash I'd brought beyond the money for the bail.

"Let's make it forty," Angus said. Angus took the twenty-dollar bill from me and pulled out another twenty of his own. "You put this money in that diver fund. You tell the sheriff the McCanes made a contribution and that we hope he finds his bodies."

"Oh, they'll float up," the deputy said. "They always do. You go on up there and get your brother out of jail."

I wanted to turn around and go home and get out while I could, but Angus was driving and I was stuck doing McCane's bidding. The rest of the way up to Huntersville the families of the dead kept appearing to me and I wondered who was caring for the wives and mothers of the two drowned men and I couldn't stop thinking about that little dead boy at the bottom of the lake.

One winter when I was a boy the millpond froze over and I walked out to test the ice. That afternoon after school Ricky Bishop followed me out on the frozen pond. Ricky had just moved in the month before and my daddy said the Bishops had lost a child to the Spanish flu. That's why they'd come up from Clinton. "They'd moved to Carlton to escape that shadow of that dead child hanging over them," Daddy had said.

Ricky and I walked out a few feet and stopped when the ice started to squeak. I stopped but Ricky walked on another dozen yards and the slick white sheet gave way and he plunged below. I turned and eased back to shore and got a stick, but I was afraid to go out on the ice far enough to use it to help Ricky. We were out at the brushy end of the pond, far from the street, so when I screamed nobody came.

Out on the pond Ricky tried twice to haul himself up out of the icy water. He never even glanced up at me. He kept his eyes focused on the icy edge like he was doing a last push-up on a fitness test at the school. He slipped once off the slick, watery edge and tried to heft himself up again right after. When he slipped the second time, he disappeared. I ran, a lot like I imagined George McCane had done, and by the time two men came back from finding help at the pool hall, Ricky had slipped under.

They had to leave him there under the ice for most of that afternoon until the fire department found a rowboat to break a trail out twenty yards. The pond wasn't that deep where Ricky drowned. They didn't need hooks to recover him. I've always wished Ricky would have looked my way before he passed under the ice. Maybe he could have told me what to do, or how to help more than I did.

In spite of Angus McCane's expectations of mountain hordes at the jail, there were no vigilantes when we arrived. The scene was peaceful. Angus dropped me off and said he'd be back in half an hour. "I'm going to see a man about a dog. I'll be down at the Hare & Hound," he said, driving off in his brother's Buick.

The jail was a cold, stone, two-story structure one block off Main Street and had not been upgraded in fifty years. It looked like something I'd expect to see in a frontier town. From the jail's front, there was a view of the mountains that cradled distant Lake Whitney and I paused there to gather in the scene before entering. Unlike most working in the Morgan Mills my origins were not in these mountains. My family had come into the Piedmont from the north, down the Great Wagon Road, much as McCane's had. We had been in Morgan since it was a district, starting out as Presbyterian farmers and then migrating to the mill when the land was played out. Somehow we'd switched to the Methodist Church. Being Methodist suited somebody better along the line.

I paid the $300 bail and the warden took me back to retrieve my boss. Mc-Cane did not seem distressed or unsettled by his situation in spite of his brother's dire predictions. When I walked up he was sitting alone, reading the daily paper. In his reading glasses he looked scholarly, like a monk in his cell. The most I could surmise in his face was the same detachment from the rabble I was accustomed to seeing in a man of his stature. As the jailer opened the door McCane began our conversation by asking about his brother. I told him that Angus had driven me up from Morgan in the Buick and had dropped me off. "He's down the block at a place he's familiar with, the Hare & Hound."

"The Hare & Hound? Well, it's good to know I haven't interrupted any of Angus's natural routines."

As we walked out I didn't have a very good feeling about things. As I stopped and looked out one more time at the lines of ridges marching west, I wondered what faith the Moreland family had, and how that would figure in to how they reacted. I don't know what Angus McCane's Roman poets would say about it, but the Bible states, "Vengeance is mine, sayeth the Lord," and up in the hills they know their Bible.

| 7 |

On Tuesday after the accident McCane's mind still seemed to be in the hills west of us and not on the working details at hand. I tried to get him to talk about Olin

Campbell and the house in Carlton he had yet to vacate. "I'll call the county sher-iff and we'll start eviction proceedings," I said. "We can have him out tomorrow —legally."

When I mentioned Campbell he flew into a rage and stormed around the office like a weak king under siege. When he finally spoke, his ire was directed strangely at the past, at some mysterious "relief" that a relative had told me had been sent down from the north in the early days of the strike the year before. "Cornmeal, salt pork, coffee, rice, and even potatoes," I related, in what I thought was passing shop gossip. "My cousin says the northern contacts even provided old clothes during the strike."

"Rice?" Mr. McCane said hours later as he stood above my desk and looked over a clipboard of invoices I'd asked him to review.

The detail was out of context and it took me a moment to track where his mind might have landed. At first I thought he was referring to the invoices and I tried to tally why and where Morgan Mills would be purchasing rice. Then I realized he was back on the union relief during the strike. "Yes sir, rice was among the provisions they sent. My cousin says it was appreciated for its novelty by the poorest of the lot."

"You call up the mill store at Carlton and tell them I want to know about anyone purchasing rice. I want to know of anyone who developed a taste for it, and I want Hester to call in his or her account. I want them collected on now."

I ignored the order to call Hester. It was my first small of act of insubordina-tion and it felt good not to do McCane's bidding for once. Early the next morn-ing I compounded my freedom by driving back to the lake. I went down to the loading dock to borrow the company pickup from the Ponder boys and when they asked me where I was going, I lied, told them I had some business in Carl-ton connected to the remodeling. Leaving Morgan, the Asheville road was foggy, and I crawled along the old turnpike even slower than usual. I almost missed the junction for the lake but recovered my bearings once I saw the railroad trestle appear ahead of me in the low clouds.

Driving around the lake it was impossible to see more than a few dozen yards, and some strange atmospheric effect bounced red lights around in the fog. The white cloud was shot through with swirling red highlights. The color enveloped me as if I were inside a cotton bale streaked with blood or, what's worse, I had caught the reflections off hell's fire itself.

As I neared my destination the fog finally burned away, and the lake opened up before me and offered a view of the various arms, coves, peninsulas, and hill-sides I had yet to pass. It's then that I saw my destination across the narrows of the lake, the search site. Red lights from the four Hunter County police cruisers parked along the edge of the road made a stain bleeding through the fog around me. As I approached the site I marveled at how twice as many people were somehow crowded behind the ski rope that remained strung between the road and the shore. The group gawked at the recovery activities on the lake, pressing against the taut ski line for a better view. Two or three other full families sat back from the shore on blankets. The women wore hats like it was church and the children ran around. The rescue workers had a full buffet of food laid out on the back of a flatbed truck. They wandered back and forth, picnicking on deviled eggs and fried chicken like it was a Sunday afternoon outing. One grown man was barefoot with no shirt and his trousers were damp below the knees from where he'd either fallen in or waded into the lake. He leaned on the flatbed and stuffed his face absently with a biscuit lathered in butter and jam.

Angus pressed against the line. He was eating a deviled egg and talking to his deputy buddy again. He waved the egg in the air and motioned for to me to come over.

"Can't stay away," he said. "Can you?"

While I stood there I heard a big explosion.

Angus could see my concern. "Dynamite," he said. "To raise the bodies."

"They'll bring 'em up," Deputy Petty said. "You'll see. They'll float up like bloated catfish."

"Like the saved rising on Judgment Day," Angus added, and Petty looked at him sideways.

"Petty, come on over here and get to work," another deputy called from the shore. Petty walked over, climbed in a small boat with another officer, and rowed out in the lake to drop more charges at various spots.

"That's where they think the three went down," Angus said, pointing out into the lake.

"Seems like it would be hard to keep from blowing yourself up," I said.

"They cut the fuses for two to three minutes," Angus explained and took a bite of egg as Petty rowed to a spot. His buddy dropped a charge and Petty rowed quickly away.

"Most of the charges consist of two or three sticks," Angus added. "Look at Petty working out on those oars."

Another charge went off. After a sharp crack, water and mud boiled up to the surface. Everybody's attention was focused on the lake.

Petty rowed back over to inspect the area. Nothing but fish surfaced with the explosion.

"This is some easy fishing," Angus joked. "Ben, you ought to go out there with a basket and collect some bass for your family. Your kids like fresh fish?"

"We don't have kids," I said. "It's just me and my wife."

"Well, maybe your wife would like some fish," Angus said. "I'll get Petty to pick up a few out there. George and me fished this lake for twenty years, but the fishing's never been this easy."

"What was your brother doing up here on Sunday?" I asked.

"He'd come up to get away I suspect," Angus said. "He uses this place as his retreat. You know George doesn't have the temperament for the hard decisions of leadership. Throwing those folks out took it out of him. You'd think he was the one that studied poetry, not me. He came up here to get away and look what found him. Three dead bodies."

"It is just like you said, a tragedy."

"I said it's a Greek tragedy, Ben. They're the worst kind because the gods are involved, and it's impossible to extract ourselves until they let us go."

"I wouldn't know much about that. I studied accounting."

"Oh, it's all accounting—on a universal scale."

"I'm not following you."

"The wheel turns—sometimes you're up and sometimes you're down—way down—like those bodies on the bottom of the lake."

Another explosion went off and Angus turned to watch. When no bodies appeared after two or three charges, Angus lost interest and went back to eating his deviled egg.

"Which one's Sheriff Orr?" I asked.

"High Sheriff Otis Orr? There he is," Angus said, pointing down toward the water. "He looks like General Black Jack Pershing standing over there, that is, if Black Jack had an insatiable taste for fried chicken."

The sheriff wore blue military trousers with a big yellow stripe down each leg and his sturdy bulk was contained in a starched blue cotton shirt with gold emblems on the shoulders. His shiny brimmed commander's hat rested on the fender of the truck while he ate his chicken leg.

"So he's out for Mr. McCane?" I asked.

"He's exerting a bunch of effort here," Angus said. "I'll bet he's blown the county's budget on this one recovery. So of course he'd like to get somebody prosecuted."

"Does he have any evidence to suggest there was a crime?"

"Only the widow's claim that George ran them over on purpose. Petty says she heard my brother yell at them about being trespassers as he came close in the boat."

"That doesn't sound like something Mr. McCane would do," I said.

"Does sound a little out of character. George doesn't like confrontations, much less raising his voice."

"I find it hard to believe he would have purposefully swamped that boat," I said. "I don't know what the sheriff is thinking."

"Well, look out there," Angus said, pointing to the raft offshore. "I think they hooked something."

Out on the raft two boys with grappling hooks pulled in an object big enough to be one of the three missing bodies. That much you could make out from the distance.

"Something's coming up," I said.

"Or somebody," Angus said.

Up out of the depths came a dark shadow flat against the gray surface of the lake behind it. The word spread quickly through the crowd and everybody pushed in hard on the rope. Petty headed over to the raft in his rowboat as one boy waved his hands and another boy reeled in what could be the first of the dead men.

The sheriff dropped his chicken leg and walked slowly to the dock, waved his arm, and motioned for Petty to come back and pick him up in the rowboat. Petty diverted from his course to the dock, where the sheriff climbed in. Petty took off again, headed for the raft offshore.

The boys wrestled what they'd hooked up on the raft and it lay there until the sheriff arrived. From this distance it was hard to make out if it was a body. The object looked like a dark, wet cotton sack. The two boys didn't want any part of it once they had it out of the water and I fought back the impulse to run, too. I stood by the rope as the boys walked to the far edge of the raft and waited for the sheriff to arrive. One of the boys held the line with the grappling hook still entangled with the mass. The sheriff pulled up alongside the raft, looked the catch over, and then had Petty paddle him back to shore.

Sheriff Orr stepped out on the dock and Petty followed behind. They both walked directly up the hill to where a small group of men were huddled near food on the flatbed. The sheriff said something to one of the men. He whispered to another one, and they told the two women behind them. I could hear the low wailing begin like metal that needed greasing.

Petty walked back with the sheriff then walked over to where I was standing with Angus McCane.

"It's Martin," Petty said.

"Looks like the sheriff's got him at least a manslaughter charge," Angus said.

I looked back up the hill and for the first time that I saw Olin Campbell was up there. He'd wrapped his arms around the woman the loudest wailing was coming from. I turned to say something to Angus but thought better of it. Olin and the two women turned with the rest of the party and walked away.

Once they had some distance up the hill Angus pointed and said, "I think that's Olin Campbell up there."

"I can't make out who else is with the women," I lied, "but you might be right. It might be Campbell."

"He's got the nerve," Angus said. "I ought to go up there and kick his ass."

"Olin will leave once the sheriff serves the papers."

"Campbell's got some nerve bucking us. I'll give him that."

"I hope that poor woman is not here when they bring up her husband and her son. Nobody needs to see that," I said.

"Ah, she'll get over it," Angus said. "She's got plenty of help."

"She'll need it all."

"I'm headed over to the Lakeside for a drink. Y'all want anything?" Angus asked.

"I'm fine," I said. "I need to get back to town."

"Ben, does my brother know you're up here watching this?"

"No," I said, "but I didn't think it could hurt."

"It's good you're here," Angus McCane said. "You heard folks say ignorance is bliss? Virgil said that in his *Georgics*. I don't usually cross swords with Virgil, but he was wrong. My brother doesn't seem concerned, but he should be. It's good we're looking out for him."

Back in Morgan I worked a few more hours. I didn't see George McCane again that day, not that I would have told him anything about the lake even if I had. I was unsettled as I headed home. As I walked I thought about the recovery of the first body, Martin's, and I was glad I was not around when they brought it ashore. It was better to remember the scene in the abstract and picture the body on the raft as simply a dark, distant shadow. I knew the family wouldn't have that luxury, and the crowd would push in to see the corpse once it was ashore, their fascination taking the upper hand. Then I thought about the grappling hook and couldn't help myself imagining the body entangled in the rope and tines of that instrument gripping deep and how the boys had turned their backs on it, seeing close-up the ghastly embrace of the hook once it performed its unfortunate task.

I walked out of my way a block or two so I could pass the Sanitary Café. I almost bumped into Coleen as I passed the front door. She was carrying two large grocery bags.

"What are you doing down here?" I asked.

"I went grocery shopping before I headed home," she said.

"Shopping?"

"They've hired me to help out with the cooking," she said.

"You're working?"

"I told you that the other night."

"You did?"

"You're not paying attention."

"I'm not, am I?"

"You look kind of bug-eyed," she said. "You look like you've seen a ghost."

"I did see a ghost."

"You must have walked by the old Carter mansion."

"Well, I didn't really see a ghost. I saw a dead body. That's close enough."

Coleen started listening more seriously. "A body? Let me take these bags on in. Then we can walk home and you can tell me all about it."

She went in the café. I hung around out front and looked up and down the street, no longer dirt like it used to be, but newly paved in the last year. Coleen came out and we started walking home.

"Where did you see a body?" She took my arm.

"Up at Lake Whitney."

"Lake Whitney, all the way up near Huntersville?"

"McCane had an accident," I said, wondering how much of the truth I should tell her.

"McCane's dead?"

"No, somebody died in an accident on the lake."

"That's why Angus McCane picked you up," she said.

"He took me up to help get his brother out jail."

"Why would he take you? Don't they have a lawyer? Oh, I forgot. You're George McCane's right hand man," she said.

Her sarcasm wasn't lost on me, and I nearly shut down and didn't finish the story. She saw her comment stung, and came as close to an apology as she often did. "I'm just kidding, honey. Go on. What happened at the lake?"

"Angus picked me up because I can get in the safe. They needed cash for bail."

"You call him by his first name?"

"He told me to," I said. "Is there anything wrong with that?"

"You are a big man. On first name basis with the boss's brother."

"He told me to."

"I learned in grammar school not to do everything somebody tells me to," she said. "Would you jump out of a window just because a McCane told you to?"

"You're making too big a deal out of this name thing."

"Well, it's a little too cozy feeling for me," Coleen said.

"He doesn't seem to mind and I don't either."

"Who died at the lake? A man?"

"There's not one, but three dead, from up in Canaan. Two men and a boy. They recovered one body and I was up there to see it."

"McCane killed them?"

"They drowned. Their rowboat was swamped. They all spilled out."

"So how was McCane involved?"

"His boat passed by. They charged him. Maybe manslaughter . . ."

"Nobody would kill three people in a boat on purpose."

"George McCane's not guilty. He'll be cleared. It was an accident. But they charged him anyway."

"How do you feel about being in the middle of all of this?"

"I don't like it," I said. We'd been walking along for five minutes and we were almost home. "But there's not much I can do about it."

"Oh yes there is. You can back your way out right now."

"How am I going to do that?"

"You got to watch out or you'll get dragged even deeper." Coleen tried to lighten things up a little. "How's our buddy Olin Campbell doing?" she asked.

Something about the comment made me mad and I slowed down. She glanced back but just kept walking.

"I don't like you thinking about Olin Campbell," I said.

"What business of yours is it who I think about?"

"And I certainly didn't like it knowing that we're throwing him out of his house."

"Throwing him out of his house?"

"We're remodeling fourteen houses and Olin's is one. He won't leave. We're evicting him this week. We'll have the sheriff draw up the papers."

"This is a real mess. This could turn into a storm of trouble. This could be a real gully washer."

"If he'd just leave there wouldn't be any trouble."

"So it's all Campbell's fault and not a bit of it rests on the McCanes?"

"The McCanes bought that mill and the houses that go with it. They can decide who comes and goes. They want Campbell out."

"The other night you said it wasn't just about the remodeling. Wasn't it also because of who signed up with the union?"

"Well, that's what I think, but I could be wrong. McCane never said that. I know he hates the union. What mill owner doesn't?"

"I'm telling you this won't be over when Olin Campbell and his family are out the door. This is just the beginning."

We turned onto our street then walked on down to the house. Coleen went up the steps first and opened the screen door. She glanced back at me standing on the ground, brooding. She held the door open and smiled. "Come on in," she said. "You've had a rough day. I'm sorry."

When I got in the kitchen I put down the bag and turned and Coleen was standing between the door and me. She smiled. I slipped forward and kissed her, just a little brushing kiss. She responded and didn't pull away.

"Where's Snowball?"

"Still in the backyard."

"He must not know you're home," I said. "Hasn't started yapping yet."

"Ben," she said. "Don't be jealous of Olin Campbell."

I kissed her again and pulled her close. "Hold your horses," she said. "Let me shut the door."

| 8 |

The next morning I went back to the lake. When I arrived Angus was already there and was one of maybe a hundred men pressing in tight against the rope barrier for a closer view. There was a steep, muddy bank where the lake had been the day before. They'd lowered the water level by twenty feet overnight.

"They posted a patrol last night in a boat to watch for the bodies," Angus said. "About 10:30 Petty and the boys rowed over to the dock and drank a few bottles of ale with me. The night was calm. Petty didn't watch real close after the ale, but nothing floated up."

"There's a diver?" I asked.

"Tanner and his daddy came in by train early afternoon yesterday. He's been down off and on since eight this morning," Angus said, recounting the early spectacle. "He actually arrived yesterday not long after you left. See those two lines?" Angus pointed and I saw two dark lines leaving shore. I traced them back to their source where an old man tended a compressor that hissed and wheezed on shore.

"One line keeps account of where he is down below, and one's to feed the diver air from the compressor. Petty told me that on the preliminary dive yesterday Tanner landed in a submerged treetop and fell out. After that he knew what he was up against and went to work in earnest. His dives have averaged about twenty minutes, after which he comes to surface for rest and to allow the work party to shift the raft. He covers about twenty-five to thirty square feet with each dive and the raft is shifted to give him new territory to explore. As he dives on one side of the raft the boys work grappling hooks on the other side, then they switch."

Out at the raft the boys hauled on lines attached to the same monstrous hooks that had brought up Martin the day before. I hoped that it would be the diver who found the father and son so that they could bring them up with a little dignity. Snagged on a hook like a carp is no way to rise to the surface your final time.

"He's coming up!" somebody along the rope said, and I leaned out and saw that those working the raft were indeed reeling in the diver's lines. The old man on the compressor even paused to watch. "Tanner told me he's been diving for thirty years down in Charleston," Angus said. "He says it's so cold at sixty feet in a mountain lake it chills you, even in that big suit and wool underdrawers."

After five minutes the awkward creature in the diving suit surfaced. At first all I could see was the huge, red metal helmet breaking the water. The black tubes surfaced beside it in a messy snarl. As they dragged the diver to the raft on his back his arms and legs trailed uselessly along. Once they hauled him out he flopped for a moment like a landed fish, then they got him sitting up. The boys dragging the bottom with the hooks let their ropes go slack while the others tended to the diver. Soon they stood him in full view before they removed his bell helmet. We were thirty yards away but even from that distance the diver looked like something from outer space, not Charleston. He looked like a Middle Ages knight in a suit of armor, or a man enclosed in a metal insect's body. The copper helmet had multiple small round ports to see out and the boys unscrewed it from the suit and sat it on the dock like a big boulder. At that distance Tanner's head looked tiny on top of the suit.

Sheriff Orr was already on the scene that morning, and he strutted along the rope line as we watched. He pushed back anybody who bulged out too far. A fat man with a notepad followed him along, pushing everyone out of the way so he could get closer and hear what the sheriff was hearing when the deputies came up to report on the diver's latest foray into the depths. "Well, boys," he said. "Nothing to report. That's it for Tanner."

"He's quitting?" the fat man asked, poised to take down whatever the sheriff said.

"He's hungry and cold. We got another diver on the way from Norfolk. He'll cover a little more territory after dinner."

Sheriff Orr passed us on the line and Angus said, "Hey, Sheriff, I think they got some fresh fried chicken over there."

Orr spun on his heel and faced us. He looked over Angus like he was assessing a car wreck, and then his gaze landed on me.

"Wearing a tie and white shirt like that," he said, "you must be somebody important, or at least think you are."

"Sheriff, this is Ben Crocker," Angus said.

I stuck out my hand, but the sheriff didn't take it.

"You're McCane's man," he said. "I've heard about you."

I was a little surprised and unnerved that he knew me. I sputtered out a response, "We're all sorry this accident occurred."

"I don't know how it is down in South Carolina, but up here nobody's family's so big and important they're beyond the reach of this state's law," Orr said.

The Lakeside Inn was a sophisticated hangout for the rich crowd the McCanes circulated among at the lake, but that day it was like a county fair and it put me in a bad mood. Tucked among a grove of mature, sheltering hemlocks the restaurant had a fieldstone patio out front with multicolored lanterns strung from limb to limb, lit up during the daylight hours. Even though it was past two when we arrived, the patio was crowded with outsiders come up to the lake like buzzards to watch the grim festivities. There were families, men in ties, and even farmers in overalls crowding five and six to the outside tables. The air hummed like a beehive with the news that one body had finally been found. We waded through the chattering hordes and I listened in on every table's speculation on when the other bodies would be recovered and what it could all mean to mill owner George McCane.

Angus knew the hostess who was seating people. She ushered us inside and we perched on two adjacent bar stools. I wasn't used to sitting up in public to be judged by those who saw you. At the Lakeside Inn I felt like I had indigestion before I'd even sat down.

We ordered simple ham sandwiches, tea for me, and of course a beer for Angus. Angus talked with the bartender as we waited for our food and I looked around. The crowd inside was more genteel than the country folk outside on the patio. Well-heeled women nibbled at salads at the windows looking out over the placid lake. They looked like window dressing, like they'd been there every day since creation.

"See those men?" Angus said when he finally turned back to me.

I looked over toward where McCane had nodded.

"The tall man is Clarence Riding, the solicitor," McCane said. "The short fat one's the reporter from the Huntersville paper who wrote the first story."

47

Riding's face was wire-thin and sharp-featured. He had eyes too small for his face, set like little black marbles close together. "Riding looks like he knows that reporter pretty good."

"Riding likes ink. When he busted Lakeside for serving hooch back in '29 they painted the story all over the Huntersville front page. They had a picture of Riding breaking up cases of perfectly good Scotch with an ax."

"You say Riding's got it out for Mr. McCane?"

"He's always had it out for any McCane. He's the one busted me for fighting. They say he wants dead bodies so he can bring murder charges to the grand jury."

"Murder? That sounds impossible."

"Maybe he believes what Fate Moreland's wife is telling him. That solicitor's a simpleton, and he's dangerous."

We'd almost finished our ham sandwiches and Angus had ordered his third beer, when Riding and the reporter passed close by our table as they were leaving. Angus burped loudly as Riding passed and the solicitor stopped abruptly.

"You'd think a McCane would have better manners than that, wouldn't you, Sweeny?"

The reporter didn't answer, but he did pause to see what would happen next.

"Riding, this here's Ben Crocker," Angus said. "He works for my brother. I figured you two ought to know each other."

I stuck out my hand. "Ben Crocker. Pleased to meet you."

Riding took my hand and gave it a quick shake.

"This word-slinger at least have the manners to pick up your dinner bill, Riding?" Angus growled.

"I pay for my own meals."

"I'm sure you do."

"You got a good story for tomorrow developing on the lake," Angus said, addressing the reporter. "They found the first body. You better get back out there or you'll miss something."

"We've got it covered, Mr. McCane," the reporter said.

After lunch, the second diver arrived, a German man from Norfolk named Klaus Everts. His dive suit was in four wooden crates on a flatbed truck. Once the German arrived he and his young son went to work in a hurry, donning his equipment behind the police barrier line. A new ripple of excitement went through the crowd and there was some scattered laughter when the small man, birdlike in his appearance, opened his crates and began assembling what looked like a string of big marshmallows. White resin chambers fit over his legs, body, and arms, attached at the joints with flexible gaskets.

One of the crates contained another compressor and separate coils of rope and breathing tube. The German set it up and the son spooled off enough of each to get out to the raft, and then instructed one of the deputies in the operation of the compressor. The German spoke with a thick accent, each sentence stippled with "der" and "das" and "doch," and more snickers circulated among the hundred or so locals listening with each sentence he spoke.

The sheriff was still marching along the line and stared down anyone who didn't look serious enough for the crime scene. Angus poked me in the side and said, "Orr's always had a riding crop up his ass. You wait and see. He'll get at George any way he can."

The boy helped his father slip on the puffy white legs, the body, and then the long narrow chambers meant for his arms. He had long black pinchers at the end of each that gave him a little visual kinship to Tanner's insect suit. The diver's perfectly round white helmet, now out of its own separate crate, sat beside him on the ground. The helmet was made of white resin too. The boy picked up the diving helmet, placed it over the diver's head, and screwed it on as a test, then screwed it off again. Unlike the metal suit that Tanner had worn, the German's apparatus had one large clear port on the front, and once he spun it into place we could see his narrow face outlined fully within.

The German stood up and took the helmet from the boy. Officer Petty brought the rowboat to shore and the marshmallow man climbed in awkwardly. The reporter quizzed the sheriff as Petty rowed the German out to the raft. "Why do you need a second diver?" he asked.

"There was no dissatisfaction with his work," Orr said. "Tanner needed to go home to fulfill other commitments. Members of the family of the drowned men wished that diving operations be continued, so the Norfolk diver was contacted."

The diver went to work from the raft, but not ten minutes after his white helmet disappeared below the lowered surface of the lake, the boys manning the grappling hooks snagged something. From our position along the rope we could see that they had brought up one long, dark mass, too heavy for the boys to pull onto the raft.

The two other boys manning the German's lines tugged on them to alert the diver, and he surfaced a few minutes later. They pulled him onto the raft and Petty rowed the sheriff out from shore. The sheriff pulled the rowboat alongside the raft and looked for a moment at the mass floating in the water. Then Petty rowed him back to shore.

The sheriff walked on burlap sacks up the bank, holding onto the rope. He walked straight over to the reporter who stood close enough to us for us to hear. "You get this in the paper so George McCane can read it. Out there's Mr.

Moreland and his boy," the sheriff said, visibly shaken. "The man's got a grip on the legs of his son's body, bringing to light the tragic evidence of how he had attempted to hold his son so that he might keep his head above water until rescue."

"Right up there's the widow of Fate Moreland," Angus said, and nodded up the bank toward where a group stood watching the recovery.

"Which one?" I asked.

"The pretty young one," Angus said.

Fate Moreland's widow stood above us, and Angus was right. Her youth and beauty were apparent even from that distance. "But isn't her dead husband over fifty?" I asked.

"She's easily about half his age," Angus said.

As the news went through the crowd that the bodies had been found I could hear the weeping of the women in the family begin like a dark chorus of frogs starting up in springtime out of nowhere. Mrs. Moreland turned and walked away, alone this day, not trailed by Olin Campbell.

All the men turned to watch the new widow depart, but not out of condolence. My gaze was a little too long and obvious. Her beauty was an open secret. I thought about how lucky that old man had been and how he got to lie down next to her every night. Angus was watching too and he said what I'd been thinking. "Look at her walking away. She fills out that summer dress," he said. "Hard to ignore that, no matter how dark the circumstances might be."

| 9 |

Angus called late Friday afternoon. "Ben," Angus said, "the Moreland family funeral's already been set for Saturday afternoon in a Baptist church up in Canaan. Martin will be buried nearby the same afternoon at Hebron Chapel. My brother should not attend these funerals, and I wouldn't encourage it even if he did want to, since they would probably draw and quarter him and leave his remains to be eaten by the bears."

"Is it necessary for someone to go?" I asked.

"This story is the biggest up here since our father built the lake. Remember what I said. It's like having a Greek tragedy in your own backyard. Attending to the rituals is always important."

"Why don't you go?"

"I don't attend funerals. I swore them off when my parents died. I always drink too much. I don't have the constitution for mourning the dead."

"What do you want from me?"

"I want you to represent the family. And I suggest you meet with our friend, the attorney Ripley Grier, on your way up. In situations like this, connections run deep. George fishes at the lake with Grier. It might be good to renew the acquaintance. I wouldn't go alone. Get one of those Ponder boys to drive you. I think their granddaddy's from near there. Ponder can work interference if they run at you. Don't mention any of this to George."

"Should I tell him you called?" I said, trying extract myself.

Angus didn't answer the question. "One more thing, Crocker. In the minds of people up there those Friday night evictions in Carlton have somehow become linked to George's accident on the lake. They're all saying George ran them over on purpose. They're saying it was our family's way of making clear we were still King of the Hill. It's important you correct the community's assessment of our family. I know I haven't done much for shining up the family's image, but I cannot stand by and see the memory of my father sullied in the press and in the minds of the locals. You feel the same way, I'm sure."

"Thank you," I said one more time, but Angus insisted on continuing.

"Ben, you're a church-going man, so I assume you know about the resurrection? By the time they get those three men in the ground they'll have been dead a week, well beyond the three days prescribed by the Biblical story. That won't make anyone up there very happy. I think you should show up there with sympathy offerings to ease their pain."

"Sympathy offerings?"

"You know, palm grease. Walking Around Bills. Calling cards. Call it what you want."

"I know those kind of people," I said. "They don't want your money."

"Don't you want to ease things a little on down the line?"

"You want me to use Mr. McCane's money to pay them off?"

"I have my own money. Meet me at the Flats tomorrow morning. Have Ponder honk when you arrive."

When Mr. McCane came into work I told him his brother had called anyway, but I did not convey any of the conversation's details. I did not tell him his brother wanted me to attend the funerals. I claimed I had work up at Carlton. He nodded his head and went in his office, and I was glad to be rid of him. I too wanted to disappear, so I plunged into my work for the rest of the day. The mill's black and white columns were easier to balance than George McCane's troubles that were building like a late summer storm in the mountains to our west. I wanted no part in fixing these troubles, but I feared the floodgates had been

51

opened, and I would not be able to stay out of the current, that what I wanted would be overtaken by what the McCanes needed.

Early next morning I left the office and walked over to the mill loading dock to meet Elray Ponder.

"Mr. Crocker, have you ever been to the beach?" Elray asked once we were in the truck.

"I drove to Columbia once for Mr. McCane, but that's as far east as I ever got."

"Is the beach far below Columbia?"

"About another hundred miles, I think. It depends on which beach you mean. You know there's a bunch of them."

"A hundred miles," he said, as if he had just been told about some place was in another galaxy.

"What's the farthest you've ever been from Morgan?"

"Asheville, and we're almost halfway there," Elray said and honked the horn.

Between the towns of Irby and Kendrick we had a moment of rare silence and it allowed me to do some thinking. I knew we'd arrive a few hours early in Huntersville and I had no solid plan but to go to the two funerals. I thought I might stop at the library and look over the coverage in the paper before proceeding. After that I'd try and call the lawyer and see if he was in.

After a few minutes Elray spoke again: "Oscar says he's going to Myrtle Beach. He says he's going down there to work as a lifeguard someday. Nothing against Mr. McCane, but Oscar says he's had it working on the dock at the mill. I think throwing those people out the other night got to him."

"Can he swim?"

"He says he's got the spring to learn. If he don't learn to swim he'll work in a hotel. He says people in a hotel don't stay long enough to get thrown out usually."

"What got him on to the lifeguarding and hotel work?"

"Oscar went to Greenville with the flying squadron during the strike and one of those northern union men was with him in the car. He was from New Jersey and he told Oscar about Atlantic City on the ride over—pretty girls, the boardwalk, swimming, and good money. In Atlantic City you can get a union job in a big hotel, he said. We don't have no place like that, do we Mr. Crocker?"

"We don't have Atlantic City, but we got Myrtle Beach," I said. "Oscar was with the flying squadron?"

"He rode with that big one that came out of Morgan. They say it was the biggest in the state."

"Wasn't he a little young?"

"That was two years ago. Oscar was fifteen. He'd been in the mill for two years by then."

"Was that the one organized by Olin Campbell?"

"That's the one. They had a big American flag on the lead truck. They were riding two cars back. Oscar says it was like a parade. They drove over to Greenville and called everyone out of the mill. That was a good two days. But then it was bad over in Honea Path, wasn't it?"

"I wouldn't go bragging about Oscar's union exploits too far and wide. That's not likely to help him move up."

"He never joined the union, so nobody has the paper on him. He sure had a good time riding to Greenville though. I'm glad he wasn't over in Honea Path. You know they killed a bunch over there. Those were bad times, weren't they?"

"Yes, Elray, those were bad times. And they weren't that long ago."

"Roosevelt sure let us down, didn't he?" Elray said, turning a little more serious.

"How so?"

"Roosevelt could have done something to make the bosses stay with the code. President Roosevelt was our fixer, and he let us down, didn't he?"

"It's a matter of opinion."

"Well, that's what Olin Campbell says."

"Olin Campbell got a bunch of folks in trouble."

"My mama wrote twenty letters to Roosevelt, and she says she'll never write again. She says those letters are piled up in an office somewhere and he never read a one. Somebody's using them to start fires in a stove in the White House."

A few minutes later we pulled into the Flats. "Honk the horn, Elray," I said. Elray honked and Angus opened the door and motioned for me to come inside.

We sat down in a booth and Angus pulled out two envelopes. "One for Martin and one for Moreland." Angus wrote a name on each envelope in his distinctive penmanship and pushed them toward me.

"I don't want to get involved this way."

"Just tell them we hope this gift will soften the blow of their tragic loss and that," Angus paused and considered his words carefully, "another gift will follow if the accident recedes as it should below the horizon of these legal proceedings."

"Another gift?" I raised my eyebrows.

"Another gift."

"What if the Martins or the Morelands throw the envelope back in my face and tell me to kiss their butts or take the money and refuse the terms?"

"That will be up to you."

"I'll just say that Angus McCane will enforce the details of what he considers a fairly drawn deal, money for your dead relatives."

Angus laughed a little and scratched his chin, surprised by my insolence. "I would prefer if you would keep our family name out of the conversation."

"Should I imply there might be legal action of our own?"

"Just put these in your pocket," he said and stood up, handing me the envelopes. "You want a beer for the road?"

"No, I just need to use the john," I said.

"Right there," he said.

Standing before the trough I opened the first of the envelopes, then the other. How much were the lives of three mountain men worth to help clear George McCane's name? There were five crisp twenty dollars in the first envelope marked Martin, but before I got a chance to look in the second someone came in the privy and I put the envelope back in my jacket pocket.

When I got back in the car Elray asked, "Why'd we stop here?"

"My business shouldn't be any of yours," I said.

"Yes, sir," he said and tooted the horn one more time as we left.

We were up the grade and into Saltilla in a half-hour, and fifty questions and ten miles later we were on the outskirts of downtown Huntersville.

"We're going to the library first, then I'm going to two funerals back up in the hills."

"Funerals?"

"You'll stay with the truck," I said. "I don't want you asking any more questions about what we're doing here. It's none of your affair. Turn here, the library's right down this street." Elray pulled the truck over and parked on the street out front.

"I like the library." He pronounced it "lie-berry." "We used to ride the trolley into Morgan to go. It looked just like this 'un. Then Oscar lost two books, and they never let us back in."

"Well, you just stay here with the truck," I said. I could tell he was disappointed when I told him he had to stay outside. I think he liked the idea of going into a foreign library forty miles from Morgan, doubling the ones he'd visited in comparison to his brother.

I got out of the truck and Elray did too. He leaned on the front of the Ford. I walked a few steps then turned and went back and handed him a nickel. "Go over there to that station and get you a Co-Cola. I'll be out in a half-hour."

Elray was right. The Huntersville Carnegie Free Library was just like the one in Morgan, only smaller. They must have drawn them from similar plans. The square stone building looked like a Greek temple covered in ivy. I mounted the single step out front, and upon entering asked the woman at the circulation desk about newspapers. She pointed me to a corner with an easy chair in front of the big windows. She said the current paper was spooled through an oak rod but I had to ask for out-of-date issues. They were piled on a shelf behind the counter.

"Are you reading about that rich man who killed that child and his daddy and the other man on the lake? That was a terrible tragedy," she said. As she handed over the papers she said, "I hope he gets what he deserves."

"And what does he deserve?" I said, smiling.

"They say he ran them over on purpose. He should go to the electric chair."

"What if it was an accident like it sounds here in the paper?"

"He'll have to live with it his whole life. That will be punishment enough."

"It sounds like you don't believe it though."

"No, I don't believe it was an accident. My boy was run off fishing at the lake one time. Run off by somebody like the McCanes in their fancy powerboat. The rich people lord over that lake like they own it."

"Ma'am, they do own it."

"Own the water that flows out of God's hills and down the Canaan Valley?" the librarian said. "Pishaw."

I sat down in the easy chair with the newspapers. Through the big window of the library I could see Elray leaning on the hood of the truck and nursing his soft drink as I read the week's worth of coverage in the *Huntersville Times* written by the reporter I'd met at the Lakeside Inn. On September seventh there was a summary story on A-1 about the accident on the lake. The details stayed close to what I'd seen myself, but I still fell victim to the reporter's florid prose and lurid descriptions of the lake's depths, the grappling hooks, the long hours after dark by the searchers committed to the effort. "The young lady, Mrs. Moreland, and her ten-year-old daughter, Floride, were saved from drowning," the reporter had written. "They were able to hold onto the overturned boat and kept from drowning until the powerboat owned by George McCane of Morgan, South Carolina, came back to their aid."

He went on to describe the scene: "Mrs. Moreland and her daughter were near collapse last night and were given medical attention at the Lakeside Inn. They were more composed this morning and were able to talk of the accident to solicitor Clarence Riding."

I stayed calm as I read, but the picture accompanying the article tore me up. There stood Mrs. Fate Moreland a day after the accident. Her hair was straight and unadorned in the black and white photo. Her eyes were deep pools of darkness as she stood alone and gazed out at the lake that still held her husband and child. She looked strong but hollow like a crude, stoneware pitcher emptied of its usual libations.

I folded the paper over and had to sit for a minute. I was affected in a way I had not been through Angus McCane's recounting of the accident. As I'd read about them the drownings became real and full of a common tragedy that I was not expecting. I felt like my sympathies were shifting a little and I didn't like that. I knew I could not let that happen. In a few hours I'd be listening to a preacher I didn't know committing these two Morelands to their eternal rest. Soon after I'd be talking with his wife, hoping to smooth some of the grief and anger with Angus's blood money. This was far from over and I would be in the middle until it was. Like it or not, I had taken on the role of McCane's fixer, the way the workers had seen Roosevelt as theirs. I knew disappointing my boss wasn't an option, but even the librarian was against him.

I gathered myself to read further. I picked up the next paper in the pile. A short article the next day on A-1 reported how the Huntersville chief of police had asked the Charleston police department to send a diver. Another story on the tenth talked about the dynamite and confirmed what I had witnessed, that they'd found the body of Thomas Martin. On the eleventh a final story reported the scene I'd witnessed with the two divers and how they'd searched for the bodies of the two missing Morelands in the deepest part of the lake in sixty feet of water "near the spot where the boat had sunk." The paper reported how "the bodies of Mr. Moreland and his ten-year-old son, Fate, Jr., were found wrapped in each other's arms," and how "they were located with grappling irons."

When I finished the series of articles I was surprised, and admittedly pleased, that the story only mentioned Mr. McCane one time. The last story ended with the simple declaration, "The bodies were sent to Huntersville for burial preparation."

I'm not heartless. Not now, and not back then when I was closer to my own origins. The vicissitudes, accidents, and actions of life often lead one into dark, unexpected places, no matter whether you are rich or poor. The actions on that Saturday morning by my employer George McCane caused ripples through mountain generations that I cannot track and don't care to.

Ripley Grier sat in a burgundy leather armchair with a high back in an office behind the Huntersville courthouse downtown, his full figure surrounded by a set of glass-fronted, oak bookcases that covered the entire wall. There were framed prints on the walls of old-time judges in powdered wigs. In this formal setting I expected us to talk in a sort of gentleman's code about legal outcomes, but Grier was forthright and even a little aggressive, and I could see he was deeply agitated and maybe a little irritated by the whole affair.

"You tell Angus McCane he's lucky his brother wasn't lynched," Grier said. "From what I've heard George McCane could be killed by somebody's daddy or granddaddy on that road to the lake."

"It was an accident as we understand it."

"I'm not just talking about that messy affair on the lake. We don't know yet what will come of that."

"Will there be more to it?"

"The grand jury convenes next week and they'll do their investigation."

"What else is there?"

"What about the Campbells and their boy Olin? Olin's granddaddy hates the mills and what he thinks they've done to the people down there in Carlton. He's a well-known hothead and I've had to deal with him several times. George acts as if his actions down there have no ramifications up here. He can't be that dumb. Carlton and Huntersville are communities connected by deep blood lines."

"Mr. McCane terminated Mr. Campbell from his position at the Carlton Mill. That's company business."

"I don't care whether he fired him for being in the union or stealing cloth. It's gonna be everybody's business if Campbell or his granddaddy takes a potshot at George or his brother on the Asheville road."

"A man of Mr. McCane's social standing…" I said, but Grier cut me off before I could finish.

"This is the mountains, Mr. Crocker," Grier said. "The McCanes' social standing doesn't count for much once you get past that honky-tonk at the state line."

As we headed to the funeral I watched the passing scenery on the road out of Huntersville. Ponder drove a couple of miles on the main Morgan/Asheville road and I put Elray off every time he tried to ask a question. "Turn here," I finally said, and he turned just as we'd passed a sign that said, "JUMP OFF ROCK."

I'd been to Jump Off Rock a time or two, and I knew its story. For a hundred years the Huntersville landmark stood shrouded in the kind of legend that clings to high exposed places in the mountains, a spot where locals claim a Cherokee maiden had jumped to her death after her lover had been killed in the Battle of Horseshoe Bend by the Creeks. The long road to Jump Off Rock crawls into the sky on a dozen tight switchbacks, and the spot had become quite a tourist attraction in the 1920s. The flat expanse of dark-stained granite tilted downward to the east. Before the wrought iron handrail was built it could just as easily been Fall Off Rock.

But this was no tourist trip, and though Elray mentioned how he'd like to see the rock, we turned in the opposite direction up a dirt track through the lower Canaan Valley. The way got darker and narrower with every mile off the main highway. A bold creek kept close to our side the whole way. We finally came around a tight corner and another fork in the road and another creek came in from the right. In the fork there was a white-shingled church on the hill with a small, square steeple. A pod of people in their Sunday best stood out front, and several turned to look at us as we drove up. All the church's windows were thrown open, and as we drew close I could hear that the singing had already started, the hopeful hymn "Amazing Grace." It was being sung in the old shape note style that had originated in the flatlands but infiltrated many mountain churches in earlier days. On each side of the road the bubbling creeks competed with the hymn for attention.

As Elray parked on the narrow shoulder I was glad we were in the old blue company Ford truck and not a sedan. There were only a handful of other vehicles. Most of the mourners must have walked from the surrounding small farms up and down the holler that opened up beyond the church. One of the cars looked familiar, and as I mounted the stone steps to the church I realized that it was the burgundy Ford coupe I'd seen out front of Olin Campbell's house in Carlton on Saturday night. After I'd taken one of the last seats at the rear of the small sanctuary I spotted what was unmistakingly the back of Campbell's head. Campbell sat in the family section next to the widow. What was his connection to the Morelands? He'd seemed intimate with them at the lake and now here he was, cheek and jowl with Mrs. Moreland at her husband's funeral. Looking to my left I saw that one of the union men who had backed Campbell in Carlton was there too. The car out front must have been his. He was the tall man with the bad eye, and he sat three rows over and had already glanced my way when I sat down.

The two raw wood caskets rested on sawhorses up front. One box was full sized, and the other was a little smaller. Here lies Fate Moreland and his son, Fate, Jr., I thought as I stared at the boxes waiting for the last hymn to wind down and the preaching to begin.

They had closed and nailed shut the casket tops, unusual for a Baptist funeral. Four days in the lake had probably done some damage to both man and boy. Everybody would be thinking about that as they stared up front. Theirs was still a complex, old-timey faith compared to the ones back in Carlton and Morgan I was familiar with. Angus McCane had pointed out how important it was to get the bodies into the ground in three days, mimicking the resurrection of Christ, and they'd missed that by forty-eight hours. "Look for everyone to be a little edgy," I remembered Angus had said.

The two raw wood caskets looked white the way the light from the open windows fell on them. Large bouquets of late season wildflowers—Joe Pye weed and white asters—sat in Mason jars in front, but there was little else as far as funeral decoration. The flowers added a subtle aroma to the close quarters of the sanctuary, but after sorting through the complex smells I realized it wasn't just the flowers. The bodies packed in tight, all mingled together, made for the complexity.

Something ominous hung about the mountain preacher standing tall and thin behind the dead. He was dressed a little more informally than I would have expected. Instead of a shiny black funeral suit he wore a gray and white pinstriped one with a blue striped tie, as if he'd been called away from a gangster social. He stood half hidden by the caskets and the pulpit, and he leaned on his spindly forearms as the last of the hymn bounced around the small sanctuary and a moment of silence finally engulfed us.

After a beat or two the preacher straightened up and began his sermon. It was one of the finest sermons I'd ever heard. I was expecting good, honest country preaching to go on for hours, but this man offered up a brief, complex reverie on early death and the pleasures of heaven. He ended with asking for forgiveness on the just and unjust. He wasn't a shouter. He kept his voice in range and kept eye contact with the family on the front row. I couldn't tell from what he said if he knew the dead or not. I took it he was a circuit rider, and so maybe he was new to the area. Whatever the case, I was moved to tears as he quoted from Matthew about the poor in spirit. He blessed the family and friends, and blessed the two caskets, and then asked for another hymn as the family walked out.

The pallbearers carried the caskets through the front door and the preacher and the family followed. I fixed my gaze on the woman sobbing in front, Mrs. Fate Moreland. She walked slowly with her head down. Dressed in her mourning clothes she was even prettier than before. She wore a dark blue dress and clutched a young girl to her side. The girl I took to be Floride, the surviving daughter. Mrs. Moreland looked even younger up close than she had at the lake. She couldn't have been more than thirty years old. Blond and heavily freckled, she had her fair hair pulled up in a bun and her beauty warmed me up from rows away. She was radiant, a full figure in the blue pattern dress, and I was surprised by a flush of desire in the widow's presence. This feeling hit me so strong I almost had to sit down. Instead I pressed against the pew in front of me and tried to coax the feeling to pass.

Olin Campbell and his wife fell in behind the widow and walked mournfully out of the church. As Campbell passed he glanced over my way and put a quick end to my little fantasy. There was more than a hint of surprise in his face when he recognized me. I tilted my head in a nod to acknowledge him when we made eye contact.

Then I remembered the envelopes I'd brought up from Morgan. They were snug in the breast pocket of my jacket, and it was when I made eye contact with Campbell that the thought of them stirred in me for the first time since that morning. After seeing Mrs. Moreland I knew that I wouldn't deliver the money. There would be no way to separate her from the family and make my little speech.

As soon as the row beside me cleared, I filed out of the church. The procession was already snaking up the holler to the nearby cemetery where the man and boy would be laid to rest, but I didn't follow. I paused next to a maple in front of the church, reached inside my coat and pulled out Angus McCane's money. I opened the envelope marked Martin again and counted the five twenty-dollar bills inside. I opened the one marked Morelands, and counted. It had six twenty-dollar bills. "That cheap son of a bitch. He discounted the boy," I said to myself. After that, I stuffed the opened stationary envelopes in the outside pocket of my suit coat and headed down the steps to the truck where Elray waited. "Take me back to Morgan. My business here is over," I said.

| 10 |

On Sunday I didn't go to church. I figured I'd heard enough preaching for one week at the funeral. I told Coleen I wasn't feeling well and stayed around the house until she returned home a little after noon. I still wasn't telling Coleen enough, but she hadn't stopped asking.

I was sitting on the porch when she returned. As she mounted the front steps she glanced around at the distance and said, "I never noticed you can see the mill stack from here."

"There's no place in this town you can't see it from," I said.

"You might say it kind of lords over us wherever we are," Coleen said.

"A dark cloud chasing us when the wind shifts," I said, knowing how melodramatic it sounded the second it was out of my mouth.

"What's brought this dark mood on?" Coleen asked. "That stomach bug?"

"Nothing," I said and put my feet up on the rail.

Coleen sat down next to me. I could hear Snowball scratching at the screen door behind us and Coleen got up and let the dog out onto the porch. She patted at her white skirt and the dog jumped up. "Have you extracted yourself from McCane's troubles yet?"

"Clear as a bell," I said. "All that's hanging over me now is this renovation project out at Carlton."

"Wouldn't it be great if you could quit someday," she said. "We could move some place far off like Charlotte or Charleston."

"You sound like Ponder. He said his brother wants to move to Myrtle Beach."

"What's so funny about that?"

"What do you know about the beach?"

"I been—well, I almost been. My rich uncle drove me and my cousin to Charleston for high school graduation and we stood on the Battery and looked out at the ocean, out past Fort Sumter."

"Why didn't you get to the beach?"

"He took us down and back from Morgan in one long day. We were only in Charleston for two hours. He isn't really rich, just tight. He wouldn't pay for a hotel room. He said that the trip down was our present."

"What's the point of that?"

"I don't know, but it caught me on fire to travel."

"Who would keep care of Snowball?" I thought about reaching out to pet the dog, but then thought better of it.

"We'd take Snowball with us."

"It takes money to travel. Something we don't have."

"We could still go places. You could work for somebody else."

"You dream us a path out of here," I said.

"Well, one of us has got to dream."

"Right now I'm dreaming of Sunday dinner."

I went into the office after eating lunch and thought I could catch up on some work. I opened the ledger book, but instead of working with the numbers I thought about the day before. I'd decided that I'd lie to Mr. McCane and say I just couldn't stay away if he heard through the grapevine I'd been at the funeral. After I'd sat at the desk an hour and done no work I got up and drove myself back up to Huntersville and retraced my way out to the Jump Off Rock turnoff and then down the road to the church in Lower Canaan Valley. When I pulled up out front the services had been over maybe an hour, but there was still a boy sweeping the churchyard, so I rolled the window down.

"Boy, you know where the Morelands live?"

"The dead Morelands?"

"That's the ones."

"There's two houses down at the end of the holler. Theirs is right before the road peters out."

"You don't know his widow's name, do you?"

"The widow? Miss Novie Moreland."

I drove on the rutted red clay road through stubble cornfields where the mountain creek had widened after dropping down off the backside of the steep sheltering ridge. The hill farmers had already harvested and the stalks were cut down and bundled away in pole barns on the field edges for the winter's fodder for livestock. A few crows worked what was left of the crop on the ground and a buzzard circled above.

I crept along over the ruts and wondered what I would say if she came to the door. I wondered what Novie was short for. Was it Novinia? Or Novilinda? Or maybe even November?

I guess I was a little surprised when the houses weren't the tumbledown shacks I expected. At the end of the road there were two matching homesteads on each side, two-story farmhouses a century or so old, in need of paint, but in good shape. I pulled over to the right. A woman in her Sunday best was standing in the shadows on the porch, and it looked like she was watering a dark wisteria vine growing up a trellis.

"Mrs. Moreland," I yelled from the road as I stepped out of the car, taking off my hat and holding it in my hands.

"Yes?" she said.

"I'm William Kirby and I work for Prudential Insurance." Until that moment I had no idea what I would say, and I was a little surprised at what came out. There was a Kirby worked as a mechanic at Morgan Mill. It was the first name that came to me.

"Insurance? On a Sunday?" she said.

"Well, there's work to do every day," I said. "Sometimes it runs over to the Lord's Day."

I'd expected her to look sad like she had in the newspaper picture, but there was something about standing in that cave of darkness that made things so much worse. She was a shade bled of all color. I almost couldn't even make out her form. "I'm not trying to sell, Ma'am," I said. "I drove up here from Greenville on orders from my boss. Your husband, the late Mr. Moreland, had a small policy and I have a settlement here for you." I held up the envelope.

"Settlement? To settle what?"

"Ma'am, may I come up on the porch?"

Then Novie Moreland finally put down the watering can and patted her pretty dress and walked to the front edge of the steps and into the light. Her blond hair was down and the sun lit it up like a fireworks display. Her dress was dark for mourning still but it was open at the neck and it accented her young figure. I could not help it, but I paused and stared longer than I should have at her there above me on the porch in the afternoon sun.

"Well, come on up, Mr. Kirby," she said. "I don't bite."

When I mounted the steps and stood before her she stepped back into the shadows to keep the right amount of space between us. I still didn't know exactly where I was going with this charade. She looked me over and said, "From Greenville, you say?"

"Yes, Ma'am." My eyes adjusted to the shade and up close she was even more beautiful than I had originally perceived. She looked a little like a scrubbed clean, mountain version of Jean Harlow.

"I grew up in Greenville, outside of town. My daddy's a sheriff's deputy down there."

"Well, isn't that a coincidence," I said, my confidence lagging noticeably the more I stole glances at her and the thinner my story got. I couldn't help but wonder what had brought her up from Greenville. In her present state she was a sad, young widow woman in her full bloom. How she had married a man in his fifties was hard to imagine.

"Your husband was one lucky man," I said. Novie Moreland seemed a little embarrassed that I would bring up her relationship with her late husband but I continued, "and it's good that he saw after you from even beyond the grave."

"He was a good man, and a good father," she said, dabbing back tears with her sleeve.

"Yes, I have heard that around."

"When you walked up you said you have a policy?"

"It's a small policy, but it has this payoff of 120 dollars." I handed her the envelope.

"Do you have the policy as well?" She looked inside, and then she closed the envelope up again. "I can't take this cash."

"Please," I said. "It's a settlement . . ."

"Then why isn't there a check?"

"I know it's a small amount . . ."

"Mr. Kirby, I don't understand," Novie Moreland said and backed off farther into the shadows. "Are you sure you are from the insurance company?"

"Oh yes, Ma'am. I know this seems a little irregular with me coming up on a Sunday, but the company now pays out all its settlements in cash to make things easier on the beneficiaries."

"How so?"

"You know, with the bank failures and all," I said, getting deeper and deeper into the ruse. "It might be difficult for someone to find a bank, or to cash a check if there are many failures in your area. How is your area? The banks, I mean."

"I'm not sure I could tell you. We generally had little business with banks before Fate died."

"Yes, Ma'am," I said. "A real tragedy that accident."

I paused and took a deep breath. "It's the first in a series of payouts," I said.

"Payout?" she said. "Who is paying?"

"The company. We offer it as a gift in your time of grief," I said.

"A gift? I thought you said it was a policy that Fate took out." She took another step back and held the envelope loosely in both hands.

"There's a good payout in there," I said. "See it has your name on the outside."

She looked at the envelope and at "Moreland" in Angus's script on the outside. "120 dollars?"

"Yes, Ma'am. The first in a series of payouts over time. The company wants this tragedy to end here as much as you do," I said.

"And what do you want in exchange for this payout?"

"I'd like to buy your farm, Ma'am. I'd like to purchase your house and land and offer you and your daughter a life estate on it. You can stay here rent free until you die, Ma'am."

"You or the insurance company? Who wants to buy my farm?"

"Yes, Ma'am," I said. "We would, over time."

"Mr. Kirby, if you don't get off this porch I'm calling my neighbor," Novie Moreland said, her voice lowered an octave. "He'll hear me scream. A matter of fact, here he comes now."

I turned and saw a tall man making his way though the yard at a fast clip. The neighbor was dressed in a white shirt with a tie loose at his neck. A brown dog followed at his heels. "Novie, is anything wrong?"

"Mr. Kirby was just leaving," Novie Moreland said.

The neighbor looked me over from the bottom of the steps and put his hand on the rail. "You was at the funeral yesterday," he said and came on up the steps. "Ain't your name Crocker?"

"No, I think you have me mixed up with somebody else. I was just leaving," I said, and I knew I shouldn't have come. I was ashamed to be there and knew that I had probably deepened the very grief I'd hoped to soothe. I felt dirty, offering money in a deal for the dead, and at that moment the remaining envelope stained my pocket from within. I felt the neighbor could see this crimson stain in my suit pocket and I turned awkwardly to my side when I started down the steps with my hand over the pocket as if I were protecting a wound.

"You listen here, Crocker," he whispered behind me as I approached the car. "Don't come up in here no more."

| PART II |

Malice Aforethought

Wednesday, December 10th, 1935

THE JURORS FOR THE STATE UPON THEIR OATH DO PRESENT, that George S. McCane, late of Hunter County, on the 6 day of September A.D. 1935, with force and arms, at and in the said County, feloniously, willfully, and of his malice aforethought, did kill and murder Fate Moreland, Sr., and two others as named as following, contrary to the form of the statute in such case made and provided, and against the peace and dignity of the State.

Clarence O. Riding

Solicitor

The Honorable Horace Tucker

Judge Presiding

| 11 |

In the first few weeks after George McCane was freed from that mountain jail he finally fixed his focus on the ambitious plan to renovate the Carlton Mill and nothing else seemed to distract him except the problem of Olin Campbell. There was little conversation between us that was not related to the project or Campbell.

"So he has not left?" McCane asked. I was hoping he'd forgotten. "Weren't the papers served?"

"I called the magistrate and he tried to serve him two weeks ago," I admitted.

"Get in the truck and drive out there and throw him out," Mr. McCane said.

"One of those union men is a lawyer," I said. "When the magistrate came out that lawyer said he had to prove Olin is behind on his rent, or that he's been laid off. He said those eviction papers wouldn't mean a thing in a court of law."

"Well, he obviously doesn't know what county he's in."

"The magistrate is Campbell's cousin."

"His cousin?"

"And they played together on the mill league team."

"Turn his water and his power off, and then get the sheriff out there next time. He isn't related to the sheriff, is he?"

"I can try one more time," I said. "Then I'll call in the sheriff."

Driving out to Carlton that morning I didn't think much about Campbell. I wasn't that worried about him or his housing situation and I didn't plan to turn off his utilities. In the big picture it really didn't matter whether Campbell left or stayed. The Carlton project was much more complex than Olin's defiance and not as easy to assess. On the surface Mr. McCane's Carlton project was a renovation as he claimed, an attempt to restore an aging mill, to bring the efficiency of an out-of-date industrial property up to modern standards, but in light of three years of unrelenting labor troubles at Carlton it would be impossible to believe that Mr. McCane did not see an opportunity to build loyalty in a new workforce out there as well. He blamed the Carlton troubles on management, but he was also convinced that the isolation of the mill allowed the "unreasonable elements" from below to gain power. "If we can make our operatives more dependent on Morgan and its amenities, then they'll come along."

It was hard to argue with Mr. McCane about the need to modernize. The road was only paved for the first five miles. At the Carlton junction the trolley and the hard-top road ran parallel and then the dirt road continued the final mile out to the village. Right outside of town the trolley crossed a small creek on a low trestle, but there wasn't a bridge for the road. There was a water crossing and it was always exciting to go through with a vehicle. The crossing was a wide slab of rock where the small tributary of the Palowee River—we always called it Mill Pond Branch—braided into trickles. The Carlton Road wasn't a bad road except when it rained and turned to mud. On those days the creek rose and cut the village off from Morgan until the water dropped, which was five or six times a year, mostly in the spring. There was always the trolley though, which I rode often with Coleen to see her parents. I always got a thrill out of driving the company truck though, and the creek crossing was the best part of the trip.

After I'd crossed Mill Pond Branch I saw a man walking up the road toward me with a fishing pole. He was most likely headed for what we always called the Other Pond, a small impoundment on the tributary creek just upstream from the crossing. When I got closer I saw it was Olin Campbell and he held up his free hand. I pulled the truck over, stepped out, and we both leaned on the fender. Olin Campbell put the cane pole on the hood and offered me a cigarette, which I took, though I didn't often smoke.

"Where's your goon squad, Crocker?" Olin asked.

"You mean the Ponder boys?"

Olin laughed. "No, not the Ponder boys. Angus McCane and his Two Musketeers."

"They're probably some place fishing, just like you." I stepped away and stood at the front of the truck and looked down the road.

"Not much else going on," Olin said. "With the mill shut down it's fishing, feuding, or fighting."

"I understand the magistrate's been out to see you."

"Yeah, Tommy came by last week. We talked about old times with the textile ball club. You know he was a hell of a first baseman." I could hear a bullfrog croaking in the distance, maybe up at the Other Pond. "You ever gig 'em?" I said, nodding off toward the sound of the croaking frog.

"Naw," Olin said, but I could tell he was listening to the croak. "I feel sorry for them in a way I never felt with fish. Something about their eyes and wide mouths."

"Tommy's paid to serve papers, not talk baseball," I said.

"Well, talking about one thing just sometimes leads to another among friends."

"Can you eat 'em? I can't. Even though when you batter up the legs they look a little like chicken. I couldn't even eat 'em."

"Friendship shouldn'a have been the point of his visit," I said, taking a drag off the Lucky Strike.

"Sometimes a man just forgets what he's there for."

"Especially if he's your cousin." I stepped around to the driver's side of the truck and opened the door.

"I thought it was McCane tried to serve those papers."

"I made that call to Tommy. Obviously I didn't get the right magistrate."

"McCane doesn't have nothing on me. I'm paid up in my rent," Olin said.

"You're not stupid. This is not about your rent," I said, walking around and putting one foot up in the truck cab.

"He can't throw us out. At least that's what my attorney says." Olin followed me around the front of the truck. I got in and closed the door.

"Your attorney? That makes it sound like you got some New York lawyer on a retainer," I said through the open window of the truck.

"Maybe I do. Maybe I got all sorts of fish on the line."

"I hope you've got a coffee can full of twenty dollar bills instead of worms if you start in with the lawyers."

"Legal representation is one of the perks for my high status with the local."

"Is the Other Pond full?" I asked.

"Much as I know."

"You know they pull it down about this time to clean it out."

"Well, if that's the case I'll just walk out on the flats and pick up some catfish."

"You're not leaving, are you?"

"Not anytime soon."

"I saw you with the widow up there in Canaan. I thought maybe you would move up there," I said, and started up the truck.

Olin stepped closer to the open window. "What are you insinuating, Crocker?"

"I noticed your wife wasn't with you at the funeral."

"I've known Novie Moreland since she married Fate."

"Is he kin?" I asked, putting the truck into gear.

"You didn't know Fate Moreland coached me one time? I thought you knew everything."

"I didn't know that."

"Back when I played that one year up in Hunter County."

"You know I can't stop Mr. McCane from calling the sheriff."

"I heard McCane has his own fish to fry," Olin said and picked up his pole, stubbed his cigarette on the truck hood, and tossed the butt in the ditch.

"Mr. McCane's business is none of yours."

"I guess he's out of jail by now."

"He was out that day."

"Of course he was."

"He didn't do anything."

"I'll stick with what I said. I imagine pretty soon my housing status will be the least of George McCane's worries."

"Hope that pond has some water in it," I said, and pulled away.

I continued down the road into the village. As I drove, the trolley clanked past. There were only two old men on board. I knew them both and we waved.

The village was indeed shabby and in need of repair. I could see that as I drove slowly down the main drag. There weren't many people out and about. Once as we discussed the improvements to the mill McCane commented on how parts of Carlton looked like pictures of the plains of Africa he'd seen in *National Geographic* as the village women carried buckets of water on their heads back from a communal well. "If they ask," he had instructed, "you tell them that modernizing the houses will improve everyone's lot in life."

I slowed down even more in front of the closed mill, which I knew had been built in 1898, a decade or so before I was born. The design was the standard three-story, baked brick box with one four-story stair tower in middle of the front facade. I counted. There were one hundred and twelve windows across the mill's front and each white-framed unit had forty glass panes. The big windows opened but I knew little air circulated.

The old mill was illuminated from within. In those days a cotton mill glowed like a magic lantern, but behind the dark brick walls in the high-ceilinged weave room the clack of the long, parallel rows of out-of-date looms created a monotonous cacophony. I didn't like to go in the weave room. The noise was like someone stuck your head inside a bucket and beat it with a stick. People who worked in the weave room always talk loud. About ten minutes in the weave room was all I could stand.

Belts hummed overhead, powering all the machines from a central machine shop where two huge steam engines labored. Several decades earlier George Mc-Cane, Sr., had brought grid power down from the lake for the Morgan Mill, but Emory Carlton's water power source—the bold stream beside the mill—had not been updated since the mill opened in the nineteenth century. Inside the mill, cotton dust swirled in the light from bare bulbs, and the air was hot and stale.

As I sat and looked at the mill I remembered the smell of old motor oil that hung in the air, the floors coated once a month with the black oil to keep the lint down. A mill was a dirty place back then. Lint not only swirled in the air but came home on the heads of the workers, earning them the nickname "lintheads" in those long ago days, a derogatory term like redneck or hillbilly. "Linthead?" my daddy always said, "I think it's a term of honor, a title like being knighted."

The promise of the new-fangled air conditioning probably would have lifted the hopes of the workers if they'd heard the changes were underway, but McCane didn't send out a memo or call a village meeting to explain his modernization. That just wasn't the way they did it back then.

Driving back to Morgan I admitted to myself that I did not doubt Mr. Mc-Cane's surface interests to improve the lives of those for whom he felt responsibility. I worried though that the turmoil and chaos of the strikes had turned my boss toward fear for his position and away from village altruism. My father had described his father George McCane, Sr., as a sort of benevolent king of the shire. The workers were his children and they loved him. The textile world was full of such paternalistic leanings in the 1930s. Had George, Sr., lived things might have been very different out in Carlton.

It's too early yet to see these paternalistic ways as positive or negative. To tell the truth, back then a sort of disturbing yellow utopian light leaked through many of the stories of textiles in the South. Behind the organized street designs and welfare initiatives such as day nurseries and brick school houses there was always the sense that if the workers were given enough perks they would not (and should not) fall victim to the call to organize. It was funny to me that the mill owners feared Communism, but they funded a sort of homegrown communal experiment in their own backyards.

There were whole villages in South Carolina that had been built as utopian playpens by local textile tycoons, but what the mill owners were mostly looking for back then was "cheap and contented labor," a term mentioned as often as "linthead" in the histories of textiles. The owners probably could have made more money had they left these utopian leanings behind, but most of them did not. There were villages where the workers lived cheaply and even contentedly. That cannot be denied, but Carlton was not one of them.

Who knows how George McCane, Sr., would have reacted to the unending union activity of that decade in Carlton? His frequent letters to the editor (most of which my daddy preserved) offer ample evidence he would not have tolerated the unrest either. Whether or not he would have suffered the missteps of his son will never be known. There was in George McCane, Jr., a weakness I've tried to understand and that the troubles of '34 and '35 irritated.

When I got back to the office Mr. McCane didn't ask about how things had gone in Carlton. He launched right back into the project at hand. "My plan to modernize Carlton will be expensive and difficult. I've asked Angus to be crew chief," Mr. McCane said as we finalized the plans for the renovation. He stood before my desk with several new file folders.

"Your brother? What's his experience with mills?" I asked.

"He has people experience," McCane said. "That will get us through."

"I think you would be better off hiring someone local to oversee this job."

"Angus is local."

"I mean someone from the village."

Mr. McCane continued, "Arrange for a paving crew to lay down a macadam surface on the road from the main highway to the Carlton Mill gates," he said. "I want easy passage for the replacement equipment that has been ordered and will arrive in a month or so." From one of the folders he pulled out pictures of the new machines ordered from Monroe Machine Works up in Massachusetts, the black and white sketches of the machines on a sheet of paper outlined in red. "I've hired skilled mechanics from Massachusetts to come down and install the machines, but we'll need a crew of a dozen loyal laborers each week. That's where your locals can come in. A wage of one dollar will be fair and sufficient."

"That rate is only a third of what most were paid working in the mill," I said.

"This is not skilled work and they will be paid as unskilled laborers," was Mr. McCane's reply.

| 12 |

On Sunday Coleen insisted I go to church with her in the village. Right after we got married we'd stopped going home every week. We'd joined the Methodist congregation in town, but Coleen still liked to go out and see her mama and daddy at the old church at least once a month. I'd been to Carlton enough lately, but Coleen insisted I go with her, so after breakfast she put Snowball in the backyard and we walked down to the Main Street trolley stop. There was only one car to Carlton and I knew the gripman, a childhood friend named Hayden Hall. He wore a vest and a cap with a shiny black brim and stood at the front of the car. He had duel responsibilities, working the levers and brakes and collecting the fares. He tipped his hat to Coleen as we boarded but didn't greet me by name as usual as I put our two nickels in the fare box. He seemed irritated when we sat right behind where he stood.

We were silent and alone in the car as we left town, but at the next stop, the Morgan Mill, we picked up six other folks, all of whom we knew. There was my third cousin, Tim Williams, and two Warren girls Coleen had gone to high school with. Then there was the sulky, hollow cheeks and the worn-out Sunday clothes of the Rogers family. I wondered when Frank Rogers had come up with the three nickels to ride. I knew he was out of work. He'd moved down to the Morgan Mill about the time I had, but hadn't done as well. He was worthless and drank too much. I would have guessed he didn't have two pennies to rub together. Maybe he made some money selling moonshine in the village.

Everybody sat near the coach's front. They each nodded our way when they sat down, but only Tim Williams, sitting directly across from us, spoke. Tim's mother, my first cousin Emma Fine, lived in New Canaan. His daddy and my daddy worked together twenty years. He went to our church too. When he sat down he took off his black Sunday fedora and placed it in his lap. "Y'all riding out to church?"

"Going out to see Coleen's mama and daddy," I said.

"Ben, I hear you're working out there," he said. "You ought to rent a place. I hear there's a house or two vacant."

"Ben's renovating the mill," Coleen said and I gave her a hard look, but she didn't care. "He's carrying out McCane's big plans."

"I'd heard about that too," Tim said. "My daddy says Olin Campbell's got his own plans."

"You sure can't predict what a man like Olin Campbell might do," Coleen said.

"Is your mama cooking supper?" I asked, turning toward Coleen and trying to change the subject, "or are we going over to your aunt's again?"

"I think we'll be at Mama's this week," Coleen said and turned away from me.

"Tim, are you still working in the picker room?" I asked.

"They put me in charge of the boiler room. I'm busy as it runs flat out all the time."

"I'm glad you've got steady work. It's hard on everybody right now," I said. "I know it looks bad to shut down the Carlton Mill but you won't believe the improvements Mr. McCane's going to make. He's air conditioning the whole thing."

"Imagine that," Coleen said. "It might look like heaven up there on the hill when George McCane gets done with it."

"Right now I'd say it's more like Frankenstein's castle," Hayden Hall chimed in as he changed gears. "It's a damn mess I'd say. We were better off when the Carltons owned it."

"They say opinions are like assholes. Everybody has one," I said, getting a little hot under the collar.

"Ben, it's Sunday," Coleen said, putting her hand on my knee.

Hall flashed my way. "Your nickel doesn't buy my respect, Crocker. It's a fact that we were better off with the Carltons," he said. "Just because your paycheck comes out of McCane's pocket don't make you better than all the other ones he let go."

After that exchange everybody around us went silent and listened to the rails clacking. I looked out the window and tried to gather my composure. We passed through the stripped cotton fields between Morgan and the Carlton cutoff where a storecropper's shack stood in one field and laundry flapped from a clothesline in the early breeze. I didn't expect that what McCane and I were doing in Carlton would remain a secret but I hadn't seen that coming: challenged by my own people in public. If a gripman on the trolley felt that way, how would those in the village really feel? Maybe I wouldn't even be welcome in my own church. Maybe my own mother-in-law would attack me once she passed me the butter beans. This was our first time back in church since the evictions had begun. I'd find out soon enough.

The trolley stopped in front of the Carlton Mill store on A Street. When I stepped off the car the late September air was fresh and light, unlike the stifling heat and humidity of summer. I helped Coleen down from the trolley and everyone else got off after us. The Warren girls and the Rogers family left without saying a word, headed up the hill on either side of the closed store. Tim Williams was the last off. He shook my hand and looked me in the face. "Good to see you, Ben. If you ever get hungry go up to Mama's. I'll tell her I saw you."

The car clanked off. Tim crossed the tracks and walked down A Street in the direction of New Canaan. We walked up Hill Street toward Boss Line. Coleen's parents lived near the ridge of the steep hill ahead of us, so we had quite a climb. "Let's take the short cut through New Town," Coleen said once we'd passed several of the two-story houses where the managers lived. We turned up a narrow alley that crossed B Street and then C Street. Then when the alley started to rise I could see New Town ahead of us. Some things in the village looked different in the stark autumn light, but some things still looked the same. The houses ahead of us in New Town had been thrown up slapdash and they hadn't been painted since they were constructed.

"Are we going to see your mama and daddy before church?" Coleen asked.

"We'll see them in church. That's enough for one trip," I said.

"If you're afraid to see your people it will just egg your daddy on."

"I'm not afraid," I said. "I'm just avoiding the questions that come in the living room, that he won't ask at church."

There were three or four dogs barking already as we walked along the alley. I could hear a Bible radio show playing through a back porch window and a couple arguing inside one of the houses. The last time I'd been on the edge of New Town it had been dark, but as I looked around I had a sinking feeling we might pass right behind Olin Campbell's house on our route to Coleen's mama's.

The alley curved before entering New Town and I saw I was right. We were beside Olin's house and I could hear someone in the kitchen. As we walked past, the back door opened and Olin's wife Reeba cracked the screen to throw out some grease. "Ben Crocker?" she said. "What are you doing up here again?"

We paused and I tipped my hat. "We're taking a short cut up to Coleen's mama's. Coleen, this is Reeba Campbell, Olin's wife."

There were others in the kitchen and when Reeba stepped out on the narrow stoop Olin filled the frame of the back door. He was dressed in a suit and tie for church.

"Reeba, who you talking to?" he said. "We got to go. The kids' Sunday school starts on the hour and it's five till."

"It's Ben Crocker," Reeba said, shaking the grease can until one more dribble fell in the dirt.

Then Olin looked out and saw me. "Well, Mister Crocker. You checking on your boss's property?"

"Olin," I said, nodding my chin. "I was just telling your wife we are on the way to Coleen's mama's and then to church."

"Hello, Coleen," he said.

"Reeba, Olin. It's nice to meet y'all."

I could see there was one more adult in the kitchen behind Olin, but couldn't make out who it was, and then she slipped into view. As Olin turned and cleared some space I saw it was Novie Moreland and her little girl. My heart jumped just like it had in the mountains.

Novie stepped out of the dark and Olin introduced us, not knowing we were already acquainted. "Novie Moreland, this is Ben Crocker."

"Miss Moreland," I said.

"Novie's down for a memorial service at the church for those who died at the lake," Olin said. She looked out at me with a little surprise but I was relieved when she didn't let on about my insurance scheme. Just nodded her head and puffed what I thought was a little smile. Her girl hugged one leg, holding on like it was a life preserver.

"Miss Moreland, this is my wife Coleen," I said.

"Pleased to meet you," she said.

"I'm sorry about your loss," Coleen said.

"Thank you," Novie said and the little girl buried her head deeper in her mama's skirts. Novie patted her girl's golden hair and pulled a fold of fabric loose from her little fist.

"Mama's expecting us," Coleen said.

"You be careful walking through New Town," Olin said. "It might be better to stick to the street."

"It's steeper than the alley," Coleen said.

"They're still smarting up there from the evictions," Olin said. "That's all I'm saying. One of those dogs might break off a chain. There are some mean dogs up in New Town."

"We'll take our chances with the alley," I said.

| 13 |

Mr. McCane did not accompany me out to Carlton when the work began. He stayed back in town. He was content to get updates as work commenced.

I drove the company pickup out that first morning and the idle mill and the grounds surrounding it were deserted, though around the outskirts of the village the ragged edges of life went on. Women hung wet clothes on drooping lines on A Street. A rattletrap car or two crawled up Hill Street. Dogs barked and snapped at the passing tires. Water flowed over the mill dam. There were dozens of children pouring from the houses into the streets, headed to school. These were the lucky ones. Somehow their parents had steered clear of the organizing efforts of Olin Campbell, and George McCane's plan had not pinched them. Once the mill was open again they'd have access to work and what possibility of improvement it offered.

That first day Angus drove down from the lake. His pickup arrived out front and as he slipped out of the seat I wondered where the families we'd thrown out in our sweep through New Town had settled. Many had gone home to the blue hills west of us to sow some collards instead of wild seeds of labor dissent. Their children were going into school with the others up in Canaan. The Carlton troubles weren't gone. They'd probably just started. They were watching us behind curtain rags as we prepared to remodel their red brick dreams.

As Angus approached the locked mill gates I remembered the left-over money he'd given me. The second envelope had slept for weeks deep in the pocket of my black suit jacket. George McCane did not know that I had been directed to squelch the sentiments against him, and his brother had said he would not mention it. I knew the money was a mistake.

And then there was money left over from the contingency fund I'd removed from the safe. I'd put that in the same envelope as Angus's money for safekeeping. I'd made no effort to return that either. So I had over a hundred dollars of McCane money on me. When I got to Carlton I'd had every intention of handing Angus's money back to him, but to me it didn't look like he was in any mood for settling up. "Ready to get to work, Crocker?" he asked when I stuck out my hand. He took my outstretched hand then said gingerly, "I could use a beer."

I'd arranged ahead of time for Carl Norris, the old Carlton Mill watchman, to meet us out front. I knew he was already on the property because I'd seen his rusted red pickup parked in the yard outside the fence. When we approached the gate Norris rambled out from the old truck. He wore an institutional gray uniform and a conductor's cap, standard issue for mill security in those days. He looked a little like he'd just walked back from Appomattox Court House. Norris didn't look up as he approached us from the pickup. He simply rattled his hundred keys on a large silver ring tied to his pants with a length of old rope. He bent over a little more like he couldn't see, and he stared at the key ring, and finally selected a big gold one to unlock the padlock on the pedestrian gate with the spinning metal mill carousel. "You gonna let us in, old man?" Angus McCane said. "Or leave us standing out here all the damn day?"

Norris didn't even glance up. He'd heard such bantering by those in charge his whole life. I could tell he had a good sense of when he needed to move fast and when he just simply needed to move.

Once we were inside the fence a strange feeling engulfed me, like cavalry entering an abandoned frontier fort, the outside surrounded by hidden Indians. After years of union strife Carlton Mill had more than a few things in common with a fort. The barbed wire fence that circled the grounds did little to protect the three-story brick mill at its center. I could see that the wire on the top had been bent down with people coming and going at night. Everybody knew the folks in the village would sneak in. They'd meet in clandestine romances in the shadows. They'd steal coal and firewood, or cloth to carry home to make quilts. As a child there, I knew every place the fence crossed a gully and we could slip under easily and prowl the back acres. The fence was more for show than protection.

At the height of the big strike of '34 there had been a machine gun mounted on one side of the gate. Mr. Norris had manned the gun. Norris must have felt strange pointing the weapon out toward the village and his relatives. The memory of the gun still smoldered in me and I slowed down a little as I passed into the courtyard and it was almost like Norris sensed what I was thinking because he said, "Ben, remember how that there is where we put that machine gun during the strike."

"Yes, I remember," I said. "You never did have to fire it, did you?"

"I came close a time or two, but I never did," he said. "That would have been one fine mess just like they had over at Honea Path."

"You boys can talk about local history when you're off the clock," Angus said. "What's the plan?"

"Clear the mill in a month, clean it up, and then take a couple of months at most to install the new machinery," I said. "I hope we can be up and running again by the New Year." I pulled the blueprints out of the portfolio, unfolded them, and asked Norris to hold one end.

"What about the houses in New Town?" Angus asked. "Who is going to do that work?"

"I'll handle the housing stock," I said. "I've hired the three carpenters who worked in the shop. They'll go house to house and add a tin skirt for underpinning, new paneling in the living room, cabinets in the kitchen, then paint."

"I don't see any problems with that plan."

"Everything should go smooth here except for lifting the crates to the top floor. Some of them won't fit in the freight elevator to the upper floors."

"We'll set up a hoist is all," Angus said, jabbing at the plans with his stubby index finger. "That won't be no skin off anybody's butt. Simple physics."

"You'll need to hire a dozen men each week," I said.

"Blow that shift whistle, Norris," Angus McCane said. "Let's get started."

The old man shot me a puzzled look.

"You do what he wants," I said. "He's the boss man on this job site."

Norris walked to the front door, rattled his ring some more until he found another key that looked just like the first, and opened the mill's front door and disappeared inside. A minute or so later the whistle blasted through the village from the top of the tower.

I'm sure more than a few of those laid-off workers thought they were dreaming. In ten minutes, a knot of out-of-work mill hands gathered at the front gate to see what was going on. They were dressed in overalls, shiny suit jackets and dull, dusty brogans. They waited like a flock of pigeons pulled in by someone about to throw out a handful of feed.

These men were veterans of past disappointment, so they watched cautiously as the odd employment process unfolded. Angus sized them up once they'd gathered. He walked among the assembled and tapped about a third of the men on the tops of their heads with a picker stick he'd found on the ground inside the gate. "Follow me, boys," Angus said, pointing the way with the stick, and those that had been tapped went inside the fence. "We got work to do."

I turned and looked back at those left behind. The ones who were passed over hovered around the gate grumbling among themselves as soon as Angus's lucky few shuffled inside. I didn't like the look in the eyes of those who had been left out. I wished there was some way we could spread what little money we had on the labor side. I knew this picking among them would be trouble in the long run.

Once we got inside Angus lined everybody up in the mill's wide hallway. I glanced over the row of men and realized I did recognize about half of them after all. Their distress had just made them look foreign outside. I started explaining the project so that the men would understand what we were doing. I gave them as much detail as I thought necessary and then got to what they were all waiting to hear: "You'll get paid by the day in cash," I said. "It's not much, but it's something."

"How much?" one man I didn't recognize spoke out from halfway down the row.

Angus walked over to him. "What's your name?"

"Jamie Biggerstaff," he said with pride. "I worked as an oiler here last year."

"Worked . . . yes, I think that worked is the proper tense," Angus said.

"What?"

"You *worked* here," Angus added. "Norris, escort Mr. Biggerstaff to the gate. We won't be needing his services."

Norris walked out with Biggerstaff and all the other men glanced at each other and then looked straight ahead again.

Angus walked back over beside me. "Ben, I believe you can continue with the orientation. I don't think there'll be any more questions." He slapped his picker stick in his palm.

"I don't have much else," I said. "You'll each get a dollar a day. I think all that's left is to get to work." As I turned I looked into the faces of the men. There was no doubt that everybody understood the ground rules now.

Once Angus had his crew running I headed up the hill in the pickup to New Town. The three carpenters from the mill shop—J.T. Sexton, Harvey Pittman, and Jerome Floyd—met me out front at the first of the empty shacks. The door stood wide open.

All three men had their tools with them and the lumber company had dropped the first truckload of materials in one of the few flat yards on the hill.

We went inside to go over the renovations and once I'd laid it out again to everyone I walked down to inspect the other twelve houses. The first three were dirty but empty, the front doors open like the first. But then four houses down the front door was closed and when I opened it I heard something moving around in the back room. The bedroom door was closed but cracked. I opened it and looked in. An old man and woman I didn't know sat on a pallet of blankets in the corner. There was an apple crate next to it with a candle in a jar lid. An open can of pork and beans with a spoon sat on the floor next to a bucket of water with a dipper. There were empty cans in one corner. The man didn't say anything. He clutched his knees to his chest and looked away. He looked like a dog that had been caught turning over a trash can. He wore old overalls and worn-out brogans. The woman's hair was sprung like a rag doll's and she didn't have any meat on her bones.

"What are y'all doing in here?" I asked, trying to sound calm and authoritative.

"Mister, this was my son's house for two years," the old man said. "We don't have nowhere to go once McCane throwed them out."

"You can't stay here," I said. "We're renovating these houses. The carpenters are just down the row."

"Well, we don't have nowhere to go," the woman said. She turned and looked straight at me. "You wouldn't throw an old woman out in the street?"

I looked at the empty cans of beans all around the pallet. "You have any money for food?" I asked.

"Our boy left these beans but you can see, we're at the end of 'em."

"Are you strong enough to tote boards?"

"Yes sir, I am."

"Well, you go down there in a little while and help that crew." I reached in my pocket and pulled out the envelope and peeled off one of Angus's twenties. "This ought to help until your boy comes back."

I turned around, walked out, and closed the door behind me. I went back to the first house and called J.T. Sexton out and told him about the old man and woman. "Make that fifth house the last one you work on," I said. "There's an old man in there. Put him to work hauling for you. Just let them stay in that house until we're finished here."

| 14 |

The next week Angus chose a different crew, tapping the lucky twelve with his picker stick. Biggerstaff was back, but Angus passed him over. Angus paused in front of him as he looked out at the crowd to make his choices and said, "Don't I know you?"

"I'm Biggerstaff," he said.

"Biggerstaff? No work for Biggerstaffs today. Nope, we're not hiring Biggerstaffs, are we, Crocker?" Then Angus's mood shifted and he darkened. "Get the hell out of here, old man, and don't come back," he said.

After they were tapped, the anointed ones cleared the old mill's three floors of the out-of-date looms, frames, lappers, and combers. In the first two weeks crews of men cleared the first floor. They learned quickly how to work together. Each time one of the huge rooms was cleared, Angus McCane set a second crew of the same three Negro boys to sweep and mop. I knew the three boys as the sons of the man who fired the Carlton boilers, Isaac Moore. Moore might not have a job as a fireman, but at least his boys could make a little money if they stayed on McCane's good side.

The Moores lived down the creek in a little community called Knuckletown. Generations of Negroes who worked in Carlton had lived in Knuckletown: the sweepers, the restroom attendants, and a line of boiler men like Isaac Moore. When Angus assigned them to an empty room the Moore boys swept and mopped and then brought in buckets and reoiled the old, heart pine floors. The place smelled like creosote as the Moore boys swabbed the planks with rags. Angus even had them clean the dusty windows.

Much of the old equipment went straight to the scrap yard where young, white village boys would salvage what they could of the metal. Being kids, they found other ways to profit from the refit. They made fleets of "iron-wheel wagons" using discarded gears and steel rods from the trash heap, and they raced down the steepest streets in Carlton. The boys had no brakes and often they would end up mired in the millpond mud at the bottom of Broadway Street, the steepest on the hill.

All through the first few weeks I alternated between checking on the renovation work up in New Town and working in the mill office on the accounts I'd brought from town. The New Town work was going slow, but each time I checked in I saw the old man carrying boards into a house and scrap to the street.

As I worked in the office I could hear Angus out in the rooms raging, swearing at anyone he didn't think was working hard enough, or punishing those who didn't understand the instructions he barked. I would walk to the open door and listen and watch. Angus always carried a pint in one back pocket. I knew he was taking a big swig before work, a time or two through the morning, a big slug at dinner, and then a time or two through the afternoon; then he'd throw the empty bottle in the weeds. He hadn't been drunk the first few weeks. His words weren't slurred and he'd cut a powerful figure as he walked through the mill, always carrying that long, dark picker stick in his right hand.

The older McCane was intoxicated on what little power his brother had granted him. At the end of each day during those first weeks I came out of the office into the yard and set up a folding card table. I paid each worker in silver dollars I'd brought with me from town. I even put each man's meager pay in its own envelope because that made it feel more like payday to me. Mr. McCane wanted it that way. He said that "the silver dollar payroll" would help us figure on how the money was circulating in the village and whether he'd need to establish some other sort of relief program to get everybody through the renovations. I don't think Mr. McCane had any idea how bad things were in the village.

I wondered how different circumstances would have been if the second son had held it together, moderated the illegal whiskey and plentiful whores, graduated an engineer from Clemson, and taken his rightful place at the head of the company when his older brother abdicated and his daddy died. Would things in Carlton have been better or worse? I imagine the situation might be better for George McCane. But it didn't work out that way, and there was nothing any of them or us could do to alter what did happen.

The next week the first man in line was my cousin, Ed Crocker. He had worked in the mill his whole life and his wife Dollie ran the Carlton "dope wagon," the cart where everyone bought soft drinks on break. Ed looked in his envelope when I handed it over and screwed up his face into a frown when he saw the silver dollar and two quarters inside. "Ben, I made fifteen dollars a week in the mill. This adds up to half that."

"This here's day labor, Ed," I said. "You're not working in the shop."

"How am I 'sposed to feed my family on this?" he said. "How am I 'sposed to do that?"

"We'll get through this," I said. "The mill will reopen in a few months and you'll be back to work. Things'll get better."

After I'd paid the eleven other men, the Negro boys fell in line. They didn't even get an envelope. I handed each two quarters like I was paying for a shoe-shine, and each boy took the change, looked it over, and walked out the gate without smarting off. I know now it wasn't right, but that's the way things went back then and, besides, they were the only ones with steady pay.

At the end of the month George McCane made a trip out to inspect what work the men had done. The paving crew had finished the Carlton Road, so there was a tar and gravel surface right down to the creek crossing, on through the village and out past it. McCane arrived midmorning. As much as I could tell, he seemed happy with the progress, though he added some new tasks. "Crocker, you need to hire us a good mason and add it to the budget."

The next week my cousin Ed was hired again and on Friday when he came through the line for his pay I asked him about a mason. "Vernon Satterfield's one," he said. "There ain't much brick work right now."

"You know how I'd get in touch with him?"

"I'll take you down there. His is the first farmhouse before you get to the Knuckletown Road," he said.

"Out in New Canaan," I said.

"Right in the heart of it."

After work Ed got in the passenger seat of the company truck and we drove out the new paved road. "How's Dollie?" I asked.

"Not doing much," Ed said. "The dope wagon's been parked for two months."

"We should be finished and running again in a couple of months. She'll have some business before winter's over."

"Ben, when did you get in with McCanes? I guess I just missed it along the way," Ed said.

"I took some accounting classes down at the junior college and Mr. McCane was looking for somebody to work with numbers," I said.

"You got lucky then, didn't you?"

"You could say that."

"You're doing all right. Much more than the numbers now," he said. "They say you're McCane's right-hand man. You're a real boss man."

"What do you mean by that?"

"You know," he said, "wearing a tie every day, riding in a company truck like this, hiring people."

I couldn't exactly catch the drift of where Ed was headed. Was he going to ask me for money? Was he fishing for a better job? "I told you I'll get you back on when the mill's working again," I finally said, hoping that would head off wherever he was going.

I understood that "boss man" wasn't exactly a term of endearment. Ed probably divided the world between bosses and workers like the union boys had taught him to do. "Like a family," sounded good, but there was no more thinking about the mill that way. A mill was a business, and in a business the bosses have some advantages because they control the capital. I'd learned that much in my two years of college and my time keeping books in the front office.

"A real boss man," he said again, and then repeated it. "A real boss man."

Down the road a-ways Ed said, "Slow down, Ben. The Satterfield place is down there. Just drive on in."

Ed pointed up a two-track with red clay gullies and cotton stubble fields on each side. At the end of the drive I could see a frame house up on blocks in a grove of pecans and chinaberries that were already starting to turn yellow. The leaves were a week or two from falling. It was a neat little farmstead for the up-country, but I thought about how barren this whole scene around the Satterfield house would look once winter set in. The hilly piedmont land had been worked so hard for over a century. Early settlers had cleared most of the big trees to make charcoal for an ironworks in the area and they'd grown cotton after that. The fields had eroded and there hadn't been any topsoil in a century. By 1935 it was becoming rare to see a farm field without a big gully growing deeper as it inched away from the nearest creek, and the Satterfield farm was no different. On each side of the road a gully formed and deepened into the distance down the hills. In heavy winter rains I'd seen the Carlton fork run so red from mud washed down all these gullies that the passing flow looked more like a moving stream of crimson oatmeal than a river.

"What does he grow?" I asked Ed as we approached the house.

"A few peaches, some pigs, turkeys," he said. "Satterfields have always made ends meet."

The Satterfields were sort of a throwback. In the early days there wasn't much need for steady labor in the small mills, so the local farmers maintained their little farms. They manned the mills when there was work.

"Here we are," Ed said as we drove up to the Satterfield house. Twin spotted beagles howled in the front yard.

The front door opened and Vernon Satterfield walked out on his porch. He was a short man with dark copper skin. What struck me right away was Satterfield's straight black hair and the way he had it combed back from his broad face. He had a sharp nose and dark eyes. "Is he an Indian?" I asked when Vernon stepped down the steps toward the car.

"There might be a pint or two of Cherokee in him," Ed said. "It's through us all from up there."

"He got more than a pint," I said. "I think he got covered with the whole gallon."

"Hey, Ed, I thought in that fancy car you was one of the government men from the CCC come to talk to me about my gullies."

"No, it's better than that, Vernon. I got you a job offer," Ed said, stepping out of the car with the beagles around him, their tails wagging.

"Get outta here," Vernon said, kicking at the beagles. "Y'all had supper?"

"Vernon, we're not here to eat. This here's Ben Crocker," Ed said as I opened my door. "He works for McCane's mill."

"I know who he is," Vernon said. "He's Boyce Crocker's only boy. I built some back steps out of block for Boyce last year. How's your daddy doing?"

"Laid off, like half the county," I said.

"Well, what can I do for you, Mr. Crocker?"

"We might need a mason up at the mill," I said. "I'd like an estimate."

"The mill? I thought McCane shut the mill down."

"We'll be open again in two months," I said. "We're renovating."

"My granddaddy laid the bricks in that mill. He was a young man then. He worked a year in 1896."

"Did he ever work for Mr. McCane?" I asked.

"No, shift work's not for us," Vernon said. "My great-granddaddy got this land early on."

"Hard to make a living farming today," I said.

"Hard to make a living working a shift. Ain't that right, Ed?"

"Damn hard right now," Ed said.

"What y'all need?" Vernon asked.

"They want somebody to brick up the windows," Vernon said. "I told him you were about the best around."

"Brick up the windows?"

"McCane's air conditioning," I said. "It's a modern thing."

"I know what air conditioning is," he said, "but why does he need to brick up the windows? They open and close."

"That's the whole problem. Somebody might just open one up and let some of Mr. McCane's expensive air out," Ed said.

87

"I can come by tomorrow," he said. "I got to feed the pigs, but I can be there right after that."

On the way back to the mill I stopped to drop Ed off at his house on A Street but as he got out of the car he said, "You thirsty, Ben? Let's see if Dollie's got some ice tea made."

"I got to get home," I said. "My wife's been all over me for coming home late."

"Oh come on, Ben. It's suppertime. You can stop your busy boss man and loyal husband life for a minute and drink a glass of tea."

Inside the house it smelled like kerosene. Dollie was at work in the kitchen on supper. She had a pot steaming on the stove and a black skillet waited on the burner. Dollie didn't seem surprised to see me when she turned around. "Well looka there," she said.

She wiped her hands on a dishrag, hugged me, and we sat down around the wood table in three of the four of their old split-bottom chairs.

"Dollie, I promised Ben here a glass of tea," Ed said, and Dollie eased back up and walked to the icebox to pull the pitcher of tea out. Ed and I sat in silence at the table until Dollie returned. It gave me a chance to look around. The floor was covered with a sheet of brick red linoleum curling at the edges. There was one bare bulb hanging on a wire and it was on. The wall behind me had two framed pictures next to each other, one of Jesus saying a blessing over a loaf of bread with a knife in it, and the other a black and white photo of President Roosevelt in a gray suit and bowtie sitting in front of a radio microphone. The Roosevelt photo looked like someone had cut it from *Life* mazine and placed it in the cheap dimestore frame. On the other kitchen wall, in contrast to the high sentiments of the two pictures, hung a funeral home calendar.

"I believe one had a little better run of it," I said, pointing up at Jesus. "And one they elected president."

"But FDR's way past thirty-three years. He got more years out of it," Dollie said, standing above me with the pitcher of tea. "Despite what McCane will tell us, it ain't over yet."

"Don't be talking bad about George McCane. Ben's a real boss man now," Ed said. "Are you going to give him that glass or not?"

"I can see that. What does your daddy think of you wearing a tie?" Dollie asked, putting down the glass of tea.

"He got me this job, for better or worse," I said. "But that doesn't mean he keeps out of my business."

"I'll bet he don't," Ed said. "I'll bet he had plenty to say about McCane and you throwing folks out."

"What is it they say?" I said, taking a sip of tea. "Something about breaking a few shells to fry some eggs?"

"He broke more than egg shells," Dollie said, putting down the pitcher on the table. "He broke some spirits and some hearts."

"McCane's got the best interest of the village in mind. He wants to bring us all into the twentieth century."

"We're thirty-five years into it, and you can tell George McCane we played it out just fine until he came along with his modern ideas," Dollie said. "Times were slower. No stretchout."

"Damn the stretchout," Ed added.

"When Mr. Carlton ran the mill we could go home for dinner every day for a half-hour or more. Nobody cared," Dollie said.

"Now, Dollie," I said. "The stretchout has proved to be of some worth. You can cover more machines at one time. The mill is more efficient now. Things run smoother."

"McCane sending men into the mill with stopwatches and timing everything we did? That made for a rough patch and there was nothing smooth about it. And then the boss told us we could do our jobs even faster. Someday McCane will find a way to get the machines to work without us. That'll be the day."

"Mr. Carlton seemed to make plenty of money without the stretchout. He built that big house in Morgan," Dollie said, refilling my tea glass from the pitcher on the table.

"And nobody with a stopwatch. And no Angus McCane breathing down your neck with a picker stick," Ed said.

"Just give it time," I said.

"Oh, time, we got plenty of that," Ed said. "We got more time than we got ice tea."

"Don't they say time is money? I think they're wrong. Money, that's something we ain't got plenty of," Dollie said. "Ed, we must have forgot to eat our greens and black-eyed peas last New Year's, because this year is almost gone and we're still broke."

"Well, you might think George McCane is a heartless rich man," I said, "but he has created his own private relief program to help folks out like you, and you are some of the first recipients." I reached in my coat pocket and pulled out the envelope of cash and folded back the flap and took out two more twenty-dollar bills and put them on the table next to the tea.

"You think you're Jack Benny, don't you?"

"It's a one-time gift," I said. "And Mr. McCane wants it to stay private. You'll soon need some money for coal."

Ed looked skeptically at the two crisp bills, over a month's labor if he had work every day. "So this is what a rich man's money looks like?"

"He gave me the authority to search out loyal workers and reward them with a modest bonus."

Ed shook his head and said, "That don't sound at all like a McCane. Maybe a Carlton, but not a McCane."

Dollie sat down and put her arm around her husband. She reached out and picked up the two bills.

"What does he want for it?"

"Buy some beans and cornmeal."

"We don't take charity."

"It's not charity. It's a private relief program, like a little Roosevelt program."

"We can't pay that much money back."

"You don't have to do anything. Just come back to work in the mill once it's open, and Mr. McCane will be happy."

"It's not like we can't use it," Dollie said. "But Ed's right, there's something off about this." She handed the bills back to Ed and Ed handed them back to me.

"Clear from the top," I said, as I stood up, leaving the money on the table. "You keep it."

| 15 |

Satterfield showed up at the Carlton Mill mid-morning. I walked him inside to count window openings. He had a little pad of paper and a stub pencil. Before we got started we ran into Angus McCane on the second floor landing.

"Vernon Satterfield's here about the brickwork," I said.

"I don't believe my brother would want you hiring a goddamn Indian," Angus said as he pushed past. "There's white men in Morgan who can do this job."

Satterfield bowed up like a banty rooster. "I'm black Irish on my mama's side."

"I don't give a tinker's damn what you are," Angus said as he turned. "You look like a goddamn Indian. Get the hell on home."

Angus disappeared into the freight elevator and the metal grate closed. The car moved to the top floor. I didn't know exactly what to do. The rest of the windows were up where Angus was working with the day's crew, and I didn't want to press the subject of Mr. Satterfield's family history any further with him.

"Mr. Satterfield," I said. "I believe Mr. McCane's brother has terminated the estimate."

"You don't have to tell me to leave," Satterfield said. "I wouldn't work with that man for a pot of the king's gold."

I showed Satterfield out the gate. Angus had complicated my schedule and I didn't know what I'd do about it. Outside the gate I saw my daddy walking past.

"Hey, boy," he said. "You wouldn't have a dime to buy your old man a hot dog would you?"

I pulled out my watch. "It is close to eleven. Let's go over the snack bar," I said, and walked across the street.

We stood at the counter and ordered. "Sheila, give this old man a hot dog and a Coke."

"Two hot dogs if he's paying," my daddy said. "All the way."

"How's mama?" I asked.

"She's worried about you," Daddy said. "I told her you'd figured everything out. It would just be a matter of time before you're running this mill, and as your mama and daddy we'd be drinking from the lemonade springs."

"And you? Are you still worried about me?"

The hot dogs came and Daddy peeled back the wax paper and took a bite. "I should have stopped worrying about you the day you started wearing long pants. You find a way."

I took a bite of mine too. "You're the one got me here."

"By the way, that's a nice thing you did for that old man and woman, letting them stay in that vacant house awhile."

"I gave that old man a job," I said. "That wasn't charity."

"Call it whatever you want," Daddy said. "I'd call it a strand of charity we haven't seen much out of the McCanes."

"You don't know a brick mason, do you?"

"Saw you was talking to Satterfield. He's the best around here. He built our steps."

"Angus McCane doesn't like the way Satterfield looks."

"Well, maybe Satterfield don't like the way McCane looks." Daddy took another bite of hot dog and looked at what was left.

"It doesn't matter so much going the other way," I said.

"Pass the mustard," Daddy said. "This dog needs some help. I think the quality has gone down since the strike."

"Can't we just have dinner?" I said. "I'd rather not talk about work. It gives me indigestion."

"Coleen told her mama you all are moving to Charlotte," Daddy said. "That's what got her worried."

"In her dreams," I said. "We're right here, and this is where we're staying. There's plenty of work to do."

I drove back to town that evening and hoped I'd arrive in time to tell Mr. Mc-Cane there would be some delay on the brick job. But when I arrived the office was already empty. I noticed Mr. McCane had left his door open, so I wandered back to close it before I headed home. Instead of closing the door I walked in and stood next to Mr. McCane's desk, one that I knew had been his grandfather's and his father's, and if he ever had a son, might be his as well. I ran my finger along the dark, polished mahogany edge and then I sat down in his hard, wooden chair.

From where Mr. McCane sat I looked out his window and saw that the tall front facade of the mill blocked his perspective. In the good days before the labor troubles he probably watched his supposedly contented labor stream through the front door and up the wooden steps into the tower, shift after shift. Now even the Morgan Mill was mostly empty three days a week and only a fool would think the laborers were content. I pondered the difference of the view from my chair. Out my window I looked directly up the wide tree-lined street. If I squinted I could see as far as the edge of the village, and even into the city beyond.

The chair springs creaked as I leaned back and impulsively opened the drawer in the center of the desk. Inside was an envelope with McCane mill letterhead addressed to George McCane at Clemson College and against all modesty and propriety I pulled the letter out, opened the flap, and read:

April 19, 1924
Dear Son,
I hope that you fare well in your upcoming exams at Clemson and prosper in your final semester there. I have received your letter asking for my blessing on your desire to move to Charleston in June where you aspire to assume an overseas sales position at your uncle's shipping company. I know this opportunity would afford you the chance to travel, something you have dreamed of doing since we first subscribed to *National Geographic* when you were only a child. I am afraid I will have to forego the blessing on this engagement. You will probably feel I placed too much pressure on your future by asking you to return home when the term ends and assume an entry-level position with the mill. I understand. You will forgive me at some point and I promise you will prosper by this request. As you know, your older brothers show no interest in textiles, and they have left me no choice but to request you return home upon graduation and postpone your plans.

I see the irony in the situation, but what am I to do? I cannot watch something as important to Morgan, or to our national industry, as the McCane family mills grow strong under family leadership for three generations then end up on the auction block were something to happen to me.

Son, enjoy your last days there at Clemson. I see no reason to ever bring this up again. Your mother sends her love.

Kindest regards,
Your Father,
George McCane, Sr.

I walked on home that night and knew Coleen would nag me about my hours. She wouldn't believe that Carlton was taking so much time. That night she was loaded for bear. "You expect me to believe every night you're getting off at ten?" she asked when I walked the door. "I ain't no fool."

"Where else do you think I might be?"

"I don't know. Why don't you just tell me where?"

"I'm working," I said, "I'm putting in every hour I need to and no more. Get off my back."

"I'll get off your back when you stand up for yourself," she said. "McCane's driving around in a new Buick every year and you're still borrowing that old Ford truck from the loading dock. Somebody's making a lot of money on that mill even during the downtime."

"I'll never be a rich man, Coleen," I said. "If you wanted to marry a rich man you should have married one."

"I don't care if you're rich," she said. "I do care that McCane flaunts it when everybody else is so hard up."

"The whole damn world's hard up. You'd see so if you'd read the paper and not just those damn movie magazines."

"What all happened with George McCane up at the lake?" she asked, and it took me by surprise. She'd sat down on the couch. Snowball jumped up and curled in her lap.

"Up at the lake?"

"They're talking about how you went up to bail him out."

"Who the hell is talking about George McCane being in jail?"

"Just everybody down at the diner. It's been two months. Harley Granger even brought in a newspaper from up at Huntersville that laid out the whole mess."

"So you do read the paper," I said.

"I read that one," she said. "Me and everybody at the counter read it. Pierce Riddle said he thought it was odd, it not being in our paper. That's when Harley said, 'Coleen, ask your old man about it. He's acting as McCane's bondsman. He ought to know it all.'"

"Harley Granger better keep his nose out of Mr. McCane's business if he knows what's good for him," I said, raising my voice so loud the dog growled.

"Once it's in the paper, it's the town's business," Coleen said, stroking her little growling dog.

"Shut that damn dog up," I yelled and Snowball jumped down and ran under the table.

"What's gotten into you?"

"It's not what's gotten into me," I said, sitting down. "It's what I got into and it ain't gonna get any better until we get this mill remodeled."

"Well, if you would just talk to me it would be better," Coleen said, and a tear welled in my eye. I knew she was right.

"I'll try," is all I could say.

"Come here, Snowball," she answered. "Come on in here to Mama."

| 16 |

Construction continued through the fall and Angus was lit up at the beginning of every day. As the job extended it became harder for the men to take him seriously as a boss man. One Tuesday my daddy's cousin Bobby Stevens came to me to complain. Bobby was an older man who'd worked as Carlton Mill's blacksmith for twenty years. His left hand had hardened into an immobile claw from early onset arthritis but he was still strong as an upcountry mule. In spite of his incapacitated left hand Bobby had been tapped by Angus's picker stick one morning and he got to work a shift. We exchanged greetings as Bobby walked in that day, and I thought it odd that he'd been chosen. I was even more surprised when he made it through till pay time.

"Cousin, how did you get along?" I asked, joking as I handed him his pay.

"Whose side will you be on if I break that goddamn picker stick over his drunk-ass head?" he said as he looked inside the envelope.

We never saw Bobby in the mill again, but the sentiments he expressed were widespread. How could anyone like Angus McCane? The side that he'd shown the men was arrogant, and when he was drunk (which was most of the time) he was sloppy, violent, and incompetent, three qualities that would not endear him with mill workers.

The modern looms began arriving at the Morgan depot in shipping crates and George McCane sent the Ponder boys and a crew from the main mill dock to transport them out to Carlton on flatbed trucks. The newly paved road accelerated the process as McCane had said it would. He bragged about how the muddy ruts of the Carlton Road had been replaced with hard tar and gravel and speculated that someday that would be the case for the whole county, maybe the whole state.

Once the machines arrived on site the crew of mechanics from up north rolled them into place on the bottom floor on heavy cast-iron dollies and the Ponders and their crew went back for more crates. The work on the lower floor went fast with the out-of-town experts there to set everything up.

When the last of the big crates arrived from the depot it was time for Angus McCane's plan to hoist them through the mill's upper windows with winches and heavy hemp ropes. Angus's crew set up the contraption, but the work went a lot slower than we thought it would with Angus in a bad mood from the beginning. This might have been a good plan when Angus McCane concocted it in mid-September, but it was cold that morning it was implemented. The out-of-town Yankees stood back and drank coffee and smoked until the crew chief, a man named Hipshire, came over to talk.

"Your men aren't very sharp this morning," he said. "Maybe they ought to set something else up and wait for the air to warm."

"We've got to get these crates moved," I said, ignoring Hipshire's comments.

"Work on those ropes. Get them untangled. Four men on each line," Angus yelled.

If a sober man were at the head of things they might not have gone so bad from the moment the crew lifted the first crate upward. The four men hauled the lead line and the crate cleared the ground, hanging in the harness of rope. The pulleys tightened above and the crate inched upward.

Even though it was cold, a big crowd had gathered outside the mill gates to watch. They'd hauled an old barrel down from somebody's yard and started a fire inside, which they fed with wood scraps from the heap beside the company store. Folks stood around the barrel and cheered when the crate broke loose from one line and pivoted, smashing the windows on the mill's first floor. The men on the second line tried to correct and swing the crate around again, but it crashed into more windows and glass flew, cutting the face of one of the workers inside the mill. The man with the bloody face came out the front door a moment later holding his cut cheek. "That drunk's gonna kill somebody," he said as he passed me.

I stood back and shielded my eyes against the early glare.

"I hope he knows what he's doing," Hipshire said. "You won't get a replacement machine for quite awhile if he smashes that one up."

"Once we get it up there y'all can go right at it," I said.

"Oh we don't mind the break," he said. "I'm just worried about your boys."

"You let us worry about that," I said.

"Your man there, Mr. McCane," he said. "He's trouble."

We could all hear Angus yelling from the second-story window where the crate was headed. He disappeared and reappeared downstairs. He raged among the eight workers manning the lines on the ground and cussed all those involved before putting his hands on his hips and watching from below.

The man with the cut face sat on a bucket and dabbed at his wound with a dirty bandana. Angus pointed at the gate, telling the man, "Go get that looked at and clean up."

I knew Angus wouldn't long tolerate the building chorus of cheers and hoots among the loiterers outside the gate. Soon he turned, pumped his fist at the crowd and pivoted with his back to us. He took a swig off his flask and wiped his mouth before he stomped over toward the crowd.

As I watched the crate stalled in mid-air I scanned those gathered near the gate and saw that Olin Campbell and Vernon Satterfield were standing next to the fire. Olin stood a head taller than Vernon. They saw me and Olin walked through the crowd to the gate and smiled like he'd seen a long lost uncle. I walked out to stop him before he got too far onto the grounds.

"Hello, Crocker," Campbell said, extending his hand. He was dressed in a clean shirt and trousers but no coat against the cold. He wore a fedora, maybe the one the union boss had that night in the village earlier in the fall. "You all got some circus going there. Those broken windows aren't helping the McCane clan's bottom line."

I was a little peeved he'd shown up and I expressed it. "I believe it's a little late for you to be concerned about Mr. McCane's bottom line," I said as I took his hand. "You've done your damage."

"Ask those Yankee boys how they'd do it up north. They'd have a union crew moving that crate and it would have gone a lot more smoother," he said.

"Well, why don't you just go on up there?" I asked.

"Supervising this job has robbed you of your usual good nature," Campbell said, and smiled easily. He was rested up now and his face lacked the shadows that I'd seen the night we first tried to extract him from the Carlton Mill village.

"Where's your posse?" I asked.

"You mean my Bolshevik associates?"

"Those would be the ones."

"Business up in the motherland."

"Why don't you organize Union County next? You wouldn't even have to change its name."

"Why don't you join us, Ben, or are you too much of a company man?"

"I do my own negotiating," I said. "I don't pay somebody up north to do it for me."

"Well, it's a fact you have done all right by yourself, Mr. Crocker, but it's a little harder for us rank and file."

"Any job prospects? Maybe these crate movers are hiring," I said.

Two small boys came up and gathered behind Campbell. They formed a skirt around his legs, clinging to his trousers, and peeked out from time to time to watch the crates rising.

"Like the song says, 'nothing but time on my hands.'"

"I thought you'd be keeping a low profile."

"Just got back from carrying these boys out to see their cousins," Olin said. Vernon Satterfield came up and joined Campbell.

"Is that true, Vernon?" I asked.

"His daddy married my mother's sister," Satterfield said.

"I believe you're related to everybody in the county."

"Look, Olin," one of Vernon's boys said and pointed. "That crazy man is heading over here."

Angus had spotted us talking and he walked toward the gate as the crate rose once again toward the top floor. The men in the window finally swung it through the opening successfully. Everybody in the crowd stopped hooting and sent up a cheer once the crate was secured on the floor; the eight men manning the ropes let loose, took off their hats, and bowed.

"If at first you don't succeed, try, try again. Isn't that right Mr. McCane?" Olin Campbell said as Angus walked up.

"It proves true in some things, but not often for dumbasses like you," Angus said. He held his picker stick tight in his right hand. "What's so funny about what's going on in there?"

"I didn't expect all this excitement," Campbell said, hugging the two boys to his side. "It's better than the county fair, ain't it, boys?"

"I'm glad we could entertain you," Angus said. "Now why don't you just get your ass back up to that little cabin in the woods?"

"You didn't hear? I ain't gone nowhere yet," Olin said. "I'm still up right where you visited that night."

"Crocker?" Angus looked my way.

"It's true. The magistrate was his cousin," I said.

"McCane don't have the papers," Olin said. "I'm staying where I am."

"Papers or not, I'd get hell out of here if I were you," Angus said. "You're just asking for trouble."

"I believe the last time I checked this was a county road, McCane," Campbell said. He pushed the boys back into the crowd as the two men faced off in the street. They eased up close, toe to toe.

Swiftly Angus swung with the picker stick and it flew free when Campbell put out his fire-shriveled hand to protect himself. Angus reached in and pulled out his billy club. Campbell's face darkened and they shuffled in a circle like dancing bears. The men on the front row of the crowd jerked back like they'd been too close to a blaze and realized it.

Angus McCane lunged again, this time with the billy club. The jab threw him off balance and Campbell stepped easily aside. I didn't realize until then how drunk Angus was, but Campbell seemed to know. Olin caught Angus in another lunge and they wrestled for a minute, then Angus seemed to lose strength and Olin eased him to the pavement, face first.

Campbell took one step back and looked for a second like he wanted to kick the down man, but I'm glad he thought better of it. The crowd didn't know whether to laugh or run. The fight ending that way surprised everyone. There was silence and then a few isolated cackles finally peppered the air, but mostly people were quiet. They knew what had happened. In our world a worker—a union worker at that—getting in a scrap with one of the mill owners could have serious consequences.

"Crocker." Campbell turned. He seemed angry for the first time, but then got control of himself. He took a step back. "I think Mr. McCane slipped and fell."

I leaned down to help Angus up. He sat for a moment, and I wasn't even sure he knew what had happened. He was so drunk his eyes were fixed on some spot of sky above him.

"There's something big cooking in the mountains," Campbell said.

"What's cooking?" I asked.

"Unfinished business with your boss man." Campbell nodded down at Angus and kicked the billy club away. "His brother."

"You best be on your way," I said.

"Let's go, boys," Campbell said and turned to gather his nephews. "There's a warm stove back at the house."

| 17 |

Angus sobered up after that. I don't know whether his brother got wind of the incident outside the mill in the Carlton Road, but Angus didn't bring his bottle back to the job. He was more direct and focused when he was sober, so the work sped up and nobody else got hurt. The heavy lifting was soon over anyway, and there wasn't much left but hooking up the electricity and bricking up the windows after that. I was glad to see the Yankee crews leaving Morgan. We fired up the boilers on one really chilly day and it was even warm in the office. We didn't speak about the incident with Campbell but once.

"He better be glad I was high," Angus McCane said one afternoon as we paid the last of the workers.

"It could have been an ugly scene," I said. "We could have killed somebody with that crate. We don't need any more of that."

"Crocker, you just don't like conflict, but it's all around us. You can't get away from it in this world. The Greeks had it. The Romans had it. All the way up the ladder."

"No, I don't like a fight when there are other alternatives."

"That wasn't a fight, Crocker. In a fight there would have been blood in the street and it wouldn't have been mine or yours."

I wasn't so sure about Angus McCane's chances against Olin Campbell. I thought he'd always underestimated him, even though he had that shriveled hand. I thought McCane was taking him (and the trouble he could mount) a little too lightly.

"What did he mean about something cooking back up in the mountains?" I asked.

"Did Campbell say that?"

"He said something about the mountains and Mr. McCane's business."

"Well, Campbell's probably right about that. I've been hearing things. I always told you that the business up at the lake's not over," Angus McCane said. "The pot's still on the stove. We'll just have to wait and see what boils."

As the Carlton project wound down, I finally drove out to the mill with Mr. McCane in his Buick. We checked in on the mill first and he seemed pleased with the progress, but once again nagged me about the brick mason.

"These aren't going to be bricked up before we open, are they?"

"There's just too much else going on," I said. "I only got one brain."

"I pay you to figure things out," McCane said.

After looking over the mill we drove up the hill to see the renovated shacks I was now willing to call houses. I showed Mr. McCane the first house on the row in New Town and he liked the improvements—the underpinning, the paint, the bathroom and kitchen. Then he wanted to see more, but I looked at my watch and lied. I told him we didn't have time. I had no idea which house the old man and his wife were living in and I didn't want McCane to know either.

Getting in the passenger's side I noticed a deep scratch on the side of the car and brought it to his attention. "A hillbilly in an old pickup run me onto the shoulder of the Saltilla Grade back in September," he said.

"Not like you to leave it," I said.

"The local body shop was backed up, so I just didn't get around to fixing it."

I didn't think much about the damage until a week later when the indictment came down from the Huntersville grand jury and George McCane was back in jail. I heard about it from one of the shift managers, Wylie Jackson, who'd heard from a cousin who worked washing dishes up at Lakeside Inn. Wylie stopped by the house around suppertime to report that the sheriff's deputies had arrested Mr. McCane at the Lakeside Inn while he was having dinner with one of his aunts. "They served the warrant and handcuffed him at the table and hauled him off to jail," Wylie said.

Coleen was working at the café that night and so I walked down to the mill and called the Huntersville sheriff's office. "McCane, McCane," the night clerk said and took his time, as if he was checking the rolls of Alcatraz. "Yeah, we got a McCane."

"What are the charges?"

"Murder, it says here. Three counts."

"Murder? Are sure you're reading the right line?"

"That's it, murder."

"Has bail been set?"

"Cash bail is three thousand dollars."

"Can we get him out tonight?"

"It's Saturday night, mister. This isn't no road house. We open Monday at 8 a.m. Come up and get your buddy then."

After hanging up I stood and looked out the window for a few seconds. The oaks were bare out front. The mill had a few lights on, but it looked bleak too. Everything was brown. Nobody had raked since the leaves fell. I couldn't think straight. My mind was as cluttered as the yard. How could this happen? George McCane was no murderer. There could be nothing premeditated about this accident on the lake. It was the judge and solicitor up in Huntersville. They had it out for the McCanes and somebody had to stop them.

I stopped on the way home to have supper at the Sanitary Cafe. I ordered off the special board—one of my favorites, liver, onions, and fried potatoes, and a cup of black coffee. Coleen brought my liver rare.

As I looked down at the plate a red stain leaked out from around the charred edges of the meat.

"I wished I had told you well done," I said.

Slicing that bloody liver I thought about Mr. McCane up there in jail. The attendant at the police desk had talked like McCane was some run-of-the-mill criminal, not the richest man in four counties. There was nobody else in the place, so I told Coleen fully about McCane's troubles.

"What got into them taking on George McCane in his own backyard?" Coleen said.

"In the end, privilege doesn't fence you off from any common indignities, so what was the use of it?" I said.

I put down my knife and fork on the plate for a moment and took a drink of black coffee.

Coleen went off to clean and I finished my meal and then she came back with a rag to wipe the counter. I remembered one more detail Wylie Jackson had recounted about the arrest: One of the officers had taken McCane's Buick and driven it back to the Huntersville courthouse. Wylie had asked me something strange, "Why do you think they wanted his car? Didn't he kill them people with his boat?"

I looked down at my bloody plate and thought about the scratch down the side of McCane's Buick.

"Time to close up in a minute," Coleen said. "We'll walk home together."

We walked the final three blocks home on that warm December evening. Snowball greeted us, tucked in the crease between where Coleen sat in the chair and the chair's arm. The dog lifted his head and growled when I came in first, then wagged his tail when he saw Coleen.

"You've had her two years. The little bastard still acts like I'm a stranger," I said.

Coleen didn't say anything, which I thought was unusual. My remark was the kind of opening she'd always taken as an advantage.

"What's wrong? In the past you'd beat me up about the hours I'm keeping or what sort of secrets you think I've hid," I said.

"What are you trying to do?" she finally said. "You're acting like this is your problem."

"It's my boss man's business, but it's mine too. It will affect the way the mills run and my future."

"The way the mills run? Are you a stockholder in McCane Mills or you simply drawing a pissant salary?"

"What do you want me to do, run off to Myrtle Beach like a Ponder boy?"

"You run off to get him out of jail. You do his business at the two mills. He's hired you to keep his books, that's all."

"I'm a company man," I said. "You'll never understand what that means."

Monday morning I was up and out of the house in a hurry so I wouldn't have to talk with Coleen. I reckoned Mr. McCane knew Angus and I would set it all up and be there soon as we could, and there was no reason to call. I went to the mill office first and filled a cotton pay sack with cash from the safe—three thousand dollars to pay McCane's bail and a hundred for other contingencies, which I put in Angus's envelope with the other bills. Then I drove up the Asheville road. Just before we crossed the state line we passed the Flats. There were two trucks parked at odd angles out front and I recognized the red one right away as Angus's. I imagined either some serious drinking was already underway, or the drinking had never ceased from the night before. I had not seen Angus since the renovation ended, so I stopped to make sure he knew about his brother.

The entrance to the Flats was a rickety wood frame with old sheet metal tacked over the outside. The door rattled like a tin drum when I opened it. Inside the roadhouse was dark, and the air was saturated with the odor of smoke and cheap, stale beer. The three booths on the back wall were empty. At the bar a man was slumped, smoking a cigarette.

"You seen Angus McCane?" I asked, approaching the man at the bar. "His truck's out front."

The man pointed behind him to where a couple was asleep, twined in each other's arms, crammed into a dark corner.

I walked over and it was Angus in the booth, passed out with his arms around a chubby girl with a rat's nest of blond hair. I could see her pudgy face in the dark. Her mouth was slightly open and a clear pearl of spit had caught on her lower lip and had been suspended indefinitely there in its journey down her chin.

"Angus," I said as the young woman's tongue slipped out like a lizard after a fly and snagged the spit pearl. She let out a little snort, but remained unconscious, though she did roll over to one side as Angus woke up.

I hauled Angus out of the girl's arms and I alerted the bar owner we'd be back later for his truck. I took him home to the lake on my way to Huntersville. He slept in my backseat the whole way. When we drove up the lake road I dragged him into his cottage and left him sleeping on an unmade bed. He was so drunk I don't think he even understood what I'd told him about his brother. I simply tucked a sheet around him and headed up to Huntersville.

After I paid George McCane's bond I told him they had his car, and he seemed relieved. "That's good. I need to go back to the lake and see my aunt," McCane said. "She's probably had a heart attack." We walked back to the desk and Mc-Cane asked for his keys.

"You can't have that car," the young officer said. "That's evidence."

"Evidence of what?" McCane said, a little perplexed. "That I drive a Buick?"

"Evidence of the murder," the man said, handing me the papers to sign. "We impounded your fancy boat, too."

"Take me over to the courthouse," McCane said, pulling the warrant they'd given him upon arrest from his pocket. "I need to get to the bottom of this with Ripley. I'll settle all this before we go home."

I know much is made of the idea that there is no king or queen in America, but in 1935 a cotton mill owner would have been about as close to royalty as you could get in the South. Back then men like George McCane were on the top of the social heap. McCane would have expected that any situation could be settled between gentlemen over spirits in a dark, paneled clubroom. Even during the Depression they had money when almost everyone else didn't. Looking back, it could be argued that they were mostly beyond the reach of petty local justice.

But the social forces of the universe had conspired in a most unusual manner to deposit George McCane in this particular criminal mess. I imagine as McCane sat in that jail for two nights he'd considered the solutions he was familiar with: Who did he know? Who owed him a favor? What backdoor was left unlatched? What was buried out there he could dig up and offer as collateral? How much effort (and money) would it take to smooth things again and get the community back to normal?

"Well, George, the first thing I'd do in your situation is get myself a good mountain lawyer," Ripley Grier said, looking down at the indictment papers.

When Grier spoke a look came over Mr. McCane's face I'd never seen before, as if a first glimmer of realization had slipped from the dark confines of his privileged mind. The fact that it had been months since the accident on the lake and George McCane had never retained a lawyer was a good indication of how immune to the local social and legal forces he considered himself and his family.

McCane said, "You think it's serious enough for a lawyer?"

"George, you've been indicted for three counts of murder by a grand jury in a county that's not your home," Grier said, glancing down at the paper before him. "Solicitor Riding wouldn't have gone this far if there were not witnesses against you. They've told you about the car and boat, so there is evidence being held by the police. You are out on low bail because of your local prominence and your long ties to the area, but yes, I'd say it's serious enough to get a lawyer."

"Well," McCane said, as if realizing for the first time how serious things were, "will you do it?"

"Be your lawyer?"

"Yes, I'd like for you to represent me in this case."

"Well, of course I'd do that, but this won't be easy," Grier said.

"What witnesses could Riding have against me? I demand to know."

"You'll see them soon enough," Grier said. "The court date's been set for the middle of March."

"Well, what have you heard?"

"I can't say."

"Ripley, you've been my friend for decades. You can tell me what you know."

"I would only be repeating hearsay, and there's plenty of that in this little town."

"Such as?"

"There's an old man out there who says you ran him off the road early the morning of the murders."

"They weren't murders. It was an accident."

"This old man says you were drunk that morning and you verbally assaulted him on the road."

"Drunk? That's a damn lie," McCane said. "It was five a.m. I was driving up from Morgan."

I thought about the scratched fender on the Buick, but didn't say anything as Grier continued. I leaned back in his big leather chair and just listened.

"Did you have an accident on the way to the lake that morning?" Grier asked.

McCane grabbed the paper off his friend's desk, stood up, and threatened to leave. "Ripley, who the hell are you, the Grand Inquisitor?"

"Sit down, George. I'm only asking questions you're going to get asked later by somebody way less sympathetic. Did you have an accident that morning or not?"

"Well, yes, I did. Some local ran me off the road on the Grade," George said, sitting back down. He retreated into himself for an instant, as if recalling the incident but then dismissed the memory with a wave of his hand. "There were words exchanged, but I drove on quickly after we settled things."

"Does your car still bear the damages?"

"Well, yes, it does. I did not have time for the repairs."

"That puts you in a fine fix."

"And what else might they have, Ripley? So far I don't hear anything that would get me charged with murder."

"I've heard they have a witness who says you have a habit of buzzing locals on the lake. They say you've threatened more than a few you think are trespassing. They even have one local boy who says that you told him if he didn't get off the lake you'd run him over with your powerboat."

"It's our lake," he said. "We can protect our property. It's in the Constitution."

"I've heard you threaten them myself. That, my friend, will sound like malice aforethought."

"What was I supposed to do? You don't want them on the lake either."

"Worst of all, they're saying the wife of Fate Moreland says you ran them over," Grier said, glancing down and reading on.

"Another damn lie. Crocker, where does this woman live?" He turned and addressed me for the first time since we had entered the office.

"She says you spotted them in the boat and came straight at them."

"Lies," McCane said. "All of it."

"Crocker," Grier said, turning to me, "I heard you were at the funeral of Fate Moreland and his son. Is that true?"

"I attended."

"There was no crime," McCane said, as if he hadn't even heard Grier's question to me.

"That's not the conclusion of the grand jury of Huntersville County, George. They heard the solicitor's evidence and they brought three counts of murder against you on Friday. That's why you need a good lawyer. You need to convince somebody besides me and your man here you're innocent."

"Who is on this grand jury?"

"I don't know. I don't want to know, and you don't want to know either. Besides, they change every six months up here. Could be anybody. I could be on it."

McCane sighed deeply and coughed. "Well," he said as he rose to his feet and put on his hat. "It's early yet, Crocker. I need some breakfast. Let's head down the mountain."

"One more thing, George. Somebody ought to fill you in on Olin Campbell and his gang as well, and I reckon it's got to be me," Grier said, standing and walking out from behind his desk to show us to the door.

"Olin Campbell?" Mr. McCane said. "What the hell does Olin Campbell have to do with any of this?"

"You're in the mountains. It's all related, just like these folks."

"I have no business with Olin Campbell."

"He's close with the Morelands. Fate Moreland was his mill league coach the year he played up here. Then soon as the indictment became public Moreland's father, Tyrone, started running around the county in his Spanish War uniform saying he was raising an army to go down to Morgan and drag your sorry ass up here for a proper lynching."

"Moreland was fifty years old when he died," I said. "His father must be seventy-five."

"He had twenty men stirred up out there near Jump Off Rock. They were ready to pile in a fleet of old jalopies and head down the Asheville road to Morgan. You better thank the Lord the Huntersville police got to you out there at the lake before Moreland's vigilantes did."

"Vigilantes?" McCane asked. "What decade is it up here?"

"A decade earlier than you'd like. You're pretty much safe down there in Morgan, but don't come back up here until your court date."

| 18 |

Later that day I looked up from my ledgers and Leland Cromer walked in. Leland was Mr. McCane's local lawyer. He handled the mill's cases and the family's affairs. I'd never liked Leland and it started way back. "That man's crawled over a lot of people to get where he is," my father once said when I mentioned that Cromer was on retainer with the mill.

Cromer's father had been assistant superintendant of the Carlton Mill when I was growing up, and Leland thought he was better than everyone else in the village. On the surface he had nothing to set him apart. He had been a pale, mousy boy with brittle bones and crooked teeth, but in spite of his frailties he was always smarter than the rest of us. One year he started in September in the third grade, but by Easter he was in the fifth. The next year he moved from fifth to seventh in nine months. I'll admit he excelled at spelling and math but that wasn't enough to move him up like a skyrocket. We children grudgingly admired his school smarts but we also resented his moving up past us. I always suspected his quick rise was because he was a teachers' pet. He cleaned too many erasers to be popular with the mill boys like me.

Leland had filled out some as an adult and he'd had his teeth fixed. He was short and wiry in build and overly pale of complexion with pointed features that made him look like a weasel. As a child he was always overdressed for any occasion. The day he walked into the office he wore a black, double-breasted, Persian lamb overcoat, though it must have been only fifty degrees outside.

"Well, hello, Benny. Good to see you as always," Leland said, looking past me as he pawed at a small speck of lint on his coat until it was subdued between his thumb and forefinger. "Mr. McCane is expecting me."

Leland unbuttoned his coat, took it off, and swept it over his shoulder like Errol Flynn as I walked with him back to Mr. McCane's door. Under the coat was a suit that cost more than I'd make in six months. I felt a little like a doorman, and I wouldn't have been surprised if Leland had handed me his coat and asked me to watch it while he was inside. Instead he simply disappeared into Mr. McCane's office, and that was that.

I don't know exactly how they planned to battle the prosecution aligned against George McCane, but Leland or his legal assistant were in our office every morning for a week, and it unnerved me to no end. I had my doubts about Angus's blood money but I trusted lawyers even less. Then on Thursday things became even more complicated when Angus paid me a visit. He came about three.

"Your brother's already gone for the day," I said as he walked in.

"I'm here to see you," he said.

"What can I help you with?"

"I thought you might want to wander one more time up into the hills and talk with some folks," Angus said.

"I didn't have much luck the first time," I said.

"Well, I was stingy in that first round," he said. "Maybe I'm feeling more generous."

"They didn't seem very interested in the deal."

"Take a little more with you this time," he said, sitting on the edge of my desk. "I've heard Yarborough is ready to help out with the introductions."

Angus reached in his back pocket and pulled out another envelope and slid it across the desk. "Open it up."

I opened the envelope. Inside was a half-inch thick stack of bills.

"Count it."

I counted.

"How much?"

"Five hundred dollars."

"That's ought to be enough palm grease for Yarborough to spread around."

"What if I say I won't do it?" I said, closing the envelope and pushing it back.

"Do what? You're just the courier," he said. "I'm the one making the deal. Besides, you're a lucky man. You get to see the widow again."

I borrowed the company truck and went out of my way a little and passed the café to look in the window. Coleen was working the counter. After that I drove home and parked out front and then walked to the backyard. I looked on the back porch for an empty Hills Brothers coffee jar and Snowball heard me outside. He ran through the house yapping, and it reminded me to look around and make sure the neighbors weren't watching. The neighbor's house was dark and a privet hedge blocked the view from the back alley. When I found a jar I screwed off the lid and took half Angus's money, folded the bills, and slipped them inside the jar. Then I placed the jar behind the ground-level door to the crawl space. Before I left I toggled the latch back to close it.

I drove through Huntersville, all the way out to the mouth of Jump Off Holler, and down the dirt road to the church. I knew better than to go on past the church to where the valley widened, opening up into barren fields patrolled by crows. I stopped short of going down to where the widow of Fate Moreland lived in the old farmhouse. That would be looking for trouble. The church was empty that day and locked up tight. I walked up to the door and shook the latch and looked in the windows. The sanctuary was simple and barren without the congregation. There was nothing I wanted inside. I wasn't a religious man and there were churches much closer to the mill if I needed them. The last time I'd driven out here it was disastrous. This time would prove more fortunate, but at first it did not seem so.

In spite of my careful stalking along the boundaries of a dangerous territory I had not noticed a dark burgundy pickup approaching and slowing to a stop beside the church. Unnoticed by me the driver had slipped out. I prepared for the worst when I turned and saw that it was the neighbor from across the street who had run me away that morning months before.

"Crocker? Why are you back up here again?" the man asked. Mrs. Moreland's neighbor Yarborough was on me in an instant, his long, raw hands hanging at the ends of powerful arms like mallets. He had on a blue suit coat, as if he'd had business in town.

"You're right," I said, hoping to avert a beating.

"A sane man would never come back. You must not be a sane man."

"I hoped to see your preacher," I said. I did not know where this was heading. "He said something that stuck with me at the funeral, something about forgiveness."

"See the preacher? He's here two Sundays a month. That don't make any sense," the man said. "You get in your truck and head on back down to Morgan."

"What I meant was I need to talk to all involved. We need to make a settlement."

"We don't want to see you no more," he said. He was still mad, but I seemed to have unarmed him somehow. "It's moved beyond us, Crocker. Whatever awaits McCane is now with the courts."

"Is it proper justice to let lawyers have it?"

"Proper is as proper does," the man said. "That young widow's husband is proper buried but far from avenged. We'll be lucky if this stops with the judge. I know that and you know that."

"Well, Yarborough, that's why we need to bargain a settlement where all feel satisfied."

"Are you trying to bribe me now with McCane's money?"

"It's not McCane's money, it's mine."

"Your money? You don't strike me as a man with means."

"I have a little."

"What's in it for you? He's just your boss man, that's all."

"I'll be truthful with you, Mr. Yarborough," I said. "I don't think George McCane is guilty. What happened was an accident, that's all. Because of that I want this incident resolved as it should have been from the beginning, between gentlemen."

"I don't believe a jury will see it that way. A rich man driving a boat too fast on that little bitty lake don't make it no accident."

"A terrible accident is all it was," I said. "I want it settled and I want you to help me settle it so we can all move on."

Yarborough looked off toward the hills, down the road toward the Moreland homestead.

"How much money you got?"

"I got enough."

"That woman down there lost her husband and her son. I only lost a neighbor. This church lost two members we'll never replace."

"The settlement should include all of that."

"There's been Yarboroughs in this valley since before the War Between the States."

109

"But there's Morelands here now and there's an opportunity to have the Yarboroughs and the Morelands both look out for the future."

"You don't have enough money to settle this thing up here. McCanes don't even have enough. He's indicted. It's going to court. You'd have to pay off half the county. I think he's going to jail."

"I wouldn't underestimate me," I said. "Is it possible for you as a friend to become the agent for the family?"

"Agent?"

"An agent for the settlement."

"I'll think about it. I'll talk it over."

"With everyone?"

"With the few."

"Good," I said. I reached in my coat pocket and pulled out the envelope in which I had put the stack of bills and counted out two hundred dollars and handed it over. Yarborough didn't even look down when he took it.

"How about the boy who claims Mr. McCane threatened him on the lake? How about the two others that were in the boat with Novie Moreland and her daughter?" I asked.

"I'll track them all down."

"Tell them we want to settle this," I said. "Tell them I'll be back a week from today."

I stuck out my hand and Yarborough finally took it after an uncomfortable second or two. The mallet I'd imagined when I thought a beating was in store for me seemed softer than it had appeared. For a farmer his grip was loose and uncertain. He released my hand, turned and walked back to the truck, and continued into town.

| 19 |

The next week I drove back up to the Canaan Valley. Before I left I slipped out behind the house and took a hundred dollars from the contingency fund in the coffee jar. I put the money in the envelope in my coat pocket just in case Yarborough had located and persuaded the witnesses. If they would attest to Mr. McCane's innocence their testimony would be worthy of the investment.

In a few months the trees would bud and some of the fields would be planted but Canaan still would not look like the promised land of its namesake. There were abandoned, falling-down shacks along the road and broken fences and skinny mules in a few barnyards. It was clear to me again why the mountain folk left these ridges and hollers in the great clearing out. They couldn't make a living farming. The subsistence farm economy had flat failed. The soils were bad and the crops vulnerable to weather. As I drove down Canaan Road I imagined what it would be like to leave there to work in the piedmont as thousands of folks did a generation earlier. My uncle Henry Bassett, my mother's brother, had worked as a labor scout in these same mountains back around 1915. His circuit had included Asheville, Waynesville, and Huntersville, where he'd scoured the hills and recruited mill hands for McCane's main mill in Morgan. I'd heard him talk about those early days and how powerful the pull was toward those distant mills when you were working the fields for nothing, or if you were a farmer who lacked the resources to sell your crops in markets.

The men and women he encountered were independent but hungry for success, so hundreds of them took Uncle Henry's free train tickets and loaded up those passenger cars and disappeared down the mountain, some never to return. Others heard the mills were hiring secondhand and simply abandoned their hard-scrabble farms and piled their few possessions into mule carts and wagons pulled by oxen. They came down the grade in a reverse migration to what their great-grandparents had endured when the Indian territory opened up a hundred years earlier.

Canaan wasn't a prosperous area and I had the feeling driving down past the Canaan church that only a proud core of people had endured the out-migration of the teens there. The Canaan community houses were neat and the fields tended unlike those to some of the surrounding valleys.

I was lucky to find Yarborough plowing an outparcel a good distance up the road from his house. Yarborough looked up as my vehicle approached, recognized it, dropped his plow, wiped his hands on his overalls, and stood in the field as I stopped the truck. I stepped out and raised my hand in greeting. He nodded. He did not walk to the road as I expected he would but instead went fifteen feet into the muddy field and waited for me to walk to him. I looked down at the mud and my nice brown polished shoes and finally tiptoed from furrow to furrow. By the time I arrived before Yarborough my cuffs were caked with muddy Canaan bottomland.

"Any news?" I asked as I stood uncomfortably in the field.

"Howry Hayes was the man on the grade," Yarborough said. "He's interested in an offer and says if it's a good one he'll help you out."

"How about the others?"

"Pink Bright's the boy McCane told to get off the lake," Moreland continued. "He's interested in what you're offering too."

"How about the Martin family? How about the other two?" I asked with some hesitancy. "How about the widow?"

"Not so much," Yarborough said. "The other two that was in the boat are long gone. I think they moved to Asheville. I haven't even asked Novie, and Martin's mama and daddy won't even talk to me. I heard Martin's nieces have seen a fancy lawyer down in Greenville and might file a civil suit."

"You tell Hayes and Bright that we appreciate anything they can do for us, and that this is for them." I handed a hundred dollars to Yarborough.

"You know those two ain't likely the key," Yarborough said. "I'm afraid it's Novie the solicitor's counting on. She's the one says McCane ran them over on purpose. She says he saw them in the boat and never slowed down a damn bit. Being a widow gives her some credibility."

"Well, we both know how unlikely it is Mr. McCane acted that way," I said. "This was a tragic accident and that will likely be proved when the case goes to trial."

"All depends on what Novie considers an advantage," Yarborough said, spitting tobacco juice into the dark soil of the field. "To her an advantage might be a world without George McCane walking free in it as a way to avenge her dead husband and son pulled from the bottom of that lake with a hook."

"I understand," I said, "but I also know that there's an advantage in this world if she could secure something for herself and her surviving daughter."

"They're hurting, that's for sure. That big note on the farm and land's probably past due."

"Then a few hundred dollars will help her out."

"She won't listen," Yarborough said, taking up his plow again. "I'll do what I can. That's all a soul can do in this world."

"Is there any way you could get me an audience with her?" I asked, grasping for some way to move things forward.

"An audience?"

"A visit, fifteen minutes alone with her to express my condolences," I said.

"She remembers about your condolences," he said. "She saw you on the porch lying about the insurance money."

"That was a mistake and I'll apologize for it, but I would like to offer that apology directly to Mrs. Moreland."

"She's not herself," Yarborough said. "I'm not sure it would do you any good to see her."

I peeled off another twenty and handed the bill to him.

Yarborough looked down and slipped the bill in his pocket. "I reckon she might give you fifteen minutes. I'll have to walk the mule back to the barn."

Yarborough and I mounted the steps to Novie Moreland's house. With the door closed, the curtains pulled, it looked like there was nobody home. Yarborough rapped on the doorframe. Novie answered and stepped back a little when she saw who stood there.

"Novie," Yarborough said, "this here is Ben Crocker. He'd like to talk to you for a few minutes. Come on out here on the porch now and set down."

Novie didn't speak. There were dark furrows under her eyes and her hair wasn't perfectly fixed like it had been the last time I saw her. Grief had finally settled like a fog in the valley and even having all that youthful beauty couldn't quite get her out of that grief's way. In spite of a visible reluctance to cooperate she did what Yarborough asked and walked out and sat in a wicker porch chair. I sat next to her.

"I gotta go tend to the mule, Novie," he said. "I'll be back in fifteen minutes." Then Yarborough stepped down off the porch and left the two of us alone.

Novie Moreland stared straight ahead, then she turned and spoke. Her face looked a little more relaxed and I even thought that her mood had lightened a little. "Here to sell me some insurance, are you?"

"No, Ma'am," I said. "I'm here to apologize and offer you that proposal again."

"Do I look like a woman in any shape to take your apology or consider your proposal?" she asked and offered a shadow of a smile.

I decided her lightness offered an opening. I thought it was best to get right to it, and I didn't hold back or make small talk. "I would like for you to consider my proposal to buy this farm and offer you a life estate as settlement."

"Don't you think justice might settle this faster than we can?"

"Justice is only one way. We don't have to see this out. There are other ways."

"There ain't no other ways for me or my family. George McCane will stand trial here for what he done on that lake. God and the judge will decide it. You might as well get back from where you came if you think it's going to be any other way."

"You've lost a husband and a son, but you still have your daughter. Don't you want to make a way for her? You'll have the money and a place for her to grow up."

"My daughter was pulled from that lake. That girl saw McCane's boat coming on with no regard for us. She still can't sleep because of what she saw up there. She's said it seemed we was like turtles basking on a log as far as George McCane cared that morning. Those three murder charges is what will be settled in a court of law."

"You know Mr. McCane is a very prominent man. He owns the mill many in this community have worked in."

"More powerful than the law? Judge Tucker said no man is bigger than the law in North Carolina."

"The law is men," I said.

"Men may be what made it," she said, "But not men like George McCane."

"I've been told justice is a woman," I said. "I've been told that's who stands in front of the Supreme Court in Washington."

"Let's hope for McCane's sake she's not a woman with a dead child."

"There is a much simpler way to go about this."

"You stay with your kind of simple," Novie Moreland said. "I'll stay with the law."

I took out the envelope. I placed it on her lap and stood up. "Novie, this envelope has $150 in it."

She looked down at the envelope in her lap and to my surprise made no effort to hand it back. Instead she stared straight at me and slipped it into the pocket on her apron.

I paused for a moment then spoke: "It was good to see you down in Carlton at Olin's."

"Olin and his wife have been good to us since the accident," she said. "He's a good man."

"Well, he might be that but he's been a thorn in my side."

"Mr. Crocker," she said. "Can I ask you something personal?"

"Go ahead," I said.

"How did you come to be on the wrong side of all this?"

"The wrong side?"

"Olin said you grew up on the mill hill like the rest of them."

"How is improving on your lot in life coming out on the wrong side?"

"Throwing Olin Campbell and his family out. That's wrong."

"Well, I haven't been very successful at that. Olin's still in his house."

"Fixing a rich man's problems."

"He's my boss. Of course I'm going to help him out of a fix."

"What does your wife think of all this?"

"What's my wife got to do with any of it?"

"You're bound together by a vow. Till death do you part," she said and I saw a tear forming.

"Well, I think of this as an investment," I said. "I'm investing in my future too."

"Maybe you should go," she said. "Yarbrough will be coming back."

"And about my wife. She's got her own ideas about how things should go," I said.

"Well, she is a woman," Novie said, looking up, and the tears were gone.

About that time Yarborough finished up with his mule and came back across the road. I watched him approach and open the gate. He walked through with confidence. Why shouldn't he? My twenty-dollar bill was tucked away somewhere. Then he mounted the two steps on Novie Moreland's porch. "Mr. Crocker," he said. "We about finished here?"

"Mr. Crocker was just leaving, Saul," Novie Moreland said. "He's completed his business."

"Good to see you as always, Mrs. Moreland," I said and tipped my hat.

"I'm sure we'll see you again," she said.

I stepped off the porch and went back to my truck. There weren't many times in my life I felt like I'd gone down a dark hallway with no windows and no door, but that was one of them. I had a sinking feeling that I'd actually done some backsliding, and besides that it was becoming clear as I saw Yarborough smiling in my rearview mirror that I'd squandered some of Angus McCane's money too.

| 20 |

A few days later Mr. McCane walked out of his office and stood by my desk. He picked up two or three files off my desk and looked them over.

"How are things up at the mill?" he finally asked.

"Almost finished," I said. "Everything's all done except bricking up the windows."

"That's an important component to our mill modernization," he said.

"Your brother didn't like the first mason I hired, but I found another one who might suit him better."

"Daddy said Angus was the best of us," McCane said. "Not much of that is showing through now. How did the men like him?"

"The men didn't like him, sir."

"Angus thinks he should have been president of the mill. He was passed over for good reasons. Did he do a good job?"

"Adequate," I said.

"Is it safe to say that the union's no longer a factor out at Carlton?"

"That's yet to be determined," I said. "They still have local number 270 of the UTWA."

"So the mill's still organized in spite of our work in the other direction?"

"Loosely speaking."

"Will they cause us trouble?"

"We won't know that until we open back up."

"And Campbell? Is he out yet?"

"No, sir," I said. "I decided to let him stay."

"You decided to let him stay?"

"Yes, sir. We would have been in deeper with the courts had we throwed him out. Why complicate the whole mess by throwing out the most prominent union boss in the whole upcountry?"

Midafternoon the phone rang. Angus was on the other end, and he sounded sober. "Crocker? Come up to the lake this evening," he said. "I've got one more errand for you to run."

"I'm afraid I'm busy," I said, lying to try to get him off the phone. "I've run enough errands."

"I don't give a goddamn how busy you are," he said. "Get your ass up here if you want George to get this mess behind him."

A little before dark I arrived at the lake and followed the gravel road around toward the McCane compound. When I was even with the dam and the dam keeper's cottage the lake opened up before me, a beautiful blue scene that perfectly hid all the trouble it had caused in September. There was no traffic. The air was too cool for boating or swimming. I thought about how easy things had been when the Canaan River was left to run free through the valley in the years before George McCane, Sr. had harnessed the power of falling water. I approached the gateposts of the McCane compound. There was little to suggest the wealth in the oaks and maples hidden on the slope above the lake, a happy hunting ground for the rich, inaccessible, peaceful. With the coming of the lake opportunities unimagined by those before had dawned and the slopes had been peopled with expectations and responsibilities. When you and your family had created something as privileged and beautiful as the lake it was hard to let it go.

I went straight up the McCane drive and knocked on the door of the little cottage right below the main house. Through the small window in the door I could see Angus sitting at the dining room table reading, his face lit by a lamp. Angus answered the door and the two of us stood in the dark entryway like boxers before the round starts. We inched closer and exchanged greetings.

"What do you need from me?" I asked.

"'Need?' You sound like a damn Salvation Army nurse. I don't need a damn thing, but I want to get some things settled," he said. "Come on in. We've got to wait until dark and then we're walking over for you to talk to the judge."

"Judge Tucker?"

"One and the same," Angus said then he walked back into the darker reaches of the cottage. "Sit down," he said. "We've got half an hour." He walked into his bedroom and emerged with a battered, crocodile satchel in one hand and a long-bodied flashlight in the other. He put both on the table before us and sat down.

"This will get the judge's attention," he said, holding up the satchel.

I looked at the battered satchel suspiciously, but Angus McCane offered no explanation and I didn't ask any questions.

When he sat down Angus poured himself a drink. He offered me one but I declined. Angus said, "Ben, do you know about power?

"Power? You mean like electric power?"

"No, power people have. The way it flows, pools, percolates, and evaporates through time?"

"I don't know where you're headed."

"Not headed anywhere. I'm just being philosophical for a minute as we wait for dark. I've been thinking about power a bunch the last few months with my brother's troubles. Power's not about money or stocks or even ownership in property. Power's about what you know and who you know and alliances and deals."

"I don't worry about George McCane. He seems to have a good bit of power."

"You know I don't really have much of that power."

"You're a McCane too," I said. "You've got a good bit, I'd say."

"Oh, I don't mean the kind of power that comes from a name," Angus said. "I mean the power to make things happen or to make them disappear or reappear."

"I'm beginning to get your drift," I said.

"Well, take a pull off this bottle and things might go crystal clear."

Angus passed the bottle over to me and I did take a long pull this time. The corn whiskey tasted strong, with a hint of peaches. Things weren't clear but they were clearing up a little.

"I've got something powerful in this satchel," Angus said. He held up the beaten-up valise. "Judge Tucker won't like that the McCanes have got what's here."

"Is there something in there he'd like kept quiet?"

"No, it's more simple than that," Angus said. "There's something in here Tucker will want cleared up. My father believed that when I was at Sewanee all I was interested in was poetry and literature," Angus explained, taking another swallow. "George might have had his engineering degree and his worthless management skills, but I took a course in history while I was up at Sewanee. Crocker, you ever heard of anthropology?"

"I've heard the word," I said.

"Well, it's the study of people," he said. "Primitive people mostly, not modern people like you or me, or so you'd expect. That history professor told us a story in class once about power. It stuck with me. He said an anthropologist had found that in some primitive tribe in Africa or somewhere chiefs got their power and wealth by what people owed them not what they owned. They give people in the village favors and the man with the most favors owed to him was the big man. It wasn't money the big man wanted when he called in what was owed to him. It was goats. He wanted a goat from everybody that owed him something so he could throw a really big party."

"So you got a goat in that satchel?"

"A goat. That's good. No, it's better than a goat. It's something to remind the judge what he owes us McCanes."

A half-hour later we were outside the cottage and Angus pointed up toward the woods with the flashlight and the yellow beam illuminated a small opening in the mountain laurel and rhododendron.

"Let's go, Crocker," Angus said. "We'll walk the old trail through the woods." We scrambled through the dark for ten minutes and I had no idea where we were going. The woods were thick and dry.

The trail was a rocky, narrow way that hugged the undeveloped ridge behind the McCane compound. Angus went first with the flashlight and I followed as closely behind as I could. There were huge oaks on either side, making the slope dense and mysterious in the dark. The path rose a hundred feet or so above the compound and then dipped as we crossed a small, noisy brook falling over rounded stones down toward the lake. The air smelled of hidden things and often I could hear a gurgle just out of sight that alerted me to small streams. At the top of the ridge McCane stopped for a moment and turned off his flashlight. Once it was dark I could see there was an opening before us.

"See those lights below?" he said, pointing down toward the cottages around the lake. "My daddy did that. Before this lake came to the Canaan Valley there was nothing here. Now our mill in Morgan gets its power from this lake. They have no idea what we did for them. Daddy used to bring us up here at night like this. He said the houses looked like a glowing pearl necklace in the dark, a necklace he crafted."

"It's pretty," I said.

"You're not still thirsty, are you, Crocker?" Angus McCane asked after a minute of silence, pulling out the half-empty pint of whiskey from his back pocket and waving it in front of my face. "I sure am."

"I'm fine," I said, pushing the pint away.

"Come on, Crocker," McCane said, offering the pint one more time. "Stop being such a prissy boy. A man never knows when the last time he'll get to take a drink might be."

I took the pint and turned it up. I didn't like being called a prissy boy. The clear whiskey burned my throat going down.

"Where the hell are we going?" I asked.

McCane took another pull on the bottle.

"There you go, Crocker, cuss a little. It's good for the soul. You know what the Roman poet said? *"Carpe diem, quam minimum credula postero."*"

"I'm afraid my Latin isn't very good," I said, wiping my mouth.

"Seize the day, then take another drink," Angus said and turned the bottle to the night sky, then handed the bottle to me.

"Seize the day," I said, turning the bottle up myself.

We came out of the woods on the dusty South Shore Drive and stood across the road from one of the biggest and nicest of the lakefront cottages. The judge's porch light was on. "That's Judge Tucker's place," Angus said, and handed me the satchel.

"What do you want me to do with this?"

"It's simple," he said. "Walk over there, knock on the judge's door and tell him you want to show him something. He'll let you in."

"What will I be showing him?"

"The deed to his nice cottage and to the two hundred acres around the cottage on this end of the lake."

"A deed?"

"A tax deed. My daddy leased two hundred acres of hunting land to the judge's daddy back in 1910. Old man Tucker's family had farmed this cove since a Kings Grant in 1770 and they owned another parcel. Old man Tucker kept the King's Grant in a drugstore frame in the front room of the cabin. It was a trade so that Daddy got the flooding rights to the two hundred acres of bottomland downstream from the Tuckers and old man Tucker got almost a mile of lake frontage and the upper end of the lake to hunt in a twenty-year lease at a dollar a year for a hundred years."

"That sounds like a deal for your daddy."

"Old man Tucker thought it was a good deal for him since he liked to coon hunt and didn't want to travel out of the cove to do it, and he didn't like dealing in cash money too much."

"So the lake is free and clear, but the land the judge's cottage is on is not?"

"The old man and his wife raised six children in that cabin and it was right on the lakeshore when the water rose. Two of his children went on to become lawyers and one is a big-time developer up in Asheville. When old man Tucker died his lawyer son who stayed tore down the cabin and built the cottage, thinking they owned the land."

"Built that big cottage on somebody else's property?"

"Well, old man Tucker didn't have a will. There's been no indication the old man told his son about the complications to the title."

"So now the judge gets the deed to the property he didn't even know he needs? Seems like a judge would be smarter than that."

"He just didn't know what he didn't know is all," Angus said.

"And someday he'll need that deed when the McCanes come calling?" I asked.

"Not just the deed. A clear title to a future, a fortune, a favorable social disposition. That half mile of lakefront up and down from his cottage will be worth a fortune."

"Your daddy was smart to work it out that way," I said.

"He thought he might need something from the Tuckers someday, and he was right."

"Why don't you take it to him?"

"I don't want it coming from a McCane. The proposal has more power coming from an alternative voice, an agent of the king, not the king himself."

Angus stood on the edge of the woods and waited as I did as I had been instructed. I crossed the road and knocked on the door. In a moment the judge opened the door. He looked surprised, but when I said Angus McCane had sent me and gestured to the satchel we disappeared inside and the door closed.

I was in the cottage for maybe ten minutes. When I was finished with the business I crossed the road, met Angus at the head of the trail, and handed the satchel back to him.

"I take it the transaction went well," Angus said.

"He said he understood," I said.

"Well, I've never doubted he's a smart man."

I turned for a moment like Lot's wife in the Bible and looked back at the judge's house. It was as if I'd escaped from a burning building and I wanted to see it collapse behind me. When the porch light finally blinked out we disappeared into the woods. I fell in behind Angus and we walked in silence, retracing our route up and over the ridge to the family compound.

| 21 |

A week later McCane left for the mountains with his company lawyer Leland Cromer to meet with Ripley Grier. McCane left in the morning and he did not return to the office in the afternoon. I stayed to tend the company's business and pay some bills for the Carlton project. There was no reason for me to tag along. It looked like what I had tried to do to free McCane from his quagmire had failed miserably. McCane and his lawyer had their own strategy for his defense and I wasn't privy to it. They'd sorted out the details behind closed doors and now they were at work on what they'd concocted with Grier. I fully expected the case to go to trial and, win or lose, George McCane's good name to come out muddied by three murder charges in every major newspaper on the east coast. I didn't even like to consider that outcome. It wouldn't be good for McCane and it wouldn't be good for Morgan, South Carolina, and it might not be good for me and Coleen, seeing as everybody saw me as thrown in with the McCanes.

That evening Coleen had to work at the Sanitary Café and I had my supper there. Wylie Jackson came in and saw me sitting in the back corner.

"Well, Ben Crocker," Jackson said. "I heard this afternoon that McCane was up in Huntersville and the fix is on. I wouldn't be surprised if that judge didn't just throw it all out before it even comes before a jury."

"What are you talking about?"

"Don't play dumb, Crocker. Your boss is facing murder charges but they'll just fix it."

Coleen walked over to fill my coffee cup.

"My husband's business is none of yours," she said.

"My cousin says you even been up there snooping around."

"We'll just have to see what a jury says, I guess."

"How's Widow Moreland holding up?" Jackson said, and Coleen perked up.

I looked down at my plate and hoped that Jackson would get the message that the conversation was over and leave. He'd said what he'd come to say and now I had to clean up the mess.

"What did Wylie mean about Widow Moreland?" Coleen asked, sitting down in my booth.

"I had to make a trip up there to talk to her," I said. "I guess he heard about that from somebody."

"Why would you have to talk to the widow?"

"Mr. McCane wanted to know if she plans to testify against him."

"Why didn't he send his lawyer?" she said. "It doesn't seem that should be any of your business. I don't want you calling on that woman."

"I wasn't calling on her for pleasure," I said. "You think it was fun to go up there?"

"I don't know what's fun for you, Ben."

"I'm sorry, honey, but I don't know what you mean by that."

Coleen leaned close and a serious scowl spread over her face. "It can mean whatever you want. I'm sorry. I'm just tired of working, and I'm tired of spending all my evenings alone wondering where you've run off to and whose business you are up to."

"I'll try and get home earlier if you'll train that dog not to growl."

"Don't let Snowball unnerve you."

"I didn't grow up with dogs in the house, and I sure didn't grow up with one sleeping in the room with us."

"Maybe you ought to feed him," Coleen said.

"Maybe we ought to send that dog on a vacation."

"I worry that you take your job too seriously. I worry that you'll wear yourself out for that mill."

"I'm wearing myself thin for us. I'm trying to provide for us in hard times."

Coleen looked over her shoulder. "I got to get back to the counter." She stood up and leaned back down and spoke almost in a whisper. "Ben, don't go back up there and see that woman. Nothing good can come of it, no matter what your intentions."

The next day McCane came in early. He shuffled around the office, not speaking.

"Did you have a good day in Huntersville?" I finally asked when I could not hold it back anymore.

"Ripley Grier assured us that Judge Tucker is a reasonable man," McCane said after my prompting. "I believe he'll see that charges of murder are preposterous once all the evidence is examined."

"Do you think there will be a day in court?"

"The circuit court is set to meet in early March," he said. "So we'll see. Let's talk about something else, Crocker. How soon can we reopen the Carlton Mill?"

"We can start hiring everyone back this week," I said. "As soon as you give me a target for the workforce."

"How about the bricking up the windows? Isn't that running behind?"

"We can brick up the windows after we get everyone hired back."

"Not everyone," McCane said. "I want you to go through the lists again. Use all your contacts. Find out all you can about allegiances and loyalties. There will be no union sympathizers working there."

"You're cutting out half our pool that way," I said. "And you're pushing out some of our best people."

"I'm sure you're aware of the savings in labor these new machines will create. They run on half as many hands as before, and those hands will not be union hands. My father passed down a decentralized concern to us, and I plan to keep it that way," McCane said. He stood over my desk and looked down at me. "Crocker, you keep the books. You know that our profit margin has always been precarious. You know our fortunes slump and surge. You know how hard it is to keep a market share. We can't afford to pay them more."

"It's not all about wages," I said. "It's also about the time clock you put on them."

"Ah, the dreaded stretchout."

"It adds more and more to them, and most of those working on the floor don't see when it's going to stop."

"It's unreasonable expecting us to pass over scientific methods just because they don't want to work."

"They're not lazy, sir."

"Call it what you want. It's our only way to make a profit, and with these new machines at Carlton we will get an efficient system in place," he said, pausing before he continued. "Say, what do I pay you, Ben?"

"You know I make twenty dollars a week."

"Yes, and that's twice what we pay someone working on the floor."

"I'm grateful," I said. "Don't get me wrong."

"What do they pay in union dues?"

"About twenty dollars a year."

"All that for nothing but strife and trouble. They'd be better off putting that money in a coffee jar."

"So you will not hire back anyone who has signed up with the union?"

"That's my preference."

"Yes, sir, we'll have everyone hired this week," I said.

A day later I was in Carlton. As I was leaving the mill grounds I saw Olin Campbell cross the street after coming out of the snack bar. He saw me and walked over.

"I was coming to see you anyways," he said as we shook hands.

"It's not always good when you come calling," I said.

"I wouldn't be so worried, Crocker," he said. "We're all reasonable men. I hear you're hiring, but the numbers are way down from when you closed up the mill."

"The new machinery needs fewer hands."

"I wanted to remind you and your boss that we still have a union here," he said.

"Who we hire back might not be union," I said.

"We still have our charter and we're acting accordingly. I'd like to sit down with Mr. McCane about all this if I could. Would you set up a meeting?"

"You think George McCane would come within a country mile of you, Dan Eliot, or John Garland?"

"If he wants to keep his shiny new mill running, he will," Campbell said.

"I think he'd say shut it down if you think you can, but be prepared to face the authorities if you illegally interfere with his operations."

"He has no idea what kind of brew's boiling, does he?"

"What do you mean?"

"It's not just the union," Campbell said. "He's got a whole county pulling against him west of here."

"That will all blow over when he's exonerated by the courts."

"Blow over, my ass."

"What happened up on the lake was an accident."

"They're saying he's bought the damn judge and the witnesses."

"Olin," I said before I turned to walk back to the car. "The union's never going to take hold any deeper in South Carolina, especially not in a McCane mill. You ought to just give up."

"Crocker, remember where you're from," he said.

"I know where I am from. I want what's best for my people," I said. "And the union's providing nothing for them but trouble."

"The union? Did the union close the mill down?"

"We hired as many as we could," I said. "We gave them credit at the company store to tide them over. They could stay in their houses and we waived the back rent."

"The union kept this village alive the last four months," he said. "Not your credit at the company store or your free rent."

I turned to head for the truck. "We're opening this mill next week."

| 22 |

George McCane wanted to throw a party for his renovated mill, so I sent the Ponder boys out with two hundred special tickets for a free pig supper to assure a partisan crowd. I'd decided we'd let anybody with a ticket in the fence and then maybe the troublemakers would have to listen from outside. I figured this was our one chance to show Campbell and the union who is in control of the mill and the village. We had to look good, and there's nothing quite like a free supper to settle everybody down.

The boys from Knuckletown cleaned up the mill yard and my cousin Ed Crocker prepared a pit and hauled in two big, slaughtered hogs to barbecue. Ed had his wife buy cabbages and prepare enough slaw to feed two hundred, and I had the Ponders buy every quart can of pork and beans at the mill commissaries around the county and round up enough white loaf bread to go along with the pig, beans, and slaw.

Ed and his wife found a big urn for sweet tea in the mill storeroom and they borrowed plates, glasses, and silverware from the village Methodist and Baptist church social halls. In the yard, they set up a long line of sawhorses and laid leftover rough-cut boards from the construction side-by-side for a table.

At midnight the evening before, Ed started cooking the two hogs, and by the time I was there in the morning the whole yard smelled like pork, vinegar, and red peppers. Ed had prepared the pit several days in advance, digging the hole, lining it with bricks, and then filling the bottom with hickory slabs, which he reduced to a foot of burning coals. Ed then placed a big rack on bricks. He placed hot rocks in the hogs' cavities and wrapped the meat in chicken wire and damp burlap bags before placing them on the rack above the coals. The cooking hole was covered with two sheets of tin and by the time I arrived smoke was leaking out from the edges.

While Ed worked on the food, the night watchman Norris and I hauled the flags up to the first-story windows and dropped them out and tacked them there. After we'd draped the flags I walked back down, stepped back, and took a look. The whole scene looked a little like a stage set for a Fourth of July celebration or a stump speech when a state politician came through.

I thought a truck bed would be a good place for Mr. McCane to stand and give a speech. This was the part of the celebration I was most worried about. All week he'd been acting like this was his big chance to clear the air with his restless Carlton workers. He told me he thought it made sense to talk about the future of textiles and how bright it looked for the industry in spite of the hard times, no matter whether that was true or not.

I said, "You don't need to tell those people anything they'll remember. In fact the contrary is true. They need to walk out of there with full bellies and empty heads." I hoped the speech would put that hard period behind us. I didn't think it was good for McCane to dwell on the details. I wanted the village back to work, and I wanted to forget about everything negative, even the pending murder trial.

"You underestimate what they will expect," McCane said.

"And you overestimate what they will appreciate," I said. "When you finish, just climb down from the bed of that truck, cut the ribbon we've stretched across the door, and open up for business. Honest work's the only thing that will cure what's ailing them."

But it was clear McCane didn't see it that way. He said, "I want to justify my actions. I will not simply repeat platitudes about hard work and progress and then let them eat the rest of the pig."

By noon there was a big crowd already inside the fence. They were milling around the food, waiting for Ed to open up the pit and haul out the meat. The Ponders were taking tickets. Most came in through the gate, but I saw a few sneaking in the back way around the mill. Even the Knuckletown boys stuck around. They stood at the corner of the mill watching uneasily. I noticed that Angus McCane had snuck in the back way as well. He hovered near the Knuckletown boys, rocking on the outside of his feet, taking a draw out of a pint every few minutes. I walked over to say hello.

He pointed up at the big flags. "This is quite a celebration," he said, taking another deep swig of the pint bottle swaddled in a paper sack.

"We wanted it to be a day we'd remember."

"George isn't too good with heights. Are you sure you want to put him up there?"

"He's not going to talk from the window," I said. "He'll be up on the bed of that truck."

"Well, keep a close eye on him. You know he'll probably feel pretty exposed up there."

"He seems strong to me."

"Where is George anyway? Shouldn't he be here circulating among his people? You know what the poets say, the wise man governs nobody but himself."

"He'll be here soon, I hope," I said.

"He never was too fond of pork. He prefers meat with French names."

Ed and two others used chains to pull the hogs up out of the hole around noon. Ed carved and dumped pan after pan of steaming slabs of the succulent pink, stringy meat on an oilcloth stretched across the end of the make-do table.

Among those shouldering up for a plate of pork I saw Olin Campbell, Dan Eliot, John Gorman, Jamie Biggerstaff, and Vernon Satterfield, all bunched together. I figured somebody must have given them tickets. Ed's wife made plates and took food over to them in the first wave. They sat on the ground and drank tea and ate pork as the line snaked past the tables.

The villagers picked the pork up with their hands like they hadn't eaten meat in months. Ed's wife kept the big white bowls full of slaw and beans. Coleen had come out from town on the trolley and she helped serve as well. She heaped the pork out in oversized metal spoons as the workers passed. They also picked up slices of white bread from the torn-open paper bags. The men, women, and children took two and three slices at a time. I could see there was no way we could feed all that was coming in on what we we'd provided.

George McCane drove a new black Buick sedan into the mill parking lot at a quarter to one. He stepped out and worked his way toward where I was standing. McCane was slowed down to a crawl by the workers sticking out their hands for him to shake like a politician. As his progress slowed he glanced toward me and he seemed surprised they didn't hate him. I thought about how false his sense of community really was. He only came out of his office to walk among his employees on special occasions, and so when his people finally saw him they all wanted to touch him, like a king or the bearer of the relics of a saint. Maybe that day they reached out to shake his hand because they remembered his father was really the one who was bigger than life and he was taken from us too soon, or maybe they did it because George, Jr., was smaller than life. Either way, coming in through the crowd that day was the happiest I would ever see George McCane.

You would have thought there would be no stopping him from delivering a real stem-winder and pouring out his heart to his people from the stage of that truck, but it didn't work out that way. As soon as McCane mounted the flatbed the day quickly turned disastrous. I don't remember the exact speech word for word but fragments of what he said have stuck with me for fifty years as I'm sure they have stuck with many of those who were there.

McCane began with a joke. "With this big crowd and two hogs I'm sure that in a few minutes we'll be in Biblical territory," he said. "I'm hoping for the miracle of the loaves and the fishes, and I hope somebody's praying for intervention from above."

Then he paused to look out over those gathered below him and his mood darkened quickly as he shifted gears: "By nature our forbearers—mine included —were mostly a barbaric border horde from Scotland, but this industry gave us all a leg up and your faces show it. Textiles brought you down from the hills, gave you all a splendid beginning, furnished you with a house, a job, and assured a future for everyone, our children, and even their children and their children's children. Textiles brought you down from a place of dirt and disease to one of clean and substantial pavements and modern lighting. In a generation this will be one of crossroads of a new South—a South hurtling toward its destiny of wealth and glory. The future when it comes will be supported by your back and hands."

After that, McCane rambled on about mental training in the local mill school as the foundations of business and industry. He talked of "that compelling spiritual power whose name is achievement. The die has been cast by our investments here. It is only now left to you to put this opportunity to use."

In the first row of the crowd—among the ones McCane had said had once been a horde—I watched the faces as he talked, the paternal tone of his words washed over them and then seeped in like a stain over their skin. As he finished any sense of pride they had towards him vanished, and they rocked like children on the balls of their feet, impatient for recess. When it was clear McCane was finished I broke the silence with clapping and one or two others joined me until something approaching an ovation finally sparked and spread like a slow grease fire through the crowd. He seemed pleased and raised his hand like Jack Dempsey after a fight.

On cue McCane stepped down from the truck bed and walked back to cut the ribbon. Not many gathered around. Most of the crowd had disappeared out the gate in depressed waves, leaving a handful for the ceremony.

"Now it's back to business," McCane said as he turned to the dwindling crowd and struggled to cut the ribbon with his brother's pocketknife. He spoke to those nearby, including his brother and me. "This should set the tone."

Once the ribbon was cut McCane looked nervous and out of place. "You always were good with words, George," Angus McCane said, slurring his words noticeably. "That should really stir them toward civic heights."

McCane listened as his brother spoke and something approaching self-awareness surfaced for a moment, but the mood was quickly deflected by his need to correct Angus.

"I hope you have one of your whores who can drive you home," McCane said to his brother.

"You let me worry about my whores, little brother," Angus McCane said. "You worry about the mills."

When the McCanes had left I stuck around for a while as Ed and his wife cleaned up what little was left of the food. They put the cans and trash in boxes on the back of the flatbed truck to haul to the dump. They gathered the borrowed plates, silverware, and glasses to clean and return to the churches. They piled the picked, clean bones of the hogs outside the fence for the village dogs.

One of the severed hogs heads was the last to go. The whole afternoon it had presided over the end of the table as people passed with their plates. The ears were huge and the roasted skin was a ruddy red, the color of Angus's face. Ed had removed the tongue and roasted it separately in the pit, and it lay next to the head, to me a grisly reminder of McCane's speech.

As he was leaving, Ed wrapped the hog's head and the tongue back up in burlap to carry to his truck. "I wish I could pay you for your hard work," I said.

"Ben, you paid us in advance that day in the house," he said, referring back to the money I'd given them. He placed the hog's head in the bed of his truck. "Besides, this is the best meat. We're county people. The cheek meat is so tender it just falls off the bone, and we all like tongue."

Before Ed left I asked him what he thought of McCane's speech.

"McCane's talk was a little like that hog's head," he said. "Not much meat on it, and what was there he'd cooked so long it just fell off the bones."

| PART III |

The Last Flying Squadron

| 23 |

George McCane's trial was scheduled for the first Monday of April, and on the Thursday before, a fast-moving snowstorm blanketed Morgan and the mountains beyond. The storm shut down the asheville road and even stopped the train from running, but the knee-high, wet drifts melted quickly away. By Friday the temperatures were up in the 60s and the routes west cleared.

The snowstorm's effects could have been worse. Work didn't stop at the Morgan Mill and newly opened Carlton Mill only lost two shifts. Norris said he recorded eleven inches of snow on the hood of his truck at the mill. Later in the day news circulated through Morgan about a tragedy out in the village: a shed roof at Satterfield's farm had collapsed with the weight of the snow and crushed his old mule. As I sat in my cozy house on Maple Street I knew that out in Carlton Mill hands worried about having enough coal for their pot-bellied stoves. My father always did. As the snow fell they'd probably huddled under quilts (as we once had) in the uninsulated mill houses and shivered and fretted until the warm weather returned a day later.

I'd hoped that the storm would postpone McCane's trial, but jury selection proceeded at 9:00 on Monday. With the roads clear, I drove up by myself to Huntersville early. McCane made his own plans. Leland Cromer had arrived early and they left from the office a half hour before I did. McCane hadn't asked me if I wanted a ride. I wasn't even sure whether he knew I was attending the trial.

I hadn't made any other trips to Canaan since I'd last seen Novie Moreland, and I had not contacted Saul Yarborough again. I had done the best I could and my only hope was that Novie taking the money from me was enough, that she would soften once she testified, but I really had no idea what any of the witnesses would say once they got on the stand, or what McCane's chances were for acquittal, though I figured with two lawyers like Grier and Cromer and the judge on his side, he had a good chance.

As I climbed the grade that morning I noted the heavy run-off from the snowmelt in the river and felt my own insides churned up and in motion as well. The current surged through the narrow gorge as the torrent ricocheted from boulder to boulder. The black trees on the ridges along both sides of the road stood out in stark relief against the snowy backdrop.

Small towns in the South in the 1930s were orderly places, at least on the surface. They were segregated by race and class, and governed by hard-won wealth such as had been accumulated by the McCanes. A man like George McCane was as clearly positioned by his family background, education, and economic privilege as a mountain dominating a horizon. To have happen to him what did in the fall of '35 was unthinkable in the tight confines of a small Southern mill town. The disorder of the indictments, the trial, and a possible conviction was beyond imagining by someone who had not experienced it, and yet, as unpleasant and unsettling as the events were, they had been successfully tamped down just like the winter weeds now bent down under a foot of snow.

I had turned twenty-eight years old over Christmas. For seven years I'd worked fourteen hours a day keeping McCane's mills solvent and his affairs in order, but I knew that what we had built could melt away if my boss went to jail for murder.

My sense of martyrdom came from unease with my own station in life. I wasn't sure exactly what I was working for during those seven years. I had been lucky and escaped the mill hill, but I was not a McCane and never would be. Through working in McCane's office I had gained financially, but I'd lost some connection to my own people, even to my own family. If McCane was a mountain, was I simply a valley below?

I arrived in Huntersville an hour before the jury selection was to begin. Turning down Main Street, I saw traffic backed up for a block, so I parked two streets away and walked past the Confederate memorial in the middle of Main. The parking spaces were full along the streets, and there were even two or three stone hitching posts with mule wagons tied up in the shadows of elms. Court day was a gala occasion and as I walked, street vendors tried to sell me boiled peanuts.

As I approached the domed Huntersville County Courthouse I could see a line of folks making their way toward the front steps. The courthouse was reminiscent of pictures I'd seen of the Capitol in Washington, D.C. The dome was the highest point on the town's skyline and the central building took up half a block; four columns supported porches on each side. I suppose the presence of all those entrances and exits could give someone a feeling of symmetry, but standing there that morning I felt uneasy. I worried that in a building with so many doors, justice could just slip out the side without anyone noticing.

When I reached the courthouse yard I paused in front of a monument made of a pyramid of river stones that I'd never noticed before. The burnished bronze plaque set in the middle was dedicated to Daniel Boone. I remembered enough history to know that we were a long way from the route Boone had taken over the mountains, so it seemed an odd thing. I thought about it and decided that Daniel Boone was the perfect hero for mountain people like those walking into the courthouse to get their revenge on George McCane. Always on the move and unhappy with settlement, Boone's memorial assured them the frontier was still open and the future was not a twelve-hour shift in a cotton mill.

When I turned from the monument I stood for a moment to watch those McCane had called "the mountain hordes" push their way inside to see him prosecuted for murder, anxious to see whether or not the hand of justice could grab a rich man by the neck and shake him.

Falling into line to enter, I mounted the courthouse steps. I bumped into a man in a hat and dark threadbare suit jacket. He turned and I was surprised to see someone I knew. "Yarborough?" I said.

"Crocker, I thought you'd be here," Yarborough said, careful to continue to press forward and not lose his place in line. "Looks like your man McCane's day of reckoning has finally arrived."

"Any hint as to the outcome?" I asked as we inched along.

"It's not a friendly crowd," he said. "McCane's only hope is these passing months put some clouds on the lake that morning for Riding's witnesses."

"How is Mrs. Moreland?"

"She's holding up."

"You give her my best if I don't see her," I said.

The hallway leading to the courtroom proper was crowded with the mountain multitudes all pushing to get through one small door. "Is there any more room?" I asked a man in suspenders and a tie guarding the door and he pointed up a narrow staircase to the gallery.

I mounted the steps and claimed one of the few seats remaining right on the edge of the railing. I looked down on the proceedings, squeezed between and surrounded by a rag-tag bunch of locals. They dressed in what passed for their Sunday best, but their rough faces and battered knuckles showed they'd spent years behind a mule. They wanted to see mountain justice served, and if they wouldn't get a public hanging on the square out of this, as their fathers would have, they'd at least like to see George McCane led off in handcuffs.

The bailiff, a balding, rotund man in his shirtsleeves, announced, "All rise. The Court of Hunter County is now in session. The Honorable Judge Tucker presiding."

Judge Tucker walked into the courtroom, stepped up to the bench, and then we sat back down. Judge Tucker looked different than the last time I'd seen him at the lake. Now he was dressed in a black robe and had an air of importance hanging about him. He pulled a pair of reading glasses onto his nose and looked down at the folder of papers he'd brought into the room. Then he looked back up and called the court to order. His glasses slid down his nose as he said, "Mr. Youngblood, what is on the docket for this afternoon?"

"The first case up today is The State vs. George McCane."

"Thank you, Mr. Youngblood. The charge as I understand it is murder and Mr. McCane has entered a plea of not guilty," Judge Tucker said. "Is that right?"

"Yes sir, three counts of murder."

A little in front and almost directly below me stood two tables. At the left table sat Solicitor Clarence Riding. I could pick him out because of his height. With his long torso his head bobbed above those below. He looked over two legal pads and a pile of papers he'd laid out on the desk. At the other table sat George McCane and his two lawyers, Leland Cromer and Ripley Grier, the flatland dandy and the mountain institution. They had McCane boxed between them.

The bailiff led a tow-headed boy about eight or nine years old into court and he stood and drew names from a hat. "I guess justice isn't blind after all," the old man sitting next to me said to no one in particular. "It's wearing short pants though."

The boy drew the first name and the bailiff called it out to the pool of jurors gathered in the room. "C.L. Nesbitt," he said. The man walked forward with his hat in his hands and stood before the court for a moment. Riding said, "Seat the juror." Right away Grier said, "Excuse the juror" after which Nesbitt walked off.

This went on for a while, some being excused and some seated. Grier struck the ones who looked the most country and Riding seemed bent on keeping those kind of men. It went back and forth. "How many strikes does each side get?" I asked the old man.

"I reckon eight or nine. That lawyer from Morgan's about played his out, I'd say."

We were up to nine seated when a fine man in suspenders wearing the black coat of a banker or a lawyer walked up, and I expected from what had gone before that Riding would turn him down, but this time the solicitor said, "Seat the juror," and Grier went into a huddle with Cromer, probably trying to figure out why Grier would want such a man sitting in judgment. They talked for almost a minute until it looked like Grier got the upper hand and finally said, "Seat the juror," and the fine-looking man proceeded to the jury box.

Over the first hour the three juror's rows below me filled up and those who had been chosen waited. I wouldn't say they looked expectant, a mixed lot of sunburned farmers and the one man in a tie and suspenders, though I was sure they were not used to such excitement. All but the man in the tie slouched in their straight-backed chairs and some picked at their nails as they waited for the end of the process.

I craned out farther over the edge to get a view, and behind a railing on that side of the courtroom I spotted Novie Moreland sitting beside Olin Campbell. Olin had his hat in this lap and Novie was dressed in black with her blond hair pulled up in a tight bun. She sat still as a marble statue. I leaned out so far I thought I might fall, though she never looked up and only sat there stone cold, far below.

I convinced myself that if I stared long enough, Novie might finally feel my gaze on her and look up. Instead it was Olin whose head tilted upward and caught my eye. I quickly leaned back, like a peeping Tom flushed from the dark.

After I recovered, I wondered if Howry Hayes, the man on the Saltilla Grade who McCane said had run him into the ditch, and Pink Bright, the teenager who had accused McCane of threatening him when he'd caught him on the lake, had been called to testify. I couldn't imagine that Riding would try to build a murder case without their testimony, so I speculated which ones they might be below me. Was Hayes the nervous man three seats from Novie Moreland with his hat in his hands like Campbell? If that was Hayes, he looked like Riding had coaxed him down from a cave high in the mountains. He looked a little like Daniel Boone himself come back from the dead. He wore a buckskin frock and his hair sprouted at odd angles around an unkempt beard. Was Bright the teenager slumped on the first row behind the solicitor's table who had smuggled in a box of Cracker Jacks?

As much as I wanted to play the game of hidden identity I was drawn back to the defense table where I knew everybody. Grier and Cromer's table was uncluttered and they talked calmly among themselves as they all waited as Judge Tucker read the indictment.

I glanced out the big bank of windows on each side of the courtroom. I could see the mountains enveloping the town like a toy village. I was a believer in progress back then, in the idea that somehow a mountain farmer had improved his lot by moving to the flatlands and working in one of McCane's mills. The courtroom was sprinkled with representatives of an older order, hollow dwellers, hermits, small claim loggers, hound chasers, and bear hunters. They sat shoulder to shoulder with the future.

In the years since McCane's trial I have successfully steered clear of court-rooms. I haven't even served on a jury. The three times in five decades that I was called for duty I managed to wiggle my way out, or I was excused by one lawyer or another, people who probably owed me a favor. In '36 I was still young and so was George McCane. I felt like our business was important and our lives maybe would last forever. At eighty I no longer believe I'll live forever. Some days I wonder if I'll make it to the next. I'm not so sure what we were doing was any more important than anything else. In the end what's the difference in plowing the same field for fifty years and manufacturing cloth to sell? Is a mountain farmer's life of any less value than that of an accountant in a textile company or his boss?

I looked down at where McCane was sitting with Grier and Cromer. McCane seemed calm, just as he had been for a week. He did not flinch as I did when the judge said murder.

"Mr. Riding and Mr. Grier, are you ready to proceed?"

Mr. Riding rose and addressed the judge. "Yes, your honor, the prosecution is ready."

Grier rose as well, nodded toward Riding, and said, "Your honor, the defense is ready as well."

"Very good," Judge Tucker said, "Opening statements."

"May it please the court," Clarence Riding began. Riding was so tall and thin that when he stood below me he looked a little like a scarecrow unfolding upward into the air of the courtroom. He wore a loose-fitting faded blue suit twenty years out of style. The solicitor stayed behind the table as he spoke and leaned forward on his spindly wrists and craned his neck toward the judge's bench, never looking at the jury. Riding's voice wasn't very loud and I had trouble hearing. The annoying click of the ceiling fans obscured about every fifth word, so I had to press forward and listen hard.

"On a Sunday last September Morgan County industrialist George McCane gunned his motorboat down Lake Whitney in the direction of a pleasure craft occupied by seven innocent citizens of this county. Approaching at a speed between twenty-five and thirty miles per hour and closing to a distance of only thirty feet, Mr. McCane's powerboat created a substantial wake that swamped the pleasure boat and resulted in the tragic deaths of two men and a boy, swallowed by the cold waters of the lake. George McCane then left the scene of the crime, only to return later. You may ask where is the murder weapon in this case? Well, George McCane used his boat as an instrument of murder as surely as if he had put a loaded gun to the heads of his three victims. The dark waters of Lake Whitney served merely as a sheet to cover the dead. It is the prosecution's position that Mr.

McCane maliciously and with aforethought ended the lives of these three and we would hope that justice would be served in this case and that he be convicted of murder."

"Thank you, Mr. Riding, for your accustomed brevity," Judge Tucker said, glancing down at the papers spread out before him. "Mr. Grier, do you have a similarly succinct statement for us?"

Grier stood and glided out from behind the desk directly below me. He crouched like a boxer as he walked up right under the judge's nose.

"May it please the court and gentlemen of the jury, you all likely know that George McCane is an upstanding citizen of Morgan, South Carolina, and here in this county where his family has kept a summer home for two generations he is known far and wide as someone who would not carelessly endanger the lives of others. My client was much distressed by the loss of these lives, and he did all he could that fateful morning to ensure the rescue of those who survived. He did not act maliciously and through the course of the trial it will become clear that there is not a scrap of believable evidence to suggest that he was responsible for the deaths of three individuals, much less guilty of their murder."

Grier turned back toward the jury and paused before jabbing a finger toward them again, then looked out toward those assembled in the courtroom. "Mr. Riding is right about one thing. This was indeed a tragedy in which three lives were lost, but unlike the story the prosecution will tell, had it not been for my client the cold waters of the lake would have claimed the lives of four more."

"Grier's a citified liar and a cheat," the rag-tag man sitting next to me burst out in a squeaky voice, speaking it seemed to no one in particular, but still quite audible to the whole courtroom below. "And McCane's guilty as charged!" A murmur circled through the courtroom.

Judge Tucker slammed his gavel down several times before lifting his eyes to the gallery. "And to those assembled here I would like to make it clear that for the duration of this trial in my court there will be no outbursts, side comments, giggles, murmurs, guttural rebukes, or careless yawns. You sir," he continued, pointing his gavel up at my row, "will be in contempt of court if I hear so much as another peep."

The man next to me sank back into his seat but there was an edge in the air that had not been there before. My neighbor confirmed one thing for me: no matter what happened in the trial there was a vast reservoir of ill will toward the McCane family in these surrounding mountains.

"Call your first witness," Judge Tucker said. Riding called Howry Hayes to the stand. A man walked down the aisle, and he was not the one I'd expected to come forward; instead of the Snuffy Smith I'd picked out, a mousy, gray-haired man walked forward, dressed in a laundered white shirt and a dandy set of red suspenders.

After Hayes took the oath, Riding pointed to George McCane. "Mr. Hayes, have you ever seen this man?"

"Yes, sir, that's Mister George McCane and I seen him one time and I wished I ain't."

"And when was that?"

"Last September, down on the Saltilla Grade," Hayes said. He seemed at ease, as if he'd testified in front of a packed courtroom many times before.

"Was it a Sunday?" Riding asked.

"Objection, your honor, the solicitor is leading the witness," Riley Grier said.

"Sustained," Judge Tucker said. "Mr. Riding, please refrain from putting words in your witness's mouth."

"So when was it?"

"Yes sir, on Sunday, too early in the morning I know that."

"And what happened on the Saltilla Grade early that morning when you met George McCane?"

"I was headed down and he was headed up. We come around that tight curve where the trucks always jackknife and we scraped a little, fender to fender," Hayes said, using his hands to mime the situation.

Riding walked over toward the jury, paused and looked directly at them, then turned and looked back at Hayes.

"Mr. Howry, did you come to a halt?"

"Yes, sir, right away because I knew it was somebody in that big car."

"And what did you observe when you got out of the car?" Riding asked, walking back toward the stand.

"Mr. McCane, that man sitting right there, was not too happy."

I looked down and Mr. McCane's countenance had not changed. He watched the proceedings with no emotion, as if he were standing in line at a bank.

"What did he say?"

"He cursed a time or two, then he asked how I expected to pay for his trouble?"

"Would you say he was agitated?"

"No, he was mad, boiling like a tea kettle," Hayes said, pleased with his elegance. A handful of those in the courtroom found Hayes's comment funny and the judge rapped his gavel to bring order.

"He was angry?"

"Yes, sir, he was hot."

"Would you say he was angry beyond the circumstances?"

"Well, it was only a scratch."

Riding approached the witness and handed him three photos. "These are photos of the damaged fender of George McCane's Buick. We offer these in evidence, your honor." He walked back a step or two and continued. "Mr. Hayes, did it appear McCane had been drinking?"

McCane's attention focused on Hayes. He seemed interested in the proceedings for the first time.

"Objection," Grier said, standing this time. "Prosecution persists in leading the witness."

"Sustained. Mr. Riding, let the witness tell his own story."

"What else did you observe?"

"I remember wondering if that rich man was drunk. It was just a scratch and he acted like I run him off the road."

"What happened then?"

"Mr. McCane dismissed me, told me to get the hell down the mountain, and that he hoped he'd never see me or my truck again."

"Mr. Hayes, when did you next hear of George McCane?" Riding asked.

"When I saw his picture in the paper after he killed those three on the lake."

"Objection, your honor," Grier said, standing with more force. "It's not for this witness to judge the guilt or innocence of my client. That is for the jury."

"Sustained."

"So you next saw Mr. McCane after the accident at the lake?"

"Yes, sir, his picture at least."

"And what did you think? That this was the drunk that cussed you out on the grade?"

"Objection."

"Sustained. Mr. Riding. It has not been established with any certainty that Mr. McCane was drinking, only suggested."

"Thank you, Mr. Hayes. That's all I have for this witness, your honor."

"Mr. Grier?" Judge Tucker asked without looking up, then continued to take notes on his legal pad.

I could see where Riding was going and I'm sure Grier did too, trying to cast aspersions on McCane's character and at least plant the idea in the jury's mind that a rich man may already have been drinking the morning of the accident on the lake.

Grier conferred with Cromer then walked forward to proceeded with the cross examination. Grier started out with a jab or two: "Mr. Hayes, it wasn't Mr. McCane who had been drinking that morning, was it?"

"That was 6 a.m. and I was headed down to a job," Hayes said.

"You didn't answer my question."

"No."

"Mr. Hayes, you had just gotten out of jail two days before for public drunkenness, hadn't you?"

"Objection, your honor," Riding said. "This has nothing do with this trial."

"Mr. Grier, what's the relevance?"

"Your honor, the solicitor, through this witness, has tried to insinuate that my client was drinking on the morning of this accident, with no proof whatsoever. I think they've opened the door to this witness's drinking habits."

"I'll allow a little more time to be sure we're focusing on the case. Overruled."

"Mr. Hayes, had you not served time for public drunkenness in the Huntersville jail two days before the incident with Mr. McCane?"

"I had served a little time."

"And that was your third offense of the summer?"

"Objection . . ."

"Let him continue, Mr. Riding, I see the relevance."

"It was 6 a.m. dang it, and I was sober as a Baptist preacher on Judgment Day."

A round of laughter circulated the courtroom.

"Order." Judge Tucker rapped his gavel.

"I'm sure you were," Grier said, casting a smile toward the jury box. "I'm sure you were. No more questions, your honor."

"Call Pink Bright to the stand," intoned Riding. I had been right about the boy. The witness was the one with the Cracker Jacks, which he left sitting in his seat as he came forward.

"Pink, what's your age?" Riding asked.

"Fifteen," the boy said and pulled himself upright in the chair.

"And where do you live?"

"On the Asheville road."

"And you like to fish?"

"Oh, yes, sir."

"What's your favorite spot?" Riding asked, walking up close to the boy.

"Where the river comes into the lake."

"The lake?"

"Yes, sir, Lake Whitney," Pink said.

"You fish from the shore?"

"No, sir, I keep a boat hid down there and go out in it."

"Have you ever seen this man?" Riding pointed over at George McCane.

"Yes, sir."

"In what capacity?"

"Sir?"

"How do you know him?"

"He's chased me off the lake a few times," Pink said, looking down at his hands.

"For fishing?"

McCane said something to Grier, and Grier nodded.

"Yes, sir."

"What did he say?" Riding asked, leaning in closer.

"He'd cuss me out."

"How old were you when he first chased you off the lake?"

"I don't know, maybe twelve?"

"And when was the last time?"

"Last August," Pink said.

"What happened?"

"I was out in my boat, all by myself, early in the morning. I heard a noise and all of a sudden McCane come roaring into the cove where I was fishing in his big speed boat, headed straight for me. Just at the last minute he swerves and sends this huge wave at me. My little boat rocked and I dropped my fishing pole in the lake. I had to hold onto the sides with both hands to keep from falling out."

"Did he say anything to you?" Riding asked. He turned and walked back toward the jury box again.

"Yes, sir."

"What exactly did Mr. McCane say?" Riding asked.

"He hollered he'd had it with me and if he caught me there again he'd make sure it would be my last fishing trip."

I was a little agitated by these witnesses appearing. Hadn't Yarborough worked out a deal with either of them? It didn't seem so.

"What did you think he meant?"

"I don't know, but I didn't want to find out." Laughs broke out in the courtroom.

"Order!" Judge Tucker said, slamming down his gavel. "Order!"

"So he threatened you that time?"

"He scared me bad," Pink said.

"I don't have anything else, your honor," Riding said, sitting down.

Grier stood and walked toward the witness stand.

"Pink, you like to fish, you say?"

"Oh, yes, sir."

"I also understand you're quite an entrepreneur."

"Sir?"

"A businessman," Grier said, putting his hands on his hips.

"I pump gas at the station on Highway 52."

"I don't mean your day job. Didn't you get caught last year for breaking into a boathouse on the lake?"

"Objection, your honor."

"Overruled. You can answer the question."

"I paid them back."

"You paid for what you stole," Grier said. "So the morning you claim you saw Mr. McCane, were you fishing or stealing?"

"I was fishing."

"I'm sure you were. No more questions, your honor."

I was glad McCane's lawyers had done their homework, as Angus's money had not seemed to do any good.

The testimony soon moved to the accident itself. "Call Defoix Granby to the stand," said Riding. A bald, wire-thin man dressed in a dark suit came forward.

"Mr. Granby, where were you on the afternoon of the Sunday under discussion last year?"

"I was near the iron bridge at the upper end of the lake about a half a mile from the scene of the drownings."

"Did you see Mr. McCane's boat that day?"

"Yes, sir. I could see Mr. McCane's boat in the distance. It's the biggest boat on the lake and I've seen it many times. He came from far away and seemed headed at a high rate of speed for this much smaller boat. I saw him approach the boat, then veer off and return in the direction he came from."

"And how fast was Mr. McCane's boat traveling?" Riding asked.

"Maybe twenty miles per hour."

"Was there a wake associated with the craft?"

"There were waves."

"That's all I have for this witness, your honor," Riding said, heading back to his table.

"Mr. Grier, would you like a chance to cross-examine?" Judge Tucker asked.

"Yes, your honor. May it please the court," Grier began. "Mr. Granby, you say you were about a half a mile away from this small boat?"

"Yes, sir, maybe less."

"Well, was it half a mile or less? Are you changing your testimony? My client is on trial for murder here."

"I didn't measure it," Granby said.

"So it could have been more than half a mile."

"Could've been, but I doubt it."

"Even a half-mile's a long way, is it not?" Grier asked.

"Yes, sir," Granby said, looking a little nervous.

"Could you see how many people were in the small boat?"

"No, sir."

"So you were too far away to tell whether there was one person or seven people in the boat?"

"Yes, sir," Granby said.

"Would it surprise you if I told you there were seven people in the small boat?"

"I wouldn't know."

"Seven people would be a lot of people for a boat that small, wouldn't it? That would weigh it down in the water pretty good, wouldn't it?" Grier said, pacing below me.

"I couldn't tell how big the boat is."

"So you were too far away to even tell how big the boat was?" Grier asked.

"Yes, sir."

"So you were too far away to judge the speed of Mr. McCane's boat, weren't you?"

"Well, I couldn't say exactly," Granby said.

"You couldn't even say it was McCane's boat, could you?" Grier walked closer to the witness chair.

"I've seen Mr. McCane's boat a good many times. He likes to roar around the lake like he owns it."

"You certainly couldn't say that he did anything intentionally to cause this boat to turn over or those people to drown, could you?" Cromer said and paused a few feet in front of Granby.

"No, sir."

"No further questions."

"Call Clyde Lindsey to the stand," announced Riding. The local district forest warden was suited up in a green, military style shirt and pants. He carried a big brimmed hat in his hands.

"Mr. Lindsey, have you ever seen Mr. McCane in his boat before?" Riding asked.

"Yes, I was on the lake in my boat on July 4th and saw Mr. McCane driving his boat."

"Was he driving at an excessive speed?"

"Objection, your honor," Grier said. "One man's excess is another man's pleasure boating. There is no established speed limit on the lake."

"Very well, Mr. Grier. Mr. Riding, refrain from using the word *excessive*."

"Certainly, your honor. Mr. Lindsey, how fast was Mr. McCane's boat going?"

"At least twenty-five per hour," Lindsey answered.

"Can you estimate the size of the wake that McCane's boat would make at that speed?" Riding continued.

"A couple of feet high," Lindsey said, touching his chin and tilting his head back.

"That's all I have your honor," Riding said.

"Mr. Grier?"

Grier approached the witness stand. "Mr. Lindsey, you're a forest warden?"

"Yes, sir," Lindsey said with pride.

"Spend a lot of time in the woods?"

"That's my job," Lindsey said, and turned his palms upward as laughter spread through the courtroom.

"Order." Judge Tucker slapped his gavel once on the stand.

"You don't spend a lot of time on the water or in boats, do you?" Grier continued.

"Well, I'm in my boat when I have a chance. I like to fish, but no, not as much time as I do in the woods."

"And on the day in question, how far away from Mr. McCane's boat was your boat when you saw it?"

"Oh, I'd say a quarter of a mile."

"And you are sure it was my client's boat?"

"Yes, sir, I've seen his boat many times. There's no mistaking it," he said, leaning forward in the chair. "There's not another boat on the lake like it."

"Did you see other boats on the lake that morning?"

"A little earlier I saw the Vermont boy fishing, but he went in about the time I put on. His family lives on the lake in the summer and he fishes out there a lot."

"Could you have mistaken Vermont's boat for my client's?"

"No, sir, Vermont's boat is a Johnboat; he's just a high school kid who likes to paddle around and fish," Lindsey said. "Mr. McCane's boat is a powerboat."

"And when you saw my client's boat, there was no other boat around other than yours and his?" Grier asked.

"That's right."

"Was he heading toward any other boat?"

"Not that I could see," Lindsey answered.

"Did you see any other boats on the lake?"

"No."

"He wasn't heading for your boat?"

"No. He was heading away from my boat," Lindsey said.

"He didn't try to run you off the lake?" Grier countered.

"No, sir."

"You've seen his boat on the lake many times, and he's never tried to run you off the lake?"

"No, sir."

"Never told you to get off the lake and never come back?" Grier asked.

"I guess he was just riding around," Lindsey said, getting a little exasperated. "But he was riding around way too fast."

"Well, Mr. Lindsey, you may know all your trees and all of the animals that live in the forest where you work, but you're not in court today telling us you're an expert at judging boat speeds, are you?"

"No, sir."

"And you were at least a quarter of a mile away from Mr. McCane's boat when you saw it, weren't you?"

"Yes, sir. But there's one thing that's different about being in the woods and on a lake." He paused. "There ain't no trees on a lake to block your view."

Riding called E.A. Griffith next. Griffith looked like a banker, wearing a fine brown suit and starched shirt.

"Mr. Griffith, where were you on the morning of that Sunday in September?" Riding asked.

"I was on the opposite side of the lake from where the drownings occurred. I was standing on South Shore Drive maybe about a half mile away."

"Was your view good from there?" Riding asked.

"I could see the two boats approaching each other. The smaller boat was about a hundred feet from the Southern shore and the large boat passed it at a distance of about twenty or thirty feet. I saw the wave strike the small boat and capsize it just as the larger boat passed. Right after that I went straight to the Lakeside Inn to get closer to where the accident had occurred."

"How high was the wave that struck the boat?"

"About knee high, I'd say."

"Thank you, Mr. Griffith. Your honor, that's all I have for this witness."

"Mr. Grier?"

Grier stood up and looked at his notes, then stepped forward to cross-examine the witness. It seemed to me his confidence was building as the trial continued. He didn't seem worried at all. "Mr. Griffith," he began, "how did you just happen to be standing by the road looking out at the lake watching the boats on that fine morning?"

"I was on my way to town and glanced over at the lake, and something caught my eye. It looked like one boat was heading straight for the other at a high rate of speed."

147

"You were a long way from the lake, weren't you?"

"Yes, sir."

"You said half a mile from the lake or something like that."

"Not a half a mile from the lake. A half a mile from the accident," Griffith corrected.

"Could you tell how many people were in the smaller boat from a half mile away?"

"No, sir."

"Could you tell what color it was?"

"I didn't notice."

"Was the boat riding low in the water with all that weight?" Grier asked, pacing back and forth.

"I couldn't tell."

"Objection, your honor," Riding said. "The witness says that he could not tell how many people were in the boat."

"Sustained," Judge Tucker said. "Mr. Grier, refrain from leading the witness."

"Did the boat have a motor?" Grier continued.

"I don't know."

"You don't know how many people were in the boat, what color it was, whether it looked overloaded, whether it had a motor, and yet from that distance, looking down on these boats, you could tell that the wave was knee high?"

"That's my best guess."

I was feeling a little drowsy and all the witnesses were beginning to run together for me, but I woke up when Solicitor Riding surprised everybody and called the daughter of Fate and Novie Moreland to the stand. Dressed in a starched blue jumper, the gangly girl walked forward and sat down.

"Solicitor Riding, this is highly unusual," the judge said. "How old is this girl?"

"Young lady, would you state your name and age for the record," Solicitor Riding said.

"Floride Moreland," she said. "And I'm just a little over ten years old."

"Your honor," Riding said, "I would ask that if it pleases the court she be allowed to testify."

"Does the defense have any problem with Miss Moreland's testifying?"

"Well, your honor, it depends on what she says," Grier said, and the courtroom laughed.

"Noted," the judge said. "Solicitor Riding, you may proceed."

Floride Moreland was administered the oath as her hand rested on the black Bible. Once she was sworn in she sat down on the high seat in the witness box and crossed her hands in her lap. Her shoes pumped back and forth like she was sitting in a swing.

"Floride, I want to begin by asking about the events leading up to your father's death. Were you having a good time on the lake that day your daddy and brother died?" Riding asked, walking out from behind his desk the first time. He approached the witness stand and stood nearby.

"Oh, yes, we'd been riding in a boat along the shore. Daddy and Junior were fishing," the girl said, fiddling with her hair and not looking up.

"Where did the boat leave from that day?"

"We left from a dock behind that restaurant on the shore. Mr. Rogers said he knew the owner."

"Were they catching anything?"

"No, Daddy said the water was too warm."

"When did you see the boat coming toward you?"

She paused and didn't say anything for a few seconds. Riding waited patiently for her answer.

"We'd been out for an hour or so," she said, looking over toward Novie.

"And how would you describe the boat?"

"There was a big boat with a little flag flying on the back."

"How fast was the big boat going?"

She didn't speak again for a few moments and kicked her feet.

"Fast, and it came so close to us."

"What caused your boat to turn over?" Riding asked.

"That big wave hit."

"What happened next?"

"We turned over," she said and looked over at Novie again.

"How long were you in the water?"

"We held onto the boat until a man picked us up."

"How long?"

"A long time," the girl said, and pumped her feet again, as if trying to tread water.

"Thank you, young lady. No more questions, your honor."

"Mr. Grier?" the judge asked.

Grier stood and walked over in front of the witness box and took Riding's place. "Young lady, have you ever been in a nice, sleek motorboat like Mr. McCane's?"

"Not before he picked us up."

"Had you ever been in a boat with a motor?"

"No, sir, not till then."

"Was it crowded in your little boat?"

"We were mashed in pretty good."

"'Mashed in,' you say?" Grier smiled. "How many were in that little boat?" She didn't answer for a long time.

"Young lady," the judge said, "you need to answer Mr. Grier's question."

"There was Mr. Rogers who took us out, Mama, Daddy, my brother, me, and the Martins."

"And how many is that?"

"Seven," she said, beginning to pump her feet again.

"Why were you out in the boat that day?" Grier asked, smiling at the girl.

"We all wanted to go for a ride and Mr. Rogers didn't have time to take us out in two trips."

"So he mashed you all in."

"Yes, sir. Mr. Rogers said it was safe."

"Could you reach over the side and touch the water?" Grier continued.

"I don't remember," the girl said.

"Was the water close to the top of the boat?"

"Pretty close, but he said it was safe."

"You say the motorboat was going fast," Grier asked. "How fast is fast?"

"I don't know what you mean," the girl said.

"Give me a number, Floride. Five, ten, fifteen miles an hour?" Grier pressed.

The little girl looked over to where her mother was sitting. There was a little note of panic in her eyes. "I don't know."

"Five miles an hour can look pretty fast if all you've ever sat in has been a rowboat . . ."

"Mama?" Floride said with a little inflection at the end of the word, hoping for rescue. She looked over toward the prosecution's table, but her mother didn't say anything.

"Thank you, young lady. No more questions from the defense, your honor," Grier said, gesturing for the girl to leave the stand.

Everybody in the room knew Grier had scored some points with his cross-examination.

"Mr. Riding, who else do you have? It's getting on."

"Your honor, my final witness is Novie Moreland." Riding stood and Novie Moreland left her seat next to Olin behind the solicitor's table and walked toward the witness chair. I was relieved that the two other passengers in the boat would not testify. I wondered if the money Yarbrough had to parcel out had helped.

Novie wore the same dark blue dress I'd seen her in at the funeral. She looked calm as she raised her right hand and took the oath.

Riding's first question went straight to the point. "Mrs. Moreland, tell us what you saw that morning, the morning your family went to the bottom of that lake."

Novie Moreland gathered herself and then spoke. "My back was to the approaching boat and I didn't see." Novie Moreland said calmly. Riding straightened up and even the judge looked a little surprised. A ripple of disapproval circulated around the courtroom and even broke into audible chatter.

"Order," Judge Tucker barked and tapped his gavel. "Order."

"What? What did you say?"

"I said I didn't see the boat pass."

"But you found yourself in the water after the wake upset the boat. How else could the accident have happened?"

"I only felt the boat tipping, and then we were in the water. That's really all I remember."

"But that's not what you said in your sworn statement." He picked up some papers and shook them at the stand. "You said in your statement that on the morning of the accident George McCane's powerboat, 'approached at an excessive speed' (he read from the papers he held with some agitation) and a three-foot wake swamped your craft and resulted in the drowning of your husband, your son, and another innocent man. Mrs. Moreland, I hope you know that justice for your husband and child is in the balance here. Please reconsider what you are saying."

Riding shook the papers one final time in her direction, then let them drop to his side as he waited for Novie to speak. The judge looked on. He even leaned a little forward in his chair for the first time. Grier, Cromer, and McCane seemed unconcerned and relaxed.

"I did not see Mr. McCane's boat. I was focused on locating my children in the water. I must have been mistaken in my first statement," Novie Moreland said. "I was hysterical. I had lost my husband and my son."

"Mrs. Moreland," Riding said, approaching the witness chair. "You do know what perjury is, don't you?"

"Yes, I do."

"And you stand by your statement here that you did not see Mr. McCane's boat approaching, that your back was to the action, and that you do not know what caused the incident in which your husband and son died?"

"That is correct."

Riding put his hands on his hips and stood for a moment. He walked back to the table and picked up several sheets of paper and walked back.

"Mrs. Moreland, what I have here is your sworn statement. Would you mind reading the last sentence of page two?"

Novie Moreland read out loud from the paper: "The powerboat approached at a fast rate of speed and turned at the last moment and a large wake swamped our boat, dumping us all in the lake."

"And so now you deny this?"

"That is not what I remember."

Riding shook his head, then turned to the judge.

"Is that all you have, Mr. Riding?"

"Your honor, because of these late developments could counsel ask for recess until tomorrow?" Riding said, approaching the stand.

"I think that's appropriate, Mr. Riding," Judge Tucker said. "Court is recessed until 8:30 a.m. tomorrow. Mrs. Moreland, you are excused from the stand. Please be here in the morning."

| 24 |

Angus's truck was parked at the Flats as I drove home. I stopped and checked in. He was sitting on a stool, nursing a bottle of beer at the dark end of the bar.

"You been up the hill to that legal circus?" he asked when he saw me come in.

"In recess until tomorrow," I said. "We had some fireworks."

"Have a seat and fill me in."

"They got any food here? I haven't eaten all day."

"Buster, give Mr. Crocker here a hamburger and put it on my tab," Angus said, waving to the bar man. "And get us two more beers."

"Can we go to a booth? I'd like a little more light than this to eat by."

Buster brought the beers and we moved to a booth closer to the door and the one greasy window. The springs under the maroon vinyl bench gave way and as I settled in I slid to the collapsed middle of the seat. With this arrangement it was most comfortable to lean forward and plant my elbows firmly on the table.

"This is one fine establishment," I said, looking around.

"Does the job," Angus said, turning up one beer to drain it and taking up the next one. "You ought to spend more time in places like this, Ben. You'd get an idea of how bad it is out there."

"I know how bad it is," I said. "I work in textiles, remember?"

"No, I mean really bad," Angus said. "These people don't have families. They don't have much to lose. If you end up a regular here you're at the bitter end of things."

"Why are you here?"

"I've got a deep itch and this is how I scratch it. Tell me about my brother. Is that judge going to give up his goat?"

"Oh, the goat," I say, smiling, and thinking back to that night in the judge's cottage and the deed and my joke about the goat.

"Well, I don't think that judge even has to be concerned about that goat now. Novie Moreland turned on the stand."

"Turned?"

"She went back on her sworn statement. She said she didn't see a thing. Claimed she was hysterical that morning."

"How about that."

"I guess Leland Cromer got to her," I said.

"That's not the way my brother does business," Angus said. "He'd never let Cromer approach the widow. That's tacky, and if there's one thing my brother won't be, it's tacky."

"Well, for some reason she did your brother a good turn," I said.

"What happened? You got any insight here, Ben?"

I took another bite and fished the pickle out. "We'll see what the judge does tomorrow when the court convenes."

"You never told me what happened to my money."

"Your money? It all went to the cause you directed it toward."

"That widow's a good looking woman," he continued. "I hope there is something in the long run in it for her."

"She's not good looking. She's beautiful," I said, and took a bite of my hamburger. "I reckon she'll do alright."

"I think you're sweet on that widow," Angus said with a little laugh. "I think maybe you did get to her."

"I visited a couple of times."

"And you, a married man."

"It's not what you think," I said. "I talked with her on the porch. That's all."

"So my money wasn't wasted?"

"Somebody settled," I said, but then I lied. "I don't know what turned her. I don't think it was your money, but it could have been."

"George won't want to know about the judge, and he certainly won't want to know about any deal we made with the widow."

"He doesn't have to know," I said. "Nobody knows anything but us."

"And the widow," Angus said. "Whatever turned her, somebody made a good investment. I should have had you handling my money all along."

"I wish I'd never gotten into all this," I said. "There's something dirty about it all and I don't like it."

"You were just the in-between-man, Ben," Angus said. "Now you can go back to balancing the books. Just forget all this happened."

"I guess numbers are what I'm best at," I said. "That's why your brother hired me."

| 25 |

The next morning Coleen put Snowball in the backyard for the day and we walked down to the café for her morning shift. Outside our house I'd picked up the paper and tucked it under my arm. Once inside she put on the coffee and filled the salt shakers as I waited for my meal and read the news.

"They got anything in there about McCane?" she asked.

"Headline says they're still finding bodies from that tornado down in Gainesville," I said. "Nothing about the trial."

"Are you headed back up there?" Coleen asked as she wiped off the counter.

"It might all disappear today," I said, pushing the paper to the side. "I wouldn't worry none about it."

"So he'll walk?"

"He should walk. That judge hasn't heard much proof McCane's done anything," I said.

"What do you want to eat?"

"Grits, eggs over easy, and patty sausage."

Coleen turned her back. Through the window the cook took the order off the spike and stuck it under his order bar. I heard the cook crack two eggs and then tend the sizzle on the hot griddle. Coleen still hadn't turned back around.

"More coffee?" she said, finally returning with a full pot.

"Just top it off," I said.

"Why are you feeling guilty?" Coleen asked, pouring coffee.

"Guilty?" I said. "I don't have anything to feel guilty about."

"There was three up there dead in that lake," she said. "There's a family without any man to support them. If it's not murder, then it's at least manslaughter."

"It was an accident, Coleen," I said. "Pure and simple."

"There's only accidents when a rich man's on trial," Coleen said.

"I don't believe Mr. McCane is on trial for being rich."

Coleen turned and yelled at the cook: "You got Mr. Crocker's eggs and grits? He's about to be on his way."

"That's the American way," I said, as she turned back towards me. "Some get rich. All the others wish they were."

"Where'd that McCane money come from?" she said with her hands on her hips. "George McCane sure didn't make it himself. Not even his daddy made it. Most of it's passed down from father to son, stripped off the backs of men like your daddy and mine."

"Honey, you sound like one of those Gastonia Communists," I said.

"That's not so bad, is it? At least not till the bosses start shooting."

I sipped my coffee and Coleen scrubbed at the counter with her rag. She scrubbed at it so hard I thought the Formica was coming up. I wanted to make a joke but I could see she was in no mood for frivolity. I sipped my coffee and watched her as she swabbed the whole counter down. She was hardworking and headstrong, and I knew she had a point. I felt guilty about lots of things, but not the ones she thought. I felt guilt for the contingency fund, for lying to Novie Moreland, and for not helping out my parents more.

The cook finally slid the eggs, grits, and sausage into the window and hit the order bell. The sharp ring pierced the silence that had settled between Coleen and me. Two more patrons had entered the café, so Coleen had others to care for. I ate my breakfast in silence and glanced down at the paper again.

Apparently the overnight recess didn't help Riding. "The State rests, your honor," he announced as soon as court resumed the next morning. Grier had obviously waived his cross-examination of Novie. He didn't think he needed to, I guessed. I think he was right.

Grier rose slowly and deliberately from his seat. "Your honor, I have a matter of law to take up with the court."

The courtroom fell silent. "Bailiff, please take the jury from the courtroom," intoned the judge. No one moved while the jury shuffled from their box, and the door to the courtroom closed behind them.

"May it please the court," began Grier, "the defense moves for a directed verdict. Taking the testimony and evidence in the light most favorable to the state, there has been no proof of malice aforethought on the part of my client. There may have been testimony implying negligence at most, but there has not been a scintilla of any intent to do harm as would support a charge of murder. The charge against my client should be dismissed."

The entire courtroom held its breath. All eyes were on Riding, and then Grier, and then the judge, turned to him. "Mr. Riding?" asked the judge.

"Your honor, we have several witnesses, in fact all of the witnesses who saw the two boats, testifying that Mr. McCane was operating his boat at a very high rate of speed, that he seemed to be heading directly for the smaller boat, that he swerved at the last moment and that the wake generated by his powerful boat caused the smaller boat to overturn and hence the victims to drown. We also have testimony that Mr. McCane had been angered in the past by those he did not consider to belong on the lake, and that he had taken actions to try to drive those people from the lake, and keep them from returning. When you put all those things together, your honor, I think we can infer that Mr. McCane was angry about this small boat and these people being on the lake and decided to teach them a lesson and drive them from the lake. Whether he intended to drown these particular victims doesn't matter. His actions were such that he knew or should have known that some harm would come from them."

"Solicitor, the court does not agree that a charge of murder can be built on inferences," Judge Tucker replied. He leaned back in his chair and chose his words carefully. "Mr. McCane may have been angry with others at other times for being on the lake. That may or may not be true."

"What about negligent homicide, manslaughter?" Riding asked. "What about a lesser offense?"

"There has been no evidence presented to this court that he had the necessary *mens rea* that is an essential element of the charge of murder or manslaughter," Tucker said. "There is no evidence that he was angry with these folks or had any intent to hurt them. There's no evidence he even knew them. As I see it, there was only one witness presented by the state who could have testified as to any apparent intent on the part of Mr. McCane at the time this happened." The judge shifted his gaze from Riding to Novie Moreland, seated just behind him in the first row of pews. "And that witness," he said, returning his gaze to Riding, "in her sworn testimony, says she saw nothing. Therefore, an essential element of the crime, malice aforethought, is missing, and the charge must be dismissed. Defense motion is granted. The defendant is free to go. Court is adjourned."

The judge rose and paused to look out at the courtroom for a moment. He even looked up at the gallery and I swear he looked right at me. Soon as he exited there was chaos below me. Some of the mountain boys rushed for the doors, but they didn't beat the reporters, who were off to file their stories. Others argued and yelled where they stood, and some pressed at the railing to hurl slurs at Novie Moreland. Olin circled his arms around Novie as they tried to exit their row. Olin pushed at the stationary crowd until the snarl broke and a path opened to the doors.

"McCane's got to her!" yelled the old man sitting next to me down at Olin and Novie as they exited, then turned to me. "It's all been set up beforehand by the bosses."

Exiting, Novie showed no signs of fear, and stepped out into the aisle to walk out of the courthouse. As she passed more people yelled and pointed. I pushed my way to the stairs and descended quickly and reached the front door just as Novie and Olin passed through out of the courthouse.

"Novie," I yelled, and it was as if the tone of my voice, so different than all those others around her, got her attention.

She turned and I was struck by how calm she seemed.

"Mr. Crocker," she said, not surprised to see me standing there, and picking up our conversation from her front porch months before, "I guess Mr. McCane might say justice was a lady."

| 26 |

After Mr. McCane's courtroom victory I couldn't square Novie Moreland's testimony. Had McCane or his lawyers paid her off in some manner, something I thought I'd been unable to accomplish? Had she been telling the truth? When it came down to standing before God and her peers was it that she just could not offer testimony to help convict a man for murders he didn't commit?

I was relieved the trial was over and had things gone well afterward I might not be picking over the bones of this story today. I thought when I returned to Carlton Mill the Monday after the trial with the name of a brick mason from Greenville things would go smoothly. The man, Fred Jewell, was to meet me Tuesday morning and look things over.

The mill was working at about half-strength, and I went out in the afternoon to check in with Harvey Bobo, the old superintendent Mr. McCane had reappointed to the mill. I went out to see if there were any payroll issues I needed to know about. We worked in the office all afternoon.

It wasn't quite dark by the time I left the mill. I was still thinking about Satterfield, the mason Angus had refused, so I drove past his farm. I was tired and worried about the resentment that had built up like rust in an iron skillet with the Carlton workers since the mill had closed. I was also concerned about what was bubbling up like hidden springs in the hills west of us now that it was common knowledge George McCane had slipped out of the murder charges.

As I drove along I was also thinking way too much about how the last few months had changed the old village of my childhood. Back in the days before I went to work for McCane my life hadn't been so complicated. Now only the blue mountains I could see out my driver's window had any permanence at all. I had a sick feeling when I looked at them. They shimmered a little, as if even the peaks were in motion. There were only a handful of the old folks of the village left—my father and mother among them. McCane had fired most of the younger workers, or he'd let them go when he downsized. If the modernization was, as McCane had claimed in his little mumbling speech, "a new day for Carlton," it was uncertain whether McCane's new day had dawned clear or stormy.

When I made the curve out front of the Satterfield farm I was met with an unexpected surprise, a country traffic jam, what looked more like a hurricane than a thunderstorm. I rolled down my passenger's side window and saw dozens of jalopies waiting to turn into Satterfield's drive. A dozen more old dusty beaters had abandoned the notion of getting fully off the road and parked with two wheels on the shoulder out front. A single-file line of men, women, and children passed my car and walked along the road and down into Satterfield's property. The men carried sacks, carpetbags, folded blankets, and cardboard boxes tied with strings. One led a nanny goat with big udders. One woman had a live chicken under her arm. A little girl trailed behind her mama, and she'd brought a kitten with her that she clutched to her scrawny chest.

Looking through the dusk down into Satterfield's place I saw dozens of campfires already blazing. In the distance the barren farm fields sloped down to the river. The fields twinkled as if fireflies had lit all over them. I could see the outline of even more people in the distance propping up canvas lean-tos and pitching old Army tents. Wisps of smoke from cook fires already rose and curled through the trees. I had a vision for a moment it was 1863 and an invading Yankee regiment was bivouacked on the river.

I pulled off the road just past the last parked jalopy and followed a flop-hatted pilgrim carrying a lighted signal lantern down Satterfield's dusty drive. When I walked in I could see into some of the lean-tos and tents. People already had pallets on the ground. These weren't overnight campers. They were here to stay a few days.

"Evening, sir," one teen-aged girl said as I passed. I paused and tipped my hat to her. She was folding a blanket into a small square for her little sister to sit on outside the opening to their lean-to. "Are you here for the strike?"

"Strike?"

"You know, shut the Carlton Mill down," she said.

I asked an old man, maybe a little frantically, what the little girl meant. My contrary tone surprised him, and also surprised several of the people working on their camps who turned and listened.

"Yes, sir," he said. "We're shutting the mill down. And getting some justice on Mr. George McCane."

I asked, "Where is Campbell?"

"Up there on Mr. Satterfield's porch," the old man said. "They're strategizing for tomorrow."

As I approached Satterfield's front porch I could see four women off to the side stirring two big black cauldrons over an open fire. They were pots big enough to scald a hog in and whatever the women were cooking had a fragrant, oily steam rising from it. On the porch sat a clot of six men circled up in straight-backed chairs with a kerosene lantern on the floor between them. The lantern cast the men in a greasy, yellow light, and they were mumbling and laughing. My first instinct was to retreat. I'd stumbled into about as uninviting a scene as I've ever seen, then or now. At first I thought they were playing cards, but when I got closer I saw how they were poring over papers laid out before them on the porch floor. They looked like Lee, Jackson, and their aides-de-camp gathered for a council of war.

"Olin," I said when I was right behind the men. The men paused their bicker-ing and looked my way.

I'd caught Campbell off guard, infiltrating his inner circle, and it took a mo-ment for my presence to register on him. "Ben Crocker?" he asked as he stood up. "What are you doing here?"

"I saw the fires as I was driving home," I said. "It's been dry lately. Hope you got a bunch of buckets. I'd hate for somebody to burn down Satterfield's woods."

"You stop by to talk fire prevention, Ben?" Olin Campbell said, recovering his balance, "Or has McCane sent you to make a deal?"

"McCane doesn't know I'm here," I said. "He probably thinks the worst is over."

"The worst is yet to come," the man sitting next to Campbell said. In the lantern light I recognized his face too. He was John Garland, the union organizer.

"Mr. Garland, glad to see you made it back from New Jersey," I said, nodding toward the man.

"We wouldn't miss the festivities," the man next to him said. I squinted into the light and I could see it was Dan Eliot, the other union man. "All in a day's work."

"Who are all those folks out in the fields?" I said. "You having a camp meeting?"

"There are hundreds of people either camped here or on the way. Most of them are down from Canaan and couldn't care less about whether McCane's mill runs or not, but there's a group led by Fate Moreland's crazy daddy down near the river gathered around a big bonfire. They're having none of it. They want blood. They'd like to burn the Carlton Mill down. They're like the Overmountain Men come down to fight the British at Kings Mountain," Campbell said. "Moreland's daddy said he hopes McCane comes up here so he can show the big man some-thing he won't forget."

"Is there anything I can do to head this off?" I asked Campbell.

"Cut back the stretchout, hire back half the workers he fired at Carlton, let all those families back in the houses he threw them out of, run back the clock on George McCane and his motorboat," Eliot said.

"That would be a start," Garland said. "There's legitimate grievances to settle here between the union and Morgan Mills."

"Let's be realistic," I said.

"You talk with them about being realistic," Campbell said, waving his arm toward the field. "You talk with them about forgiving and forgetting." I turned and in the distance saw a bonfire burning in the grove by the creek. The flames were twice as tall as the men standing around it, and ever-so-often a drift of sparks would break loose and jump toward the night sky. If I listened closely I might have heard Celtic horns and war drums, but I didn't. The night was quiet except for the whispers of those settled around their own small fires.

"So how does Old Man Moreland feel about what his daughter-in-law said up in the Huntersville courthouse?" I asked.

"Blood's blood," Campbell said. "He's mad at McCane, not at Novie."

"Well, she had a chance to turn the trial," Ben said.

"She's had several chances. Who is to say what turned her—if she turned," Olin said.

"You sound like you believe McCane wasn't guilty."

"We know it's unlikely he meant to kill them," Olin said. "Novie saw or didn't see what she said."

"So this isn't so much about the trial then?"

"This is about the Carlton Mill down there, and what is right. This is about how it should run."

"Oh, it'll run," I said. "As a business or not at all."

"One man's business is another's mule ring," Dan Eliot said.

"Mr. Eliot, what could you have possibly learned about mules up there in New Jersey?" I asked, spreading my stance and crossing my arms over my chest.

"He's got a point there," Campbell said.

Almost on cue a woman came out of the houses carrying a pot. She reached up with a spoon and rang Satterfield's supper bell. It took me a second but I could see it was Novie Moreland on the porch. She looked down and saw me and our eyes met for a moment and then she turned away to carry the pot over to the serving line.

"Is that Novie? Is she safe here?" I asked.

"She's a lot safer here with me than up in that Jump Off holler," Olin said.

Many of the scattered hundreds of Canaanites camped out in the fields headed toward us now through the dark. They carried lanterns as they slowly approached Satterfield's house.

When I turned back around, Campbell could see that I was now a little unnerved, first by seeing Novie Moreland in the camp, and then by everyone headed our way.

"Don't worry, Crocker," he said as a smile broke across his face. "They're not coming for you. They're coming for a plate of union pintos and a ladle of goat stew. You're welcome to stay and eat some with us if you want."

I ate a plate of pintos and stew with the Canaanites. Sitting on the edge of the porch I watched the people come through the line, and I hoped that Novie would pass close enough for us to speak as she came and went from the kitchen in Satterfield's house, but she never did.

| 27 |

About 7:30 the next morning I was already back up at the office in Carlton Mill. A little after I arrived the brick mason got there from Pickens, Fred Jewell. Jewell was a fat man, a hard contrast to Satterfield. But Jewell was white as Aunt Emma's sheets, so neither Angus nor nobody else would be bothered by his skin tone.

Jewell had a scheme to sell me first thing when he sat down. "I got my own brick-making machine," he said. "You can pay me to bring it over and use your mud. It will save you some money." Satterfield and Jewell shared one thing— gray mortar stuck to the nails of the fingers of their stubby working hands.

The more we talked the more Jewell irritated me. He sounded like he had gravel in his mouth and he sat and flaked off the mortar on his hands with a pearl-handled pocketknife. The concrete chips gathered in an ashy pile around his brogans. We were going over the bid for the brickwork line by line, and we were close to shaking on it and getting him out of the office. Then I heard the first shift workers clapping as they came inside. Outside I heard what sounded like a parade coming down the hill. There were car horns tooting on top of all that.

I went to the front of the office and looked out and saw a line of vehicles approaching. When I threw open the window I craned my neck and wasn't surprised when I couldn't see the end of the convoy. All the cars and trucks I'd seen the night before at Satterfield's farm were coming down bumper to bumper.

I counted fifteen cars and trucks behind the first one until the line disappeared around a curve on the Morgan road. It looked like every vehicle had at least four or five people in it.

Campbell's blue truck was first in line. He had a huge American flag flying from the back of the cab on a pole. I don't know where they got hold of it, but the second vehicle was a dull red bus loaded down with people, and the third was a rusted-out wrecker derrick for cars. Every driver and passenger had the windows down and as they pulled up they were making almost as much racket as the band. By the time they were all out front of the mill they were yelling so loud I could hardly hear my own voice.

Campbell's truck pulled into a vacant lot next to the river and came to a stop, and others pulled right in beside him. They were in no hurry. The procession was all orderly and slow. The bus pulled up broadside to the fence as close as the driver could get. I could see Hunter County schools stenciled on the side nearest the fence. The people poured out the other side into the outside yard. The wrecker had no muffler and the driver gunned the motor as he turned and backed in where he could get the hook on the gate if they needed to.

When I saw the flag on the front truck I knew there was going to be trouble. "It's a flying squadron," I said to Jewell.

"A what?" Jewell asked.

"I recognize that big flag from the strike two years ago."

"If it's a flying squadron, it'll be the last," came a voice from just inside the doorframe. Angus McCane stepped into the room. He'd come down from the lake to see how things were going and had slipped into the office while I was looking out the window. I could tell he'd already been drinking by the way he rocked back and forth and leaned on the doorway. He confirmed my suspicion when he pulled the fresh pint out of his back pocket and took a pull right in front of us.

"It's gonna be a long day," I said. "Jewell, I think we'll have to take up the issue of the brickwork later."

Angus McCane headed out of the office door. He walked down the short hall and out into the yard and continued about halfway to the fence. I followed him and we stood there and watched as more than a hundred vehicles rolled up. I counted them like they were the boxcars of a freight train rolling in.

As I counted, the night watchman Norris slipped in behind me. He was standing a little too close, like he was hiding. I imagine he was remembering those scary days two years before when he'd been asked to man a machine gun on the Carlton fence as the first round of flying squadrons had crawled all over the upcountry back in '34.

"Lock that gate down, Norris," Angus McCane said, and Norris looked at me.

"You do what he says," I said.

Norris crept out from behind me and shuffled forward, closed the gate, and slipped the padlock into place. The crowd stared him down from outside.

"Those that's in are staying in for awhile, I reckon," Angus said. "And those that ain't are coming no closer."

We watched as men, women, and children piled out of the convoy and gathered behind the two union men I'd seen the night before. The wrecker pulled up right next to where my truck was parked and Olin Campbell got out and joined them as well. I turned and looked back at the mill. Those working first shift had opened the big windows and stood staring out at the scene below.

"You stop where you are," Angus yelled as Campbell walked toward the bus. A man followed with a short, wooden ladder and propped it against the bus. With a boost from two men, Campbell climbed onto the fender and then onto the flat hood, and mounted the bus roof. He had one of those megaphone cones you used to see and he turned toward the mill and yelled at the workers in the windows, his back to the big crowd.

"Nobody's armed, nobody's carrying weapons," Olin Campbell said through the megaphone, then he dropped the megaphone from his mouth and held out his arms like somebody in a Western, showing he didn't have a gun. "We're not coming to make trouble. We just want this mill to close and stay closed until McCane meets the union's demands."

"The hell you're not making trouble," Angus yelled back. He was standing in the yard between the fence and the mill. "What's to say you're not all armed?"

"Our only weapon is moral persuasion," Campbell answered across the fence. "We want these workers to get the justice they deserve. Shut down your machines, cut off your motors, and come on out and join us," he said to the men in the mill windows.

The men gathered at the windows listened, but nobody moved toward quitting. Angus turned from Campbell and looked back at the windows. "Go on back to work or you won't have none," he said. "These Bolsheviks have nothing to say that you should be interested in. That time's over."

Some of the men at the windows laughed at the Bolshevik comment, and I could see that made McCane mad. He reached in his back pocket and pulled out his bottle and took a swig for courage.

After the laughter ran through the crowd one man spoke. I could see it was my cousin, Ed Crocker, standing in an upper window. I wished for a moment I hadn't gotten him back on with the mill.

"McCane's cut the workers in the Carlton Mill by half," Crocker yelled. "There's nothing to say he won't do it again in five years. Someday this whole mill will operate without us."

"Come on down here and join the strike," Campbell blasted through the cone when he heard my cousin's comment. "We want to show everyone the strength of our movement."

Angus walked up to the fence. "Hell, I recognize some of these men from the drownings; these aren't strikers," he said. "This is no union. These are peckerwood bandits from Huntersville."

"It's an invitation to join the union," Campbell said.

"Your union can kiss my ass," Angus said. "Nobody's coming out and nobody's coming in."

"I don't believe that's for you to say," Campbell said. "Are you men up there with us?"

"What's in it for us?" another man on the second story yelled.

"You shut the hell up," Angus yelled back.

"Yeah, we got jobs now," another chimed in.

"You got jobs but you're also working long hours for low wages and the boss man is still driving around in a big Buick and spending his weekends up at the lake," Campbell said. "Come with us and we can get you your rights."

"I know the boss man's eating steak," a short man with a bald head yelled from the front door. "But at least now I got a pan of cornbread and a kettle of pinto beans on the stove."

"Come with us," Campbell repeated. "We're coming in peacefully. We just want you out so we can shut this mill down."

"If we come, what then?" Ed Crocker yelled from a third floor window.

"We'll strike for your rights," Campbell said. "We're camped out at the Satterfield place. You can go home or you can join us. We got goat stew out there. We're prepared to stay as long as it takes. There's even tents for anyone throwed out of their houses."

"The damn mill's just now opened again," somebody else yelled. "Why would we want to shut it down?"

"McCane's not got the word," Campbell said. "It's a union world coming in. Either he complies with the labor codes or we'll shut him down time and again."

"All that union ever done was get my daddy throwed out of his house," another man yelled. "I come out there and Mr. McCane will do the same with me and my provisions will be in the street by sundown."

"You shut up, you son of a bitch," Angus yelled to the man in the window.

"What if we don't shut up, McCane?" Ed Crocker yelled back.

"I'll come up there and shut you up," Angus McCane said, shaking his fist at the whole side of the mill. He turned his back on Campbell and the crowd and staggered back toward the mill a few steps.

"You can't get the ones back he let go," another man yelled from a window. "Those jobs are gone and not never coming back. We tried the union in '34 and it wasn't no good. Let's go, boys, there's work to do here." The man turned from the windows and headed back to the floor. Some followed him. Others stayed to listen to what else Campbell had to say.

"We're coming over the fence and we're coming in peacefully," Campbell yelled. Two men held the ladder and a line of men waited to climb up on the bus behind Campbell. "We want to talk to y'all man to man. This here's Dan Eliot and John Garland. They got literature from the union." He pointed down behind him to the first two men in line to come up the ladder. The two union men took off their hats and held them up high and shook them, and everyone in the crowd cheered. "They're from the UTWA and once we get inside they'll give us a speech or two you won't forget."

"If they come in, I'm getting out of here," I told Norris. "There's a mess of people out there in the street and three of us."

"They're not coming in," Angus said. He had staggered back from the doorway and looked out at the crowd. "That chicken shit's bluffing."

"Come on," Campbell said. "It's time to go over the fence."

"I'm with you, Olin," Ed Crocker said from the upper window. "Come on in. Let's sit down and have a cup of morning coffee and take a break like a boss man."

"Dan, John," Campbell said. "You hear that? There stands Ed Crocker, a proud union man. Who else will stand with us in this strike?"

"I'm with you," another man yelled from a window.

"You can count on me," said another.

"That's three that will speak up," Campbell said.

Then Angus staggered back toward the mill and disappeared inside. Campbell vaulted over the fence and climbed down the other side. A dozen men followed him up on the bus, they came over one by one, and they all gathered on our side of the fence.

I could hear Angus yelling and arguing with those headed down as he scaled the steps. I imagined men stepping aside as Angus pushed his way upward on the crowded stairway. A few minutes later I saw Angus leaning out the third story window to yell something else down at me.

"You tell them all to go to hell," he yelled and shook his fist. "I'll deal with this."

Angus turned and paced away to where I couldn't see him in the window. He yelled and the men yelled back at him. Then Angus was back in sight, throwing his arms around. I saw him take a swig off his bottle, then he leaned out the window again to yell something else down at me, but before he could speak he began to sway back and forth. He's going to fall, I thought. He turned his back to the window again, still yelling. I could hear Ed Crocker yelling back.

"Angus," I yelled, trying to get his attention, so he'd move away from the opening.

The crowd at the fence looked up. Even Olin Campbell dropped his megaphone to his side and watched. Everyone seemed to look up at once as Angus tipped like a bowling pin and plummeted head-first out the open window. The whole place went quiet as Angus McCane's body dropped three stories to the ground.

For years people who were there that day argued whether he leaned too far forward, tipped over, and hurtled to the ground, or whether he was aided in his descent by a push from Ed Crocker. Either way, George McCane's brother was likely dead soon after he hit.

"That man's head splattered like a melon when he fell," people often said when retelling the story, but *splattered* isn't exactly the right word because his head held together when he hit in the dirt. Strangely enough, there wasn't even any blood. I was the first to get over to him and it was his neck I remember, not his head. Angus's neck was bent at a right angle to his body as if one had decided to go in a contrary direction without telling the other. It looked so unnatural I wanted to reach down and straighten him out before anybody else came up. Olin Campbell was the next to reach him.

The eerie quiet of the crowd outside the gate turned chaotic quickly. The men looking out the windows rushed down toward the yard and poured through the mill's front doors. The strikers surged back and formed a crowd just outside the gates. Some of the others, more deeply spooked, loaded back into the trucks and cars.

"That stupid drunk son of a bitch," Olin Campbell said.

"Get the hell out of here, Campbell," I said. "This is no time for partisan foolishness."

"We'll pull back till you deal with McCane," Campbell said, "but we're not going nowhere today."

"There's a dead man here," I said, standing up and facing him. "Is that what you wanted?"

"He was dead drunk before he fell," Campbell said. "It's his own damn fault."

"Let's get him moved out," I said. "I need to call an ambulance."

"McCane's dead, Crocker," Campbell said. "I need to get on with the work of the living and close this mill down."

"Norris, help me get Mr. McCane out of here," I said.

"Just carry him in the truck to the hospital," Norris said. "It'll take an hour for an ambulance to get here."

Norris reached down and took one side of Angus's broken body.

Somebody went out in front, took off the padlock and threw open the gate. The strikers stood silently by as Norris and I carried Angus McCane's body out. The crowd parted as we pushed through, opening a path toward where the company truck was parked.

As we walked with Angus's body I glanced up and was surprised to see Novie Moreland standing among those inside the gate. She stood on the front row of the gallery of gawkers. I caught her eye as we passed. She was jammed in between her neighbor Yarborough and another man, whose face was flat and emotionless as a cement block. He could just as well have been in the presence of a dead hog bound for the slaughterhouse. But not Novie. She looked grief-stricken and on the verge of tears as she glanced down at Angus's body, and the directness of her stare at the dead man threw me a little. Death was not something I could look so easily on, but she had seen plenty of death that year. She had seen her husband and her child pulled from the clinging waters of a dark mountain lake. After Novie looked at Angus's dead body she glanced back up at me, and I want to believe that her eyes were not clouded with incurable grief as they met mine, but I can't be sure. I could not call what I saw there love, or even affection for me, the man dragging a dead body through the mill yard, though I would have liked to, in spite of the circumstances.

In her presence I slowed a step, and stumbled in the scuffed-up gravel, causing Norris to drop Angus's body right there at Novie and Yarborough's feet like some fallen Celtic tribal chieftain delivered to the victors. I never let go, but I had to bend a little, as if to bow, to get a grip so I could pick the corpse up again and get us into motion. Novie's glance vanished as quickly as it had arrived soon after the unwitting bow. She stepped back and her face disappeared as the crowd surged forward for a closer look—and we went without burden to the waiting truck.

That afternoon I arrived home early and Coleen was sitting on the front porch with Snowball in her lap. I sat down and the dog raised its head, and then looked away. I tried small talk. I wasn't ready to get into what had unfolded at the mill, but Coleen could tell something was wrong just by the way I carried myself. When I sat down it didn't take long for her to start digging at it. Finally I just took a deep breath and said, "Angus McCane is dead."

167

"Dead?"

"This afternoon," I said. "He fell out of an open window at the mill."

"What happened?"

"It was Olin Campbell again. He showed up with a crowd of cars and trucks to shut the mill down and Angus tried to stop it."

"Somebody probably pushed the son of a bitch."

I stared hard at her and she stared back and just sat there stroking the dog. "Don't joke about something like that," I said.

"I'm sorry. I apologize," she said. "But I've told you nothing good would ever come from messing around with those McCanes."

| 1988 |

In his later years George McCane became obsessed with genealogy and family history, so maybe that's why he kept those newspaper clippings. In the 1950s the McCanes had even made a trip back to Scotland to find the obscure origins of their clan. When he returned, Mr. McCane showed everybody a coat of arms and began to wear a plaid scarf everywhere even out of season.

That was odd, but not half as odd as when George McCane paid to have all the gravestones replaced in the family plot with elaborate markers carved with the family coat of arms. Then he replaced his grandfather's, father's, and two older brothers' unobtrusive flat stones with ones bearing carved reliefs of four medieval knights.

But when McCane died there was no knight for him. George McCane was cremated, and for years there wasn't even a marker in the plot to commemorate his death. Before I lost my ability to walk without assistance I'd wander over to the Episcopal Church cemetery and look at those stones and wonder what exactly George McCane had meant by the erection of the four knights and the omission of one of his own. I tell this morbid story in order to show the odd ways that George McCane changed after the trial.

In the fat years with Morgan Mills I had to admit I moved occasionally among the privileged, if not elite. At the end I entertained cloth buyers from out of town at the posh Palmetto Club, in private rooms with white tablecloths.

At first it had felt good to sit surrounded by the ghosts of textiles past. When I led clients through the front hall of the Club we always walked right by the portrait of George McCane, Jr., president of the Club's board of trustees a record six times. I always pointed out Mr. McCane and recited many of his honors: induction into the South Carolina Business Hall of Fame, citizen of the year from the Morgan Area Chamber of Commerce, a lifetime achievement award from the Textile Association of America, even the cover of *American Textiles* magazine. McCane always looked most at home framed there on the wall. He always liked to hide among his own class, and the Club's gallery was a perfect place to do it.

Many in town were pleased that the house had dodged the decline of the finest Victorian homes downtown, but the rambling house turned club was always full of ghosts for me. It was in the parlor, now a private dining room, where the business of this small Southern town is discussed over lamb chops and shrimp and grits, that I had told George McCane of the death of his brother after the grisly fall from the open window at Carlton Mill on the day Olin Campbell had closed it with his flying squadron. When I brought the news, McCane paused a moment and leaned against a sofa, then he raised his right hand and waved me away as if I were a maid bringing tea. I saw a small tremor go down McCane's cheek when I told him his brother was dead.

The day Angus died is a day I've never forgotten, but then there are other days that I just can't recall a thing that happened with any detail worth repeating. Why is it that the vision of Novie Moreland standing on her porch in the October sunlight is so clear to me? And why is it the face of George McCane looking out at me from the Huntersville jail might as well be a cartoon from the local paper? Is it that Novie Moreland at that time was at the height of her vulnerability and I was susceptible to her situation more than I was to Mr. McCane's? Novie Moreland was a woman left abandoned by an accident. One day she woke up in the morning with a husband, children, and a farm. Later that day most of her life was gone. At least that's the way I assumed it happened. My sympathy went out to her the moment I saw her weeping in the church. That sympathy grew each time I saw her until that strange day in court when she changed the direction of her life.

From the cold present I can even admit now that it wasn't only my sympathy that went out to her. I was attracted to Novie's helplessness. I wanted Novie to fall for my insurance settlement story so I could come back to visit her again. When she stepped from the shadows into the light I imagined myself as her savior. I would have happily become William Kirby, insurance agent, when I crossed the North Carolina line for a chance to visit with her again. I would have lied again—and often—to be in her presence. But I didn't. I never checked on her again. My marriage to Coleen improved through the years. Her hard edges softened as we prospered.

I've never told anyone until now these silly romantic fantasies I had back then, but sometimes now when I'm alone I think only of them. Once the pleasure potential of these fantasies of an old man is exhausted, I circle back to something I know was important, like Coleen sitting beside me on the porch, something that I thought I needed to recover in order to make sense of my life.

I know what's forgotten and what's remembered (like a face) are related. As another signpost for my muddled memory, I also keep returning to what Edna McCane asked me here on the front porch: "What did it cost him?"

This question is even more complicated than my memory of Novie Moreland. Edna McCane knows that cost accounting is what I did for a living all those years. If I'd ever answer her question truthfully then maybe stirring all this up was worthwhile. That said, I wish I would have had the forethought to tell Edna McCane that the past isn't a ledger. Even for an accountant, there are no neat profit and loss columns in a life lived day-to-day with no understanding of what the future might bring or not bring.

The past is more like the daily papers I let pile up beside my reading chair in the house. The news in that pile is all pressed close and dark. Finally the pile topples over at some point on to the next and goes out to the trash. Here beside me there are layers upon layers of newsprint and I know I've read it all, but for the life of me, I can't remember what came first or last.

Mrs. McCane never sent that car for me. Maybe in the end she decided she probably knew about as much of her husband's personal history as she needed or wanted. I can't say I'm sad I missed my promised outing to the venerable Palmetto Club, but I quickly tired of sitting on the porch and decided I wanted to mount an outing of my own. I walked to the backyard, something I hadn't done in years with the little energy (and balance) I had left. I shuffled down the three front porch steps using the rail and my cane, an act of courage on my part maybe equal to Neil Armstrong walking on the moon. I opened the side gate and passed the graves of four Snowballs (each meaner than the last), and then I twisted the latch to open the little plywood door to the crawl space. Inside, as I had left it so many years before, was the coffee jar with the remains of my contingency fund. The lid was rusted so I picked up a brick and smashed the jar on the concrete seal. I reached down and picked up the money and counted: three hundred dollars in a tight ancient roll.

I made my way back to the porch and then inside with the money. I picked up the phone and called Elray Ponder. Would he come by the next Sunday afternoon and drive me to Huntersville? He'd married my niece and so I'd seen him a good bit over the years. "That's a mighty long Sunday outing, Ben," Elray said, so I confessed it wasn't just a pleasure trip. "I want to revisit some of the places I have not been in a long time." The money sat before me on the telephone table in the hall.

On Sunday afternoon after church Elray picked me up in his new red Dodge Powerwagon. Elray was over seventy and retired from cutting meat in various grocery store chains, so he was able to slip out of the mill life before it closed down and left him stranded. He helped me in the cab and stowed my cane in the back seat. "You don't want your walker?" he asked out of politeness. "We can put it in the truck bed."

"No, I figure as little as I'll be on my feet I can stand to take a step or two."

"You want to go up I-26 or the back way like we went that other time?" Elray asked once we were headed out Main Street.

"Let's go up the old Asheville road," I said. "It's Sunday. Maybe there'll be a peach shed open on the way and I can take a bag home."

"You'll be better off finding peaches at Bi-Lo," Elray said. "Most of the farms are closed up there now. There are houses in the orchards, little subdivisions, Smurf houses I call 'em. Besides, peaches are cheaper at Bi-Lo, even though they grow in California." He went silent for a moment. "Ben, why you want to drive all the way up to Huntersville? It isn't the peaches."

"I want to see if it's how I remember it," I said, fibbing.

"I fish over in Pisgah sometime and I drive through Huntersville to get up there. The hills are covered up with retired Florida people. You won't like it."

"Maybe we'll both feel right at home," I said. "Maybe you should have moved up there."

"Too many Yankees for me," Elray said. "You know they just never get it that we don't care how they did it up north. What do you think about all these Yankees moving here? Do you think we'll ever have anything to ourselves anymore?"

We weren't even to Irby yet and already Elray was asking questions, just like the old days. "You mind if I take off my tie?" and "You remember when there was two Waffle Houses here at the interstate?" and "You think that dog is a stray?" and "You enjoy watching the Baptists preach on TV as much as sitting in the sanctuary of the Methodist church downtown like you used to?" I'd forgotten how he couldn't stop asking questions, but it didn't irritate me quite as much that day. As long as Elray kept asking questions about dogs and Waffle Houses I was alright. I just didn't want him prying into why we were repeating a route we'd driven years before.

Once we were past Irby things looked familiar along the way. Around the state line I spotted a tumbled-down concrete block building and said, "Those two block walls could be all that's left of the Flats. Pull off here for a minute."

Elray wheeled his truck into the small, washed out gravel parking lot.

"You remember when we stopped here before?"

"Not really," Elray said. "I was pretty young."

"This is where Angus McCane went to drink."

"Angus McCane? I haven't thought about him in years. Did they ever find out if he fell or if was he pushed?"

"We'll never know," I said. "I like to think of it as an accident, whether it was or not."

"I always heard he was pushed," Elray said. "They say that Ed Crocker even bragged some about it once he left the mill."

"What kind of man would brag about something like that?"

"You know how Ed Crocker was," Elray said.

We pulled back out in the road and soon crossed into North Carolina. I didn't know whether Elray had ever heard the full story of George McCane's and the accident on the lake, closing down the Carlton Mill, going to trial, but I suspect he had. If he had he might understand the ambiguity of Angus McCane's death. Elray's brother was in the union and so he probably had heard all about McCane's troubles from their perspective. After the mill closed McCane had made enough concessions to open it up again and then he went to work to run out the union once and for all, something he finally accomplished in the 1950s. I've always thought that George McCane's success in squashing the union was one reason they put him on the cover of that magazine.

"Don't you think Tompkins is a pretty little town?" Elray asked as we slowed down where the Asheville road turned to Trade Street.

"I thought you didn't like Yankees," I said.

"Well, I admit up here they seem to fit in," he said. "After all, this is North Carolina."

The Saltilla Grade road had been widened since the days George McCane drove up to the lake. There were young men on bikes coming down, but very few cars.

"You know they ride those bicycles over from Greenville?" Elray asked. "They stop in Saltilla for dinner. They must be doing fifty miles an hour on the way down."

After we reached Saltilla and the top of the grade we passed South Shore Drive, the road to the lake. "Do you know if the Lakeside Inn is still open?" I asked.

"Of course it's still open," Elray said. "We come up here for Mother's Day and eat outside under the colored lanterns. The grandchildren love it."

"Turn on in there and let's go around the lake," I said.

The water was calm and blue. We passed the old stone pillars I'd turned between to visit the McCane compound. I imagined the grandchildren were there now. I looked up the driveway to where it turned but the mountain laurel was too thick to see anything.

In a few miles the Asheville road turned to four lanes as it approached Huntersville.

"Where were you thinking of going?" Elray asked. "You need to stop at Hardee's for a pit stop?"

"I'm doing all right," I said. "Just go on around town on the bypass. Go out to the Canaan turnoff where we went that time back in the 1930s."

"I remember. Are we going past Jump Off Rock? We going up to that rock this time?"

"Maybe we'll have time. Quite a view I hear."

"You think that little church is still there?"

"I guess we'll see."

At the Canaan turn-off Elray pointed to a big sign announcing "Mountain-Aerie, an award-winning private national destination golf retreat and residential community."

"Looks like the Yankees have arrived," he said.

Soon the little church where I'd attended the funeral came into view. The small, white frame building was still surrounded by big maples, but as we approached I could tell things weren't the same. The sign for the church had been removed, and the building had been converted into a sales office for mountain properties. Several flat parking spaces had been bulldozed into the hillside and paved. "Come in for your ticket to mountain views and country living," the sign out front announced.

After we passed the old church the road to the Moreland farm had been widened and bike lanes were painted on each asphalt shoulder. The country road had been lined with flowering pear trees on both sides. We passed the golf course, the holes built along the rocky creek on the passenger side of the car, converting what had once been good pasture and corn to eighteen holes of golf. In the near distance up on the slopes of Jump Off Mountain, I could see large dark mansions with steep roofs and big views out over the valley.

Soon two huge, stone pillars came into view on the driver's side. There was also a stacked stone gatehouse with a sign above made out of timbers that announced "MountainAerie." Stretching behind the gate was a large grape vineyard with houses built along the edge that swept up the gradual slope of the facing peak. Elray slowed down so I could take the scene in. The MountainAerie guard stepped out with his hands on his hips when he saw we weren't turning through the gates.

"I told you things had changed," Elray said. "It's real pretty now. This place looks like something from that rich and famous channel."

"I remember when these were farm fields ploughed by a man named Saul Yarborough," I said. "His house sat right where that gatehouse is."

"At least there's one pretty old mountain house still here," Elray said, pointing to the other side of the road at what I recognized right away was Novie Moreland's house. "But somebody's really fixed that one up, haven't they?"

"Pull up there," I said.

"Do you know them?"

"I might," I said.

"There's a car in the driveway, so there's somebody home," Elray said, pulling up out front. "Do you need your cane, Ben?"

"I think I can make it up there under my own power," I said. "It's only three steps."

Then I changed my mind. "Well, I think I'll use that cane after all."

He handed me the cane. "I'll wait here," Elray said. "You just wave if you need help getting back down."

It had been so many decades and I'll admit I wanted things settled, finally. What was it that freed George McCane from the murder charges? Why had Novie Moreland recanted on the stand? What could possibly have turned her testimony?

I knocked and a pretty young woman came to the door, about the age Novie was when I knew her. She had Novie's blond hair and figure. She wiped her hands on a blue dish towel. A fleeting shadow of recognition crossed her face.

"Do I know you?" she asked.

"Mrs. Moreland?"

"No, I'm Mrs. McGinnis."

"Is your first name Novie?"

"No, but that was my grandmother's name."

"I'm from down in Morgan. My name is Ben Crocker," I said. "I knew your grandmother a long time ago."

"Morgan? That's funny," she said. "Our Uncle George was from down there and you reminded me a little of him."

I stepped back and almost lost my balance. She reached out to steady me, and let her hand come to rest on top of my hand clutching the cane.

"Uncle George?" I asked.

"Yes, Uncle George," she said.

"I brought something for y'all," I said, reaching in my pocket but I stopped short of pulling out the handful of old bills.

She looked a little confused.

"I was in insurance back when I knew your grandmother, and I was hoping to talk with her about an old settlement. But it looks like y'all have done fine," I said. "With the house fixed up and all."

"Mr. Crocker, my grandmother died about three years ago."

"Died?"

"Cancer took her."

"I'm so sorry," I said.

"Well, thank you for stopping by," she said. "I'm sure my grandmother would have loved to see you."

"Yes, and you don't know how much I would have liked to see her one more time."

"Thank you again."

"Can I ask you one more thing? Your Uncle George from down in Morgan. His last name wasn't McCane was it?"

"Yes sir, it was McCane," she said. "Did you know him?"

"Everybody knew George McCane," I said. "Did you get to see him often?"

"Only when we were visiting from Asheville. We moved up here when grand-mother died. He stayed down at the lake mostly and he'd come to see grand-mamma."

"I see," I said. "I see."

"Mr. Crocker, I'd like to talk more but I've got some errands to run."

"Don't let me keep you," I said.

"Be careful going down those steps," she said and closed the door.

She left me standing alone on the porch. I knew George McCane was not her uncle—and I'm sure she knew it too. I imagined calling him that was just a polite Southern way of saying McCane and her grandmother had what we would call a special relationship. I looked down the three steps to the road and I thought about knocking again, but what else would I say? There was no settling things. Most of the things that had happened no outsider would ever know, and those who did know were all dead. That's just the way life is sometimes. I knew then I would go to my grave with uncertainty, doubt, and even a dose of guilt. George McCane had settled things, but not with me. He had no reason to do that. That much was for sure.

From the top of Novie Moreland's steps I could see Jump Off Rock in the distance and I thought for a second I'd just get Elray to drive me up there and do what the name commanded—jump off. But what good would that do? I was no young lover spurned in the affair of my life. I was just an old man trying to settle an impossible account with the past. Instead I took unsteady baby steps and walked slowly down from the porch, and slid in the passenger seat with no help from Elray. He drove me back to Morgan that day, where by noon I took up residence once again on my own porch and watched what was left of my old world pass by.

ACKNOWLEDGEMENTS

There are only a few novels about the Southern textile experience, so I have always wanted to write one. I did not grow up in a Southern mill village, but stories of that world were always close at hand. Three generations of my mother's family (Mabes, Bradleys, Browns, Norrises) worked in various mills from the late nineteenth century through the twentieth century. My mother competed for "Miss Textiles Goes to War" at Spartanburg's Camp Croft in 1943. She worked at Saxon Mills in Spartanburg County, and when she was named one of the mill's two representatives, she received a fancy dress and also the day of the contest off. She was runner-up. She carried the *Life* magazine clipping with her picture in her purse until the day she died.

This novel would not have been possible without my mother or my mother's stories or the backdrop of that piedmont mill world. We did not grow up anti-union in our house. My mother always exhibited great pride that her stepfather was "union" and refused to scab during the strikes of the 1930s. Though this story is set in the fictional town of Morgan, South Carolina, there are parallels between my family's real work world and the imaginary one I have made up. In the thirties Spartanburg was more of a union town than most people think. Today nearly everyone's either forgotten the strength of the unions or never knew.

There is another stream that contributed to this novel's birth, a more scholarly stream: over the last twenty years I read a series of books about Southern textiles that sketched out a clear picture of the lives of the workers and owners: among them David Carlton's *Mill and Town* and G. C. Waldrep III's *Southern Workers and the Search for Community*. These books, specifically about my hometown, Spartanburg, South Carolina, were most important to me, and to my story. One more important inspiration for me was the 1995 documentary film *The Uprising of '34*, by George C. Stoney, Judith Helfand, and Susanne Rostock, which tells the story of the general strike by hundreds of thousands of Southern workers during 1934.

In 2002 my wife, Betsy Teter, edited what I think is one of the best books about textiles in the South, *Textile Town*. I will always be indebted to Betsy for her clear historian's mind and journalist's tenacity.

I would like to thank Megan DeMoss for reading and making valuable suggestions and corrections; Mindy Friddle for reading an early draft and heading me in the right direction; Venable Vermont for listening to my endless possible plot twists as we paddled and drove around the upcountry of South Carolina; Melissa Walker for suggestions on the story; Ken Anthony for listening to, reading, and improving the courtroom scenes; and Sandra and B. G. Stephens for reading often (through several drafts) and suggesting ways to make the story more accurate. Finally, I would like to thank Jonathan Haupt and Pat Conroy for their sympathetic readings and for title suggestions that helped me clarify the story.

ABOUT THE AUTHOR

JOHN LANE is the author of a dozen books of poetry and prose, including *My Paddle to the Sea; Begin with Rock, End with Water;* and most recently *Abandoned Quarry: New and Selected Poems,* winner of the 2012 Southern Independent Booksellers Alliance Book Award for Poetry. A professor of English and director of the Goodall Environmental Studies Center at Wofford College in Spartanburg, South Carolina, Lane is a 2014 inductee into the South Carolina Academy of Authors.